COWBOY FE
ROLLING TH
HAIRS ON T
BEGAN TO

Taking the stairs two at a time, Cowboy raced back to Room 17 . . .

In the middle of the floor, arms and legs spread-eagled, lay the body. The eyes were open and staring. The hair lay in a pool of congealing blood, the stain spreading across the worn carpet . . .

In his mind he heard the words of warning they had received. 'If you want to take a friend's advice, Cowboy, forget it. You're not in the same class as this man, and you never will be. Fuck with this guy and you'll get dead.'

Sean Martin Blain was born in 1947 in Dublin, the youngest of six children. At thirteen he joined the FCA, the Irish equivalent of the Territorial Army, and in 1962 he ran away from home with a stolen birth certificate to join the British Army in Belfast. There followed a nationwide search and, once found, he was discharged from the FCA, complete with the rank of corporal in the Military Police, for being under age. Nevertheless, he joined the British Army at the age of seventeen, with his parents' blessing, and then went on to serve in Germany, Kenya, Libya, Canada, Scotland and Hong Kong.

In 1970 Sean married a Danish national, and seven years later they had a son. He was discharged from the army at his own request and moved to Denmark a year after to be with his wife and child. He spent his time working in a slaughterhouse and in a dairy, attending a five-month course to learn Danish and eventually owning and running a pub and disco. However, these ventures were not successful and he returned to England to seek employment. He was divorced in 1988 and then began writing in earnest. *Java Man*, his first novel, was published in 1995 and *The Chameleon* in 1996, both available in Signet. He is currently working on two further novels.

SEAN MARTIN BLAIN

THE CHAMELEON

A SIGNET BOOK

SIGNET

Published by the Penguin Group
Penguin Books Ltd, 27 Wrights Lane, London w8 5tz, England
Penguin Books USA Inc., 375 Hudson Street, New York, New York 10014, USA
Penguin Books Australia Ltd, Ringwood, Victoria, Australia
Penguin Books Canada Ltd, 10 Alcorn Avenue, Toronto, Ontario, Canada m4v 3b2
Penguin Books (NZ) Ltd, 182–190 Wairau Road, Auckland 10, New Zealand

Penguin Books Ltd, Registered Offices: Harmondsworth, Middlesex, England

First published 1996
1 3 5 7 9 10 8 6 4 2

Set in 10/12pt Monotype Plantin
Typeset by Datix International Limited, Bungay, Suffolk
Printed in England by Clays Ltd, St Ives plc

To Val
who changed her mind . . . or did she?

CHAPTER ONE

Seven Years Ago

STATION-MASTER CHARLIE DELANEY looked at his watch as the metallic dark blue Rolls Royce turned into the station car park, and smiled. His watch showed the time as 18:59. Had it been five minutes either side he would have changed it. The Dublin commuter train was due in at 19:07 and the Silver Shadow in the car park meant that Mr O'Brien was on board. It was the same scenario every weekday. Whatever the weather, the Roller pulled into the car park between one minute before and one minute after seven. It was Charlie's daily time-check. Although he and the chauffeur had never spoken, they always acknowledged each other with a wave. At eight minutes past the hour, the Dublin to Dún Laoghaire commuter train pulled into the station and the passengers disembarked.

Among them was a well-dressed middle-aged man. Briefcase in one hand and season-ticket in the other, James O'Brien smiled at Charlie as he walked through the platform exit, heading for the car. The chauffeur had stepped out of his car as the train pulled in and was now standing by the driver's door. When O'Brien was twenty feet away, the chauffeur produced a revolver and fired six times. All six rounds hit O'Brien in the chest and he fell to the ground, dropping his bulging briefcase. The chauffeur climbed calmly back into the Rolls Royce and drove off before any move was made to stop him.

For five seconds everything was still and silent, then a woman started to scream. Galvanized by the sound, Charlie ran to the fallen man, but he could see that it was too late. James O'Brien lay where he had fallen, arms outstretched, a look of shock on his dead face. For just one moment Charlie thought he might have been wrong as he heard a slight gurgling sound from the stricken man, but it was air and blood bubbling from the deadly wounds.

Moving back from the body, Charlie Delaney urged the six confused passengers to remain where they were while he phoned for the police. Seven minutes later a squad car, lights flashing and siren wailing, pulled up with a squeal of brakes. Five minutes behind was an ambulance. Thirty minutes later an unmarked police car arrived at the scene from the Headquarters of the Criminal Investigation Branch – the CIB. In charge was Detective Inspector Frank Mooney.

At 19:59, as Mooney was taking Station-master Charlie Delaney's statement, the man's eyes opened wide in astonishment, staring over the Inspector's shoulder. Mooney turned to see what he was gaping at. A metallic dark blue Silver Shadow Rolls Royce had just pulled into the car park.

'Jesus, Mary and Joseph,' Charlie muttered, transfixed by the sight. 'I don't believe it. He's back. That's him, Inspector. That's the man you're wanting.'

Calling to his Sergeant, Bob O'Brien, Frank moved swiftly towards the car. Seeing the two men approach, and noticing the police activity, the chauffeur got out of the car just as Mooney reached him.

'What's going on?' he asked, bewildered. 'Somebody hurt?' His tone was so innocent that for a moment it threw Mooney.

'A man has been shot. A Mr James O'Brien,' he blurted out.

'*What?* James? I don't believe it!' His face turned ashen, as he looked from one to the other, the truth slowly sinking in.

'Oh my God! Oh my God! Who did it? For God's sake, who would want to shoot James?'

'According to the witnesses who saw the shooting, you did,' Mooney replied.

'*Me!* You're joking. You have to be joking. I've only just arrived.'

'You lying bastard,' Charlie Delaney shouted as he approached. 'You were here an hour ago, and shot him as he walked towards the car! You killed him, and I saw you. Me and the rest of the people standing here.'

The chauffeur stood open-mouthed, seeming to have trouble breathing as the detectives read him his rights, handcuffed him and led him to their car. As he was bundled away from the scene he stared back at the body of his employer, apparently lost in an agonizing mixture of grief and incomprehension.

CHAPTER TWO

Vietnam 1972

SOMEWHERE IN THE JUNGLE, NORTH OF THE 17TH PARALLEL

AS THE CHORUS OF JUNGLE NOISES changed from night to day sounds, the level of the river began to fall, and the animal in the cage could relax a little. The night-long struggle to keep his head above water was over for the moment. There were wounds on his face and neck from fighting with the water rats, but a small, hairy body floating nearby showed that it had not been a one-sided fight.

The animal trussed up in the water-cage had once been a man. He had had a happy childhood, been to school, entered college, dated girls, lost his cherry and answered the call of his country. He had been proud when his country asked him to go to war. Unlike many of his contemporaries, he believed that his government knew best. He had been a patriotic eighteen-year-old boy when he had enlisted, but within twelve months that boy was dead, replaced by a well-oiled, living, breathing, killing machine. A Mechanic. The Army discovered that he was faultless at killing and never questioned the orders he was given. They were not interested in knowing that all human feeling in him had died, that now he was solely concerned with successfully executing the assignments he was given, and with his own survival.

The chest of his Number One dress uniform was not broad enough for all the medals he had been awarded

4

over the years. They lay in a tin trunk, in a room at the Long Range Reconnaissance Patrols ('LURPS') base at Nha Trang Airfield, near Saigon. LURPS normally operated in six-man teams, penetrating deep inside enemy territory, acting as the forward eyes and ears of the Army. But some members of the 5th Special Forces Group, who ran LURPS, were specialists; assassins known as 'Mechanics', who operated alone. For six years he had been killing. Once, they sent him home. They gave him Orders to Fort Bragg, to train others to be like himself. Every morning at 0700 he was to be found outside his Commanding Officer's door, dressed in his Number Ones, his written application to be sent back to where he belonged in his hand. He wanted to be back in the jungle, back in *his* jungle, with the other animals.

He now knew the jungle trails of Vietnam, in and out of Cambodia and Laos, better than he could remember the back alleys of the small town where he was born. He could go for days without food or sleep, surviving on rationed sips of water. He knew many more ways to kill than were written in the Army Manual and never hesitated to use them.

The last time he was on R & R – Rest and Recuperation – he had killed three fellow servicemen in a Saigon bar. They were nothings, pen-pushers, paper lords. They were the vultures who lived in luxury at Saigon Supply Depots, deciding amongst themselves if the front-line troops should, or should not, receive the vital equipment they repeatedly indented for. Those who could pay the most received the most life-saving equipment. The vultures believed only suckers and mugs put their lives on the line. The intelligent ones, like themselves, took what they could from life, made their illicit stack of greenbacks for when they returned home, and looked after their own interests.

He knew that he should just have walked out. He had *wanted* to walk out. To ignore their arrogant, boastful bragging. But he couldn't. He was the last surviving member of his Recruit Company which had included five of his boyhood friends. They had all flown home zipped up in green plastic body-bags, like unwanted garbage. So he stayed in the bar. He stayed and listened and drank until he could take no more. In the end he had wrecked the bar and killed the three pen-pushers.

The Military Police came in answer to a screaming telephone call from the Vietnamese bar owner, and he allowed himself to be arrested. He was released into the custody of his Commanding Officer, the charge sheets were destroyed and three more bodies went home in plastic sacks to be given heroes' military funerals. The army did not intend to destroy a perfect killing machine simply because it blew a gasket and wasted three next-to worthless small cogs that could be replaced with a thousand similar ones. So they forgave. Maybe not forgot, but they forgave, and sent the machine back to work with the barest of warnings.

He was completely at home, on his own in the jungle. The insects that plagued others, he ignored. He was the sleekest, the fastest and the most dangerous cat on the prowl. But even great cats fall into traps from time to time. So now he had to concentrate on surviving until there was an opportunity to escape.

He had been in the water-cage for fourteen days and nights. The length of time was irrelevant to him, his mind was in a state of suspension, living from moment to moment. He conserved all his energy for when he would need it. If no opportunity came, then he would die – it was not important to him – but if his captors made just one mistake he would be ready to exploit it without a moment's hesitation.

He could neither sit nor stand. His arms were wrapped round a stout bamboo pole, tied tightly together with rope, then lashed to his ankles, forcing him into a constantly crouched position. Once a day he was released to eat a few grains of food, but even with his hands free, he remained in a crouched position. To straighten and stretch was too painful to bear if he was going straight back into the cage. By staying in one position, he was allowing his body to adapt to its circumstances. There was no point in struggling until the moment was perfect.

Only one of the other cages was occupied now, by a pilot who would not last much longer. Pilots lived in luxury in Saigon at Nha Trang or Tan Son Nhut on the northern edge of the city, or at one of the other main Air Force bases spread throughout South Vietnam. They took off, dropped their bombs or strafed a jungle position or village, then flew back to the home comforts of their bases. This pilot stood no chance of surviving. Brought in three days ago, he was already in a worse condition than his fellow-prisoner. Tomorrow he would be dead. Had he been a Marine or a Dog-face – an infantry man – he would have made contact with him. It might have been possible for them to help each other to escape. Marines and jungle-trained infantry soldiers would have had some knowledge of the jungle, of how to survive, outside of the textbook theory. But the pilot would be a liability, and he had enough of those already, so he ignored him.

He heard laughter as the Viet Cong guards came for their early-morning ritual of urinating on the prisoners. He gave no reaction to the warm urine on his bare head and face, but the pilot cried. The guards roared with laughter and wandered back for their breakfast, chatting happily, the prisoners immediately forgotten. They did not reappear until midday, this time bringing some weak soup with a handful of noodles floating in it, just enough sustenance to keep the prisoners alive for another day of pain and fear. The routine had been the same every day, but today was to be different. He was being sent up country, probably to Hanoi, to one of the prisoner compounds, built near the airfields, factories or ammunition depots.

'Hey, American Dog, you are going home,' one of the guards shouted in sing-song English. The others laughed. 'It's true, American. Uncle Ho has decided that you are all really such nice boys that you can all go home.' This was greeted with more laughter.

The pilot had heard and started to cry. Home! He was going to make it. After all the terrible suffering he had endured over the last couple of days, he was going to make it. He would *never* be back. If God gave him this one chance, he would never, never *ever*, come back again.

The tone changed. 'Come on, American. Out.'

The lid at the top of the cage was removed. Rough hands reached in to grasp the bamboo pole he was attached to. He was heaved up out of the river and dumped on the ground at their feet.

He struggled to his feet, still bent at the waist, apparently humble and respectful, ignoring the pain in his arms. He slurped the soup and noodles from the bowl like an animal, balanced on the edge of the makeshift jetty. Looking round he could see signs that they were breaking camp. They were all moving. As they led him away like a dog on a lead, the pilot began to scream.

'What about me? You forgot me. I wanna go home too.'

The guard who spoke English turned and called back to him. 'You are home, American. Not home and *dry*, but home and wet. There you will stay.' They all laughed. The one who had spoken laughed loudest and longest at his play on words. Oh yes, he was very good at the English language.

The pilot screamed and cried and pleaded, but they ignored him. He was already dead as far as they were concerned. Over the next few days the rats would finish off the job they had started. His bones would fall through the bars of the cage, down into the mud at the bottom of the river. In a few months the bamboo cage would rot and fall to pieces, floating away like other jungle debris. The place where they had built their hut would be overrun by the undergrowth once again, and no trace would remain. Nobody would know they had ever been there.

Shortly after noon, a motor launch was heard coming up river. There was a brief argument among the VC guards over who would go in the boat and who would take the prize American north through the jungle to the first base camp. Eventually it was decided, and nine of the ten irregulars boarded the boat along with all their equipment and several wooden crates. As the boat moved off, they stood at the stern waving and shouting at their lone comrade. He stood on the jetty watching until they disappeared, then, removing the bamboo so that the prisoner could walk, he pushed him roughly towards the jungle trail. It would be several days before they would arrive in Hanoi and he didn't expect the prisoner to make it. It would be simpler for him if he died sooner rather than later. Ignoring the doomed shrieks of the caged flyer, they entered the gloom of the jungle.

The trail was narrow and barely visible. Whenever they came to a division in the path the guard would tap him on the shoulder with a thin stalk of bamboo, indicating which trail to take. Over the next few hours his back began to straighten itself. The pain was excruciating, but he blocked it out like he blocked out the insects that swarmed around them and the thirst and hunger gnawing at his insides like rats. By night-time he was able to walk upright once more. The animal was turning back into a man.

In the evening, the guard managed to catch a squealing wild piglet. Lighting a fire, he roasted and ate it, tearing at the hot burnt flesh, his face and hands dripping with fat. When he had eaten his fill there was still plenty left of the carcass. He looked across the fire at the prisoner who was ignoring him, not allowing the tempting smell of the roasted flesh to reach his brain. Eventually the guard tore some more flesh off the bones and took a tin plate across to where the prisoner was trussed up. Untying one arm, leaving the other lashed to the tree, he pushed the plate towards him. 'Pig,' he indicated. 'You eat pig.'

Flexing his freed arm, the man looked up at him with expressionless eyes. Pointing to the food, he made signs of cutting with his hand. He wanted a knife and fork. The guard grunted impatiently, but crossed back to his kitbag to get them. As he handed them over the prisoner caught his wrist like a cat pouncing on a mouse, jerking him off balance. The startled guard fell between the wide open legs of his prisoner which closed as tight as a vice round his neck, cutting off his air supply. The prisoner's free hand smashed down onto the man's nose in a lethal slicing action while the legs turned and snapped the victim's neck. Finding a short, sharp bayonet in the scabbard on the dead man's belt, the prisoner cut free his other hand. After rubbing his wrists for a short time, he attacked the roast pork with his fingers.

When the meal was finished, he took a long swig of

water from the guard's canteen, and belched in satisfaction. A full stomach brought him another step closer to being a man again. Turning to the body, he searched every pocket of the uniform, then the rucksack that lay close by. Spreading everything he found out on the ground, he checked his new possessions. A Russian-made rifle and fifty rounds of ammunition, the bayonet, a water-bottle, some matches in a damp-proof container, thirty cigarettes, a small bag of cooked rice, a tin plate and cup, a knife and fork and a rucksack to carry them in. He secreted the body in the jungle vegetation, crawled up into a nearby tree, and slept properly for the first time in two weeks, his body soaking up new energy from the desperately needed rest.

He woke to the sound of grunting. Parting the foliage very carefully he looked down to the ground. Three full-grown pigs were tearing at the body of the guard which they had pulled out into the open. As he dropped to the ground, the pigs bolted back into the jungle, but he knew they would return as soon as he left and finish their interrupted meal.

Before setting off he swallowed a mouthful of rice, took two gulps of water and ate three cigarettes. The nicotine would help to keep hunger pangs at bay. He did not know where he was, nor how far he was from his own lines, but if he travelled south he would eventually get back to civilization. Breakfast finished, rifle checked and loaded, he pulled the rucksack onto his back and set off.

It was his concentrated will to live that had kept him alive in the water-cage for so long. Now he was free of the cage and had eaten some proper food for the first time in weeks, his will power wanted a rest. As it relaxed he slowed down, and nature herself set out to stop him. On his third day of freedom a fever began to take hold of him. It started as hot and cold flushes, and pretty soon he was burning up. His thirst was enormous and impossible to ignore. His water-bottle had been emptied, replenished from shallow pools of rain-water, and emptied again. It was hours since he had last had a drink when he came across the pool. He neither saw nor cared about the body of the forest deer that lay on the opposite side of the water-hole. To his fevered mind, water was water. He did not care if it had been poisoned to keep the Viet Cong from it, he had no choice but to drink. He drank his fill and replenished his water-bottle before setting off once more. Now he was stumbling over every root and branch, his head spinning and his muscles refusing to obey his weakened mind.

It was one hour and one mile later that he knew he could not carry on. It was painful to put one foot in front of the other and his double vision made it impossible to stay on the path for more than two steps at a time. The trail was narrow and he found himself wandering off into the wilderness around him. He knew he had to rest or he would make a fatal mistake. He had just enough strength to leave the trail and cover himself with vegetation, holding his rifle beside him, before he sank into a feverish sleep.

How long he slept before he woke he had no idea, but he could hear voices. The imminent danger brought his highly trained mind and muscles back under control. His will to survive had returned and was using every last ounce of strength it could summon from the almost-defunct bodily system. He drew the rifle nearer and quietly cocked it. The voices came closer, and then stopped. Now he could hear whispering, and a noise like somebody creeping about, somebody who was not very good at disguising their presence. He brought the rifle across his chest, aimed it in the direction he felt they would come from, and waited, hardly breathing. When the foliage parted he found himself looking up into the face of an angel. Then he fainted.

When he woke he was in a smoke-filled hut, lying on a bed of reeds. Somebody was washing his body with something cool and refreshing. Whoever it was realized he was awake and bent low over him. He saw the face of the angel once again. She looked into his eyes, smiled, and left him. He heard voices and almost immediately a man appeared beside him.

'You have the fever, American. You have been drinking bad water.' The voice was friendly and through his blurred vision he could see an old man looking at him.

'Where am I?' he asked, his voice weak, barely above a whisper.

'You are safe. You are in my village. I am the Pholy – the village headman. This is my daughter, Thu Suong. She and the other children found you not far from here.' The old man smiled, showing rotten teeth. 'The other children thought you were a devil. Perhaps they were right.' He smiled again to show he was only joking. 'For the moment you are safe and we are safe. Do you want something to drink?'

The man nodded weakly and the girl went away, returning with an earthenware jug. She raised his head gently with one hand, holding the jug to his mouth with the other. Whatever it was, it was cool and thick and nourishing and he wanted to drain the jug.

'No, no, American,' she stopped him. Her voice was soft, and as cool as the drink. 'You ill. Must wait until weller. Better little bit now, little bit later.' She took the jug away and laid his head back down. 'You sleep now. I come again later.' With that she and the Pholy left him, and once more he fell into a deep sleep.

For four days and nights the fever overcame him. Every time he came close to the surface he saw the same angelic face bending over him, her hands washing him with the cooling liquid he later found out was called Ternum – a home-made rice alcohol much favoured by the Moi people, in whose village he lay. On the fifth morning, when he woke, he felt strong enough to lift himself out of bed and grope his way to the door. His eyes were dazzled by the bright sunshine after so long in the dark, smokey hut. The fresh air cleared his head at first but then made him feel weak. He had been alone when he woke and was cautious about showing himself at the hut entrance, but it appeared safe enough. The womenfolk were going about their daily chores and everything seemed peaceful. The hut was built about ten feet from the ground, the support poles resting in cans of water in an attempt to keep the termites at bay. Resting against the opening was a log ladder, made by hacking steps into a tree trunk and leaning it at an angle on the hut platform.

It was the children who spotted him first as he crawled slowly and dizzily down the log. They began giggling and then screaming, running for the other huts. The women stopped their work and turned to look in his direction, but none dared to approach him. The old man, the Pholy, came out from another hut in answer to the children's screams and saw him. He descended elegantly to the ground and walked across to the other man. 'You should still be in your bed, American. You are not strong enough to move yet.'

His first thought that morning, on waking, had been fear of the unknown. Then he had realized where he was and the memories returned, some recent and some long suppressed. He remembered the young man he had once been, before he had first entered the jungle, and all that had happened to him since. His body, which had gone off guard as he slipped so close to the comfort of a peaceful death, had immediately tightened up. The moment he was back in control, he shut out the painful memories of everything he had suffered and lost, and forced himself to concentrate on the present and what he should do next. He knew that he had to leave this place, to get away as quickly as possible. Not for himself, although he knew he was in great danger, but to protect the people who had saved him. If the VC came and found him there – or even found traces that he had been there – then they would crucify the Pholy in front of the entire village, rape all the females over the age of ten, slaughter all the children under that age, and chop the right hand off every adult male. Then they would burn the entire village and any food stocks they could not take away with them. Word would soon spread of what had happened to a village that had given help to an American. Any more of his kind, escaped prisoners or shot-down airmen, would be handed over to the VC immediately. He *had* to leave.

'I must leave your village,' he replied in answer to the Pholy's remark. 'It is much too dangerous for you and your people for me to stay.'

'There are no soldiers or VC anywhere for two days' march. I have people out watching and listening. Had there been any danger we would have moved you sooner.' The American nodded. There was nothing more to be said on the subject. He did not ask why they had helped him. Maybe the old man would not have been able to answer anyway.

That night he ate solid food for the first time since the pig, some sort of roasted meat, with a spicy sauce, vegetables, and goat's milk to drink. There was also freshly baked bread and piles of fruit. He ate where he had been cared for, in the Pholy's hut, meeting the rest of his family for the first time. The Pholy had four wives, the youngest of whom was the mother of the girl who had found him. It was obvious that she was his favourite child from the way he picked the choicest cuts of meat to share between her and the American. As well as seven daughters he had four sons. All of them were married with families of their own. Thu Suong was the last of his children and soon it would be her turn to leave the family hut.

After the meal he and the Pholy sat and talked into the night. He learned it was a three-day journey through the jungle to the American lines. In about a week's time he would be fit enough to make the journey. The Pholy offered one of his sons as a guide, but the American declined the offer. It would be safer for him to travel alone, and he knew the ways of the jungle. He did not want to be responsible for someone else's life as well as his own. He would find his own people. He determined to begin his preparation the following morning. He needed to be in the best shape possible for the journey.

He woke early the following morning and started some limbering-up exercises to get his slack muscles back into shape. The children watched him, amused. It was only when Angel, the name he had given to Thu Suong, began to copy him that the other children lined up and joined in, laughing and screaming with delight at his antics.

Thu Suong had passed her twelfth birthday and was considered a mature woman in the village. All that could be taught by her mother and stepmothers she had learnt to perfection. Soon she would have to find a husband. Several of the young men in the village had already spoken with her father about this, but she refused to choose. She did not want to get married and, because she was her father's favourite, he did not insist. Now that the American had come, the Pholy knew it would be even harder on the girl. It was obvious from the way she cared and looked after the American that if she could, she would choose him as her husband. She made new sandals for him. She made new clothes for him. She made sure he did not tire himself with his exercises, that he rested, that he ate and drank. She was never far from his side. It would, the Pholy knew, be a sad day for his daughter when the man left. But leave he would, never to return. He would probably never think of the child/woman who had found him in the jungle, but she would think about him, dream about him, wondering if he would ever return. Eventually, the Pholy knew, she would accept that he was gone for good and on that day she would begin to die.

For the remainder of the American's time with the Moi, Thu Suong was his constant companion. He could not remember the last time he had smiled over innocent pleasures, but she got him to smile, and to laugh. It was as if, for a short time anyway, the last six years had faded away and he was once again the young college boy, joking and laughing in the Californian sun. He never wanted to leave, but knew he must. Every day he stayed was more dangerous for these people. On the sixth day he told the Pholy he would be leaving in the morning.

Once again they sat talking, long into the night. He told the old man; 'When I return to the soldiers I will tell them of the help I received from your village. If you wish I will return with the soldiers and they will move the village down over the 17th Parallel.'

'No,' the Pholy shook his head, 'we have lived in this area for many many years. My people were here when the country was little known to foreigners, and was known as Nam Viet – the land of the Southern Viet

People. We were here when the Chinese conquered Nam Viet, and ruled the country for hundreds of years. By the time of the Tang Dynasty we were free of the Chinese. We held off in turn the Mongols, the Sung, Ming and Manchu emperors. Then the French came. Then the Japanese, and after them, but only for a short time, the English, who handed the country back to the French. Then our country was divided into two and the French were driven out. Now the Americans are here. They too will leave one day and the land will be re-united into one country, the land of Nam Viet once again. And my people will still be in this clearing. Invaders have come and gone, and will do so again, but in the end the people will be the same as before. Thank you for the offer, but we will stay where we are. This,' he indicated the jungle clearing and his village, 'is home.'

In the morning the entire village turned out to say goodbye to him. Before he left, he gave Angel a gift. It was a large wildflower of many colours that he had picked at the jungle edge before collecting his things together. The Pholy wished him a safe return to his people, and then it was time to go. His rucksack had been packed with food and his water-bottle filled with fresh drinking water. The Russian rifle had been cleaned several times over the past few days and was now loaded and hung from his shoulder by the canvas strap. There was nothing more to be said except thank you. Just before he entered the jungle he turned back. Only the old man and his daughter stood where he had left them, looking after him, she with the flower held gently in her hands, the old man with his arm round her shoulder. It was too far away for him to see that she was crying. He raised his hand and slowly waved from side to side. They waved back, and watched him disappear.

It was three hours before he took his first rest. Settled on his haunches, back against a tree, sipping from the water-bottle, he heard them coming. A long way off in the distance, like the humming of a swarm of angry bees. He knew these bees. He had called them often enough himself. These bees were armour-clad and carried many stings. In a few minutes they flew in battle formation over his position, the noise now more like thunder. They flew low, just above the tree-tops, two full squadrons of American gunships. Their 'stings' were .50 calibre armour-piercing rounds fired from the Browning machine-guns mounted on either side of the flying ships. With sudden clarity he realized where they were heading. Quickly packing his gear together he turned back, jogging at a pace he could once have kept up for hour after hour with a 50 pound pack strapped to his back. By the time he got there it was all over, the helicopters having passed him an hour earlier on their way back to their base.

All that remained of the village were burning ruins and dead bodies. The Pholy lay in the middle of the clearing, shot down with his arms spread wide in a futile effort to stop the slaughter of his people. Lying in a row, as they had tried to flee to the protection of the jungle, lay the bodies of his wives. All round the clearing were the bodies of the rest of the villagers, including the chickens and the goats. He didn't notice the tears at first and it was only when he had to wipe his eyes to see better that he realized he was crying. He moved from body to body, finding her eventually. She was lying on her stomach near the ruin of her father's hut, her head a mass of blood. At first he thought she was dead, but as he turned her over gently, she moaned. Clutched to her stomach, as though to protect it, was the flower he had given her that morning. Using water from his bottle he washed the blood from her head wounds and discovered that most of it was not hers. It came from the carcass of a nearby goat that had exploded on being hit by the .50 calibre rounds. She had been struck on the head and neck by a large chunk of wood that had been shot off the nearby hut. From her entire village of over 100 men, women and children, she was the sole survivor. Injured, but alive. Picking her frail body up in his arms he headed back into the jungle. They could not stay. It would not take the VC long to come investigating. But he no longer headed south. His new direction was west, towards Laos, then further west towards Thailand.

Several months later a letter-gram was delivered to a middle-class family living in a small coastal town in the State of California. The Department of Defence of the United States of America regretted to inform them that their son was 'Missing in Action', presumed dead, somewhere in the jungles of Vietnam. The letter-gram went on to explain how proud the President was of their son, and of the great sacrifice he, and they, had made for the country. Their son had already been awarded many military decorations which would be forwarded on to them shortly and the President was proud to tell them that he was also to be awarded the Congressional Medal of Honour, the highest award that could be given for valour. That was the last the family heard of the fresh-faced college kid who had done his country's bidding, and gone to war.

CHAPTER THREE

The Baltic Sea 1979

IT WAS 01:35. The dockyards and ferry terminal were ablaze with lights. The Danish passenger and car ferry, the *Kalundborg* was due to sail in fifteen minutes. The passengers were on board and the vehicles chained down, ready to sail. All that remained to be done was for the East German border-guards to disembark the ship. On his bridge, Kaptajn Larsen watched the activities of the guards with a weary smile. It was the same thing every trip. Before any ship could leave harbour it was searched for 'criminals', as the East Germans termed anybody who wished to defect to the West. The *Kalundborg* made the round trip four times daily and was subject to the same search each time.

She sailed from the town of Gedser on the Danish island of Falster, the most southern island in the Danish archipelago, to Warnemonde in East Germany. During the holiday season most of her passengers were Western, travelling to and from the Eastern Bloc countries on organized tours. Today the majority of the passengers were truck drivers, taking their huge articulated trucks and trailers to the East, delivering Danish products and returning with whatever the East had to offer for export. Sailing time from port to port was about 2 hours and 5 minutes, depending on weather conditions. On this trip the *Kalundborg* was due in Gedser at 04:00. At last

Kaptajn Larsen received the All Clear from the shore control. His ship had been searched, his passengers and vehicles checked, and nothing out of the ordinary found. He waved to the senior officer on the dock and gave the order to sail.

Easing her way slowly out of the harbour the *Kalundborg* headed for the open seas. It would be a quick crossing and the weather was clear and fine, with a full moon in a cloudless sky. It would not be all that long before Kaptajn Larsen and his crew would be tucked up in their beds at home.

They were half-way home. Larsen was still on the Bridge drinking coffee with 'Matros' – Able Seaman – Hansen. Behind them at the radar scanner was 'Styremand' – Mate – Steensbeck. All were silent, thinking of various mundane events in their lives, looking forward to getting ashore.

'Kaptajn.' The silence was broken by Steensbeck. 'I'm beginning to pick up something on the screen. Directly in front, very small, and stationary.' As the Captain crossed to look at the radar two more dots appeared on the screen. 'Two more, Kaptajn, travelling fast from our stern, on course for the first one.'

To both sailors the vision on the radar screen was as clear as a television picture. In front of them somebody was making an attempt at crossing from the East to the West. They had been spotted by the shore radar, and the other two 'dots' represented fast, East German patrol boats heading out to pick the smaller one up. 'What's our position?' Larsen asked.

'We are in international waters, Kaptajn, and so is he. The Germans will be entering it shortly as well.'

Hansen, the Matros, had turned and was watching the other two men. He heard the conversation and knew what it meant. A decision had to be made, and made fast. Time was running out for whoever was in the small boat in front of their ship. Larsen turned and smiled in his direction. 'Okay, Hansen, full steam ahead. Give her all she's got.' Turning back to Steensbeck he ordered him to keep a sharp eye on the approaching patrol boats. 'Sound the fog-horn, Hansen. Let's give whoever is in that boat a bit of encouragement.'

Both Hansen and Steensbeck smiled back at him. 'Aye Aye, Kaptajn,' they chorused together.

What Kaptajn Larsen intended was both tricky and dangerous. The patrol boats were closing fast and there was not going to be enough time to stop and lower a rescue boat to help. They were going to have to attempt to pick the escapee out of the water while still moving. The danger lay in the fact that they might run him down. The tricky bit was getting him out of the water from under the noses of the East Germans. Quite apart from the fact that they wished to help whoever was trying to escape, the Danes liked to tease the Germans – both East and West – as much as possible. The Danes had long memories, not only dating back to when they were occupied during World War II, but further back, when they lost a great portion of what had once been Denmark to Bismark.

Picking up the phone on the Bridge, Larsen rang down to the crew's quarters. Those not active for the crossing would be sitting drinking beer or coffee. He ordered two of them to the Bridge immediately. Pulling a switch near the phone, he turned on the huge spotlight mounted to the roof of the Bridge, playing the light out on to the water in front of them. It was too soon for those on the ferry to see the smaller boat, but the boat would be able to see them, and know help was on the way. Beside the Kaptajn, Hansen was playing with the fog-horn, smiling as it made its mournful wail. The two sømænd – seamen – ordered to the Bridge arrived and received their orders.

'Right lads, we've got ourselves a runner. He's floundering in a small boat directly in front of us. He's also got two hound-dogs on his tail. We don't have time to stop, so we're going to pick him up, using the hooks. Mortensen, you go forward and take the first one, Nicholaison, you go below to the car deck. Take up your position. Get the platform set up and get strapped in. If Mortensen misses, then you've got one, and only one, chance. We can't turn back, and if he enters our wash, he'll be swept aside. It's all we can do for the poor bugger. If we don't catch him, and we don't drown him, the Germans will get him. Go to it. We haven't much time.'

As the two seamen left, the Radio Operator arrived with a message for the Kaptajn. It came from one of the patrol boats, and warned the *Kalundborg* to stay clear. They were on their way to assist the smaller craft.

'Give that "Tysker" our position, our *exact* position, then repeat it. Tell him we are in international waters. Thank him for his concern and offer of assistance, but assure him that we can manage on our own. They'll ignore it and keep coming, but send the message anyway. Got it?'

'Aye, aye, Kaptajn.' The operator grinned and returned to his radio shack to send the message.

'I'll take over, Hansen.' Larsen moved over to take control of the wheel. 'I want to get as close as possible. Keep your eyes peeled and watch for him.'

Hansen now took over the searchlight, peering out into the darkness, moving the beam backwards and forwards in a narrow, tight, arc. As the light floated across the water he saw something, moved the light back, and there it was.

'There he is, Kaptajn,' he shouted, keeping the searchlight on the tiny rowing boat. A figure, dressed in black, stood in the middle of the small, black-painted boat, waving a white flag from side to side. Hansen reached once more for the fog-horn and played a tattoo on it.

At the bar on the passenger deck they had all heard the sound of the horn. As the night was clear, with no fog, the passengers drifted out on to the deck to see what all the noise was about. It was not long before they guessed what was happening. Looking to the rear of the ship they could see the lights of the speeding patrol boats, coming up on the port and starboard sides, closing fast. Seeing where the spotlight hit the water in front of the ship the passengers, almost all of them truckers, began to cheer.

Below on the car deck, just above the water-line, Nicholaison had removed the last porthole. Nearby stood a large wooden platform, which he dragged forward, placing it just under the porthole opening. On either side of the porthole two large metal rings had been soldered to the side of the ship. From a recess beneath the wooden platform he extracted a wide, heavy canvas belt, with two hooks stitched into the canvas, and a long length of rope with a three-pronged hook fitted to one end. A trucker, checking on his load, asked what was going on, and, when it was explained to him, asked how he could help. Nicholaison told him to take the end of the rope and secure it round the axle of a nearby truck. The seaman warned him to stand well clear of the slack. If they were lucky and caught the rowing boat, the slack would play out very very quickly. A leg caught in it would be broken like a matchstick and the attached body would be smashed against the side of the ship. While the trucker was fixing the rope, Nicholaison fitted the canvas belt round his waist, pulling it tight. He then connected the hooks hanging from the side of the belt to the rings by the opening. This was his own safety harness. Very soon he would be leaning out of the opening, attempting to catch a small boat from a fast moving ship. He had no desire to be dragged out of the porthole and into the Baltic! Satisfied that everything was ready, the seaman leant out of the ship, the rope with the pronged hook dangling beside him, to his right.

On the upper deck, at the bow, Mortensen was speaking through a megaphone. The wind was blowing his words back at him but he hoped some were getting through. He shouted in German, Danish and English. 'LIE FLAT IN THE BOAT, FACE DOWN. HANG ON TIGHT TO THE SIDES. WE ARE NOT STOPPING. I REPEAT. WE ARE NOT STOPPING. WE ARE GOING TO TRY AND HOOK YOU. LIE FLAT IN THE BOAT.'

At first the figure in black did not understand. He had seen the lights of the Danish ship and had heard the foghorn. Then, on either side of the larger ship, he could see the pin-pricks of light of the patrol boats, and his heart had sunk. So near, yet so far away! The Danish ship was not slowing, and looked like it was going to run him down. He could not believe it. Then he caught some of the words, distorted by the wind. He understood some of them. 'Lie down.' 'Not stopping.' 'Hook.' Then he realized what they were going to attempt to do. They were going to 'fish' him out of the water, or drag him all the way to Denmark.

On deck Mortensen saw the man get down into the small craft. It seemed like he understood. Dropping the megaphone he reached for a rope, similar to the one his crewmate Nicholaison was holding. With the pronged hook hanging over the side, the other end had already been lashed to one of the ship's bow restraining pins. He looked up at the Bridge and signalled with his arm that he was ready, then indicated to the Kaptajn that he should move the ship slightly to the port side. At that moment the Kaptajn ordered 'All engines stop'. This would slightly reduce the speed of the ship for a few vital seconds, giving the two seamen a better chance to catch the boat. He saw Mortensen drop the hook. He gave the order to 'Start all engines', then 'Full speed ahead', and smiled as Mortensen punched his fist in the air. They had a catch!

Below on the car deck, Nicholaison saw the boat come into view. The wind blew spray up into his face but he ignored it. He had been at sea all his life and had learned to peer with half-closed eyelids into the wind and rain. The ship's swell began to sweep the small boat further away from them. It was now or never. He threw the hook.

As he lay face down in the boat, the hook hit the man on the back, bounced off, then caught the side of the boat. He was praying it was strong enough to withstand the pressure of the 'pull' and would not fall to pieces. It held. Both hooks were caught fast. From merely bobbing on the calm water the boat now took off like a racing car from the grid. As it gathered speed, being pulled forward by the first hook caught in the bow, it was being dragged nearer and nearer the ship by the hook caught mid-stern, which was steadying it slightly. He hung on tightly. The muscles in his arms were screaming with pain but he would not let go. Never. Just as he thought he could no longer bear the pain, the boat slowed slightly and he could hear the cheering. High above him, men were leaning over the deck-rails, shouting at him in German.

'Hey, Fritz, why don't you buy a ticket like the rest of us?'

'Come on Fritz, the beer's getting warm and we have a few ready for you.'

While Mortensen pulled the rope taut at the bow, Nicholaison and the trucker began to reel in their catch. Nearer and nearer they dragged the small boat, until they had it beside the ship, just below the opening. Tying the rope fast, they helped the man crawl into the Danish ship. Both were smiling and clapping the man on the back. 'Welcome aboard, Tysker, you've made it. You're free.'

On the Bridge, Kaptajn Larsen instructed his radio operator to send two messages. The first one was to the East German patrol boats. 'Tell them the man is a Dane who went fishing and got swept out to sea. They won't believe it, but who gives a shit.' The second was to Gedser, asking for the police to be informed that the *Kalundborg* was arriving with an unexpected additional passenger.

In the small police station at Gedser, 'Betjentten' – Constable – Nils Sean White of the Danish Police was about to call it a night when the phone rang. After the call he put his jacket back on, secured the leather holster on his hip, took his hat, and went to his police car. He never minded these types of arrests. The man would be held in detention until the Criminal Police, who dealt with all foreigners in Denmark, came from Copenhagen to collect him. After an extended interview in the capital, the man would most likely be allowed to stay in Denmark, or apply for asylum in another Western country if he so wished. Whatever the outcome, the Danes had put one over on the Germans – again!

CHAPTER FOUR

Århus, Denmark, July 1994

THE NEWLY PROMOTED DETECTIVE SERGEANT
'COWBOY' JOHNSON had arrived that morning at
Copenhagen, from Dublin. He had almost missed his
connection to Tirstrup, in the north of Jutland. Nobody
had explained to him that while he had landed at the
International Airport, his connecting departure would
be from the Domestic, and that he had to walk or catch
an airport bus to get there. When he eventually found
out, he had made the flight with only minutes to spare.

He was in Denmark as the Irish representative for the
third annual conference of the International Police Federation, the IPF. This year the conference was being
held in Århus, Denmark's second largest city, and
Cowboy, along with many other delegates, was booked
into the Atlantic Hotel. In marked contrast to the more
'political' Interpol, the IPF was more effective and helpful to member countries. It had no headquarters, no
full-time staff and no red tape. While not officially
recognized by any government, neither was it frowned
upon by any, and each year one member country would
host the conference.

While, like Interpol, the IPF had no powers of arrest,
it got results by cutting through the political paperwork
by the simple use of the telephone and the fax. If, for example, a known criminal was spotted boarding a plane

from London to Düsseldorf, this might result in a faxed message to the Düsseldorf Police Headquarters telling of his imminent arrival. His previous form and illegal inclinations might, where possible, also be sent. Requests for assistance in surveillance could be made from country to country. In some cases criminals were met at their airports of destination, informed that they were not welcome, and sent back to their ports of embarkation by return flight. In other words, the IPF worked as a large 'Old Boys' network. The conference was a way of bringing together representatives of member states to air their problems and find areas in common where they could work together. Ideas were discussed and exchanged, new contacts made and old ones renewed.

His hotel room was on the fourth floor with a view over the harbour and ferry terminal. The Copenhagen ferry sailed from here to Kalundborg, on the island of Sjælland, where the Copenhagen train awaited. The room was similar to millions of other hotel rooms throughout the world, functional and reasonably comfortable.

After showering, dressed in his own towelling dressing gown, he was reading the information pack and drinking coffee sent up by room service, when there was a knock on his door. On opening it he found himself looking at a tall, casually dressed, smiling man. Cowboy's police-trained eyes gave him the once over. Late forties to early fifties, mousey-blond hair with streaks of grey in it, slightly puffy cheeks, brown eyes, and the mark of a policeman, boxer, or roughneck criminal – a broken nose.

'Detective Sergeant Johnson?' the man asked in fluent English.

'Yes,' he replied.

The man stuck his hand out. 'Welcome to Denmark. I

am what they call "Kriminalassistant", which is basic-ally Inspector, and my name is Nils Sean White, Danish Criminal Police. Better call me Sean – it'll be easier on your tongue. I'm your host for the next few days.'

Cowboy smiled in return and grasped the proffered hand, asking Sean to come in.

'Thanks for calling by – and what sort of a name is that for a Dane to be using? Am I mistaken, or do I actually hear a hint of an *Irish* accent? Dublin, in fact.'

Sean laughed. 'Spot on. I'm half-Irish, half-Danish. My father was Irish, from Dublin. They call me Nils here in Denmark, but I use Sean when in England and Ireland. It's easier.' They both laughed as Cowboy closed the door behind him.

'I saw your name on the list of Reps and I thought I'd offer my services as your host. I was actually waiting for you to arrive downstairs, but I got called to the phone. Missed you as you checked in. I thought I'd leave it a bit, give you time to unpack and shower before I came up. Looks like I came a bit too early.'

'No problem. I was just reading the information pack, wondering whether to eat in the hotel or take a look at the city and eat out. So, thanks for calling. Fancy a drink?'

Sean smiled and produced a half-bottle of Irish whis-key from his jacket pocket. 'As the host, I insist on buying the first round. Got any glasses?'

Cowboy got the two mouthwash glasses from the bathroom and Sean poured a generous measure into each of them. Handing one to Cowboy he raised his own glass in salute.

'Céad Mile Fáilte, Sláinte, and as my Danish half would say, "Skol" – One hundred thousand welcomes, and health.'

31

'Sláinte Leat,' Cowboy replied – 'the same to you.' They drained their glasses.

Cowboy indicated the armchairs by the coffee table and both men sank into them. Sean topped the glasses up.

'So, what's a half-Mick doing in the Danish police force?' Cowboy asked.

'Well, I'm a fully fledged Dane now. I took Danish nationality on my eighteenth birthday. Felt more at home here, having spent all my life in the country. I spent most of my school summer holidays with my Irish grandparents in Dublin, which would explain the accent with my English. As for being a policeman? Seemed like a good idea at the time. Haven't regretted it so far.'

'Are you married, Sean? Kids?'

'Was, am sort of, and yes – in that order.'

'Now that *is* the Irish side of you coming through,' Cowboy laughed. 'Ask a simple question and get a riddle in reply.'

'Yea, I know,' Sean replied, also laughing. 'I *was* married, but it didn't work out. I have a son, sixteen he is now. Lives with his mother in Copenhagen. She married a second time and the guy's nice enough. Treats my boy like his own, so I have no complaints. I get to see the boy about twice a month, and he spends a few weeks with me each summer and at New Year. He spends Jul – Christmas – with his mother, but comes to me for the New Year. That's a big thing here, New Year. Fireworks going off all through the night, all over the country. It's a really festive time.

'As for the "sort of", that means I have a live-in girl-friend. We've been together about five years now. What they call in Danish a 'papirløsægteskab' – a paperless marriage. Mette and I like things as they are, and as they

32

say, if it's not broken, don't fix it! Mette's a nurse at the city hospital. What about you?'

'Pretty much like you, but without the marriage and the kid bit . . .'

'*Now* who's being Irish?' Sean laughed.

'Okay,' Cowboy laughed in reply, 'but I'm *fully* Irish! But yea, there's a great woman in my life too. Her name's Marlane. We've been together for several years. We're not married, but it's on the cards we will be some day. We each still have our own apartments, but that's mainly because of our work. She's a model and goes off on assignments all over the world. We never seem to get enough time to find a place we both like. But, like you say, what's not broken doesn't need fixing. The relationship is a bit unusual, but it works for us.'

'A model, eh? Some guys get all the luck.'

Cowboy laughed. 'It's not all that great, believe me. She's away quite a bit, working as hard as she can before her career ends. But . . . I must admit, I do enjoy the looks I get sometimes when we're out, like the "what the hell's he got that I haven't?" glances from some blokes you meet. I love watching some of them trying to move in if I go to the loo. Lane – that's what I call her – has a great way of putting them down. Cracks me up sometimes. But enough about that. Are you hungry? Expected home, or can we eat together?'

'No problem,' Sean replied. 'Mette's on night-duty this week, so I have to look after myself. Do you like Italian?'

'Love it.'

'Great. Get dressed and I'll take you to the best Italian restaurant here in town.'

Two hours later the two men had finished one of the best Italian meals Cowboy had ever eaten and were having *cappuccinos*, while Sean smoked one of his small Danish cigars. Cowboy declined a cigar and lit a cigarette. 'Mamma Mia's' was located on Clems St., one of the narrow side-streets off Søndergade and Clements Torv, the main shopping thoroughfare of the city, known as the 'Gå Gade' or pedestrian precinct. Most of the small side-streets were filled with intimate bars, restaurants or boutiques. On arrival, Sean was treated as a long lost son, despite the fact that he and Mette had eaten there only a week or so earlier. Cowboy watched in amazement as his friend conversed in fluent Italian with their host, introduced to him as Francisco. The waitresses and barman also smiled a welcome to the Danish policeman.

During the meal the two men had got to know a little bit more about each other. 'How did you get the nickname Cowboy?' Sean asked.

'I got it from my father's best friend, a man I always refer to as Uncle Ron,' he explained, 'because of my childhood preference for always playing Cowboys and Indians. Despite the fact that the character I always chose was the Indian, he called me Cowboy and it stuck. My background is unusual for a policeman. My father was pretty wealthy and always assumed that his only son would follow him into the family business. With that in mind he had encouraged me to study law. I did it willingly – but not for the reasons he believed. As long as I can remember, I had wanted to be a policeman. My ambition was to join the ranks of the Criminal Investigation Branch, the CIB, of the Garda Síochàna, the Irish Police. I never had to break this to my Dad because he died of a heart attack before I finished my studies. I inherited a considerable amount of money and could have lived quite comfortably, but I still had this ambition. I got my transfer to the CIB from uniform and my later promotion within the CIB through hard graft, same as everybody else.' What Cowboy did not mention to Sean was that he was considered something of a celebrity policeman by the newspapers in Ireland, being invited to all the right places and parties. Having a beautiful girlfriend had only served to amplify his newsworthiness.

Eager to stop talking about himself, a subject which he always found embarrassing, he asked Sean about his language ability. Coming from a lazy race, who often couldn't even be bothered to learn Gaelic, their own native tongue, Cowboy was impressed by the other's ability.

'Languages are rather my speciality,' Sean admitted. 'Having been reared in a bilingual household, they seem to come easy. Swedish and Norwegian are merely dialects of the original Scandinavian language, just like Danish. In school I took French instead of English, and German, and became fluent in both. I can also converse fluently in High Spanish, and can understand and be understood in the South American dialects. It came in quite handy when I was stationed in Copenhagen. Over the years Denmark has accepted many political refugees from the dictatorships of South America. Some of these refugees had been involved in drug-running. I operated for a while as an undercover policeman in bars and nightclubs around the city, and I was able to pick up a lot of useful information. I also spent many nights locked up in city jails as a "drunk", listening to conversations between the South Americans. I took up studying other languages as a hobby and now I'm pretty fluent in Hungarian and Czechoslovakian as well.'

'What the bloody hell are you doing in the police?' asked an astounded Cowboy.

Sean laughed. 'The police is my *work*, and languages

35

are my hobby. I enjoy both of them. I could have gone further with my education, possibly studied to be an interpreter, but it wasn't a field I was particularly interested in. I love my work, and as long as that lasts I'll stay a copper. Maybe, when I retire, I might do something with my language abilities.'

They sat drinking several *cappuccinos* and glasses of Sambuca which, despite Sean's protestations, Francisco had insisted were on the house, before going back to the Atlantic, where Cowboy invited Sean for a nightcap in the hotel's bar and he accepted.

The bar was filled with policeman from all over Europe, plus several bewildered businessmen. As they pushed their way through to the bar, Cowboy heard his name being called.

'Cowboy! Hey, Cowboy. Over here.'

Turning in the direction of the voice he gave a theatrical groan, slapping his forehead with the palm of his hand. 'Ooooh no. Not *him*.' But the smile on his face belied his displeasure. 'Bang goes an early night, Sean. Come on over here and meet a London gorilla.'

Detective Inspector Jimmy Douglas of New Scotland Yard was sitting in a window booth, waving in their direction. He and Cowboy greeted each other with handshakes and punches to the shoulders. Introductions were exchanged and room was made at the table for the two newcomers. Jimmy had spent the last hour trying to converse with two Swedish businessmen who shared his table.

'Thank Christ for somebody who can speak the Queen's English, even if it has to be with a bloody Irish accent. I've been trying to get a pint of best bitter here for the past hour, and all they keep shoving in my glass is lager. Never mind. What'll it be, boys?' With foaming

36

glasses of draft Carlsberg in front of them, Cowboy, Sean and Jimmy relaxed.

As the drinks flowed, the stories began. First it was jokes, several of which seemed to be international. The Irish told the same jokes about the Kerrymen that the English told about the Irish, that the Americans told about the Poles, that the Danes told about the people from the city of Århus. But some were new and the laughter was loud. Jimmy was coming off worst in the joke line, because Sean and Cowboy had teamed up together. Eventually Jimmy gave up. He couldn't compete with one-and-a-half-Irishmen!

After the jokes, they moved on to funny incidents which had occurred during arrests and trials. At some stage one of them asked about the easiest arrest, trial and conviction, the other two knew of or had been involved with.

'That's an easy one for me,' Cowboy replied. 'Couple of years before I joined the CIB there was a dilly of a case. Murder. Made all the headlines at the time, English as well as Irish. Big financier in Dublin got himself shot to death by his chauffeur in front of about a dozen witnesses. Not only that, but the chauffeur arrived back on the scene an hour later, even before the police had finished taking statements! He denied everything and said he had just arrived. Witnesses called him a liar to his face – and in court – saying they had watched him shoot his boss as he got off the train, and then drive off before anybody could stop him. The weapon was found in the chauffeur's home and the motive also.'

'What was the motive?' Sean asked.

'The victim – O'Brien I think his name was – had been a Major in the Irish Guards during the War and the chauffeur, Connelly, or something like that, had been his batman. After the war, O'Brien gave him the job of chauffeur. In point of fact, there was more to the relationship than employer/employee. They were friends. O'Brien was best man at his driver's wedding and godfather to the daughter that followed after. An only child. She died in London when she was about sixteen years old. Accidental drugs overdose. First time she tried some really hard stuff. The motive was the daughter. Really explicit pornographic photographs of the girl, taken when she was only about eleven or twelve, were found in O'Brien's den. Along with the gun, the photos were enough to send him down. He's doing life in Port Laoise maximum security.' His tale finished, Cowboy drained his glass and placed it in front of Jimmy.

'Okay, okay, I get the hint. But I vaguely remember that case, and the reason I remember it was my Governor at the time said that he had been involved on a case a couple of years before where the killer returned to the scene of the murder almost immediately. I mean, they do say that a murderer always returns to the scene of the crime – but an *hour* later! That's truly *begging* to be lifted. Same again? Right. Back in a minute.'

While Jimmy went to get the drinks, Cowboy decided to visit the loo, so neither of them noticed the frown that creased the brow of the Danish policeman. With his mind slightly fuzzied with alcohol Sean couldn't quite put his finger on what was bothering him. It wasn't something either of the other two had said. It was something another man had told him, quite a few years earlier, that he was trying to recall. He pushed it out of his mind when the others returned and they continued drinking and telling more stories until 3.00 a.m. While Sean staggered off to find a taxi home, the other two swayed their way to the elevator, hoping that they could find their rooms.

CHAPTER FIVE

Denmark, July 1994

IT WAS TWO DAYS LATER that Sean remembered what it was that had bothered him that first night at the bar. After making a couple of phone calls he went to see the others.

'Listen you guys, tomorrow is the end of the show and most of it will be taken up with everybody saying how nice we Danes are and how well we've looked after you all, blah, blah, blah. Do you fancy doing something that I think you will both find very interesting instead?'

'What's up?' Jimmy asked. 'Porno movies?'

'Better than that, Jimmy. I promise.'

'What've you got up your sleeve, Sean?' Cowboy asked.

'I want to take both of you for a drive. To meet somebody. On the way you'll see a nice bit of Denmark, and I guarantee that the story you'll hear will make you both sit up and listen. Are you on?'

It was agreed.

The following morning, sharp at 10.00, Cowboy and Jimmy were standing in the hotel foyer when Sean arrived, tooting the car horn from outside the main door. A few minutes later Sean's Volvo reached Viby, a suburb of the city, and was heading towards the E45 motorway going south.

Shortly before 11.00 they stopped at a petrol station

with a cafeteria, just south of the town of Vejle. Here they had coffee and Danish pastries. 'This pastry,' Sean explained, 'for which Denmark is so famous, is not in fact Danish at all. Here we call it "vienerbrød" – Viennese bread, or pastry. Many years ago the Danish bakers went on strike, so their employers imported bakers from Vienna. After the strike many of them stayed and married Danish girls. They also taught the Danish bakers how to make the pastry. They then went on to make it world-famous. So, everywhere, except here in Denmark, it is known as Danish pastry.'

'That has a ring of Irish-ness to it, Sean. No wonder your old man felt at home here.'

'For that remark, Jimmy, you get the pleasure of paying the bill!'

Coffee finished and car tanked up, they set off again. They left the motorway at the Vandrup exit, near Kolding, continuing their journey on the back roads, passing farm after farm, driving through the lush pastureland of Southern Jutland. They could have continued further by motorway, but Sean, spending most of his time in the city, loved to drive through the countryside. At Toftlund they turned south for the village of Agerskov, and were now only 40 kilometres from the land border with Germany. Turning right into the village by a large furniture store complex named 'GG Møbler' they drove through the main street, pulling into the driveway of a small, two-storied house with a sharp-sloping roof. As Sean applied the handbrake, the door to the house opened and a smiling man in shirt-sleeves stood waiting to greet them. Getting out of the car, Sean took his hand.

'*Goddag Nils. Velkommen til Sonderjylland, og Agerskov.*'

'*Goddag, Jens, Tak. Jeg tror vi må heller snakke engelsk. Mine to venner snakker ingen danske.*' Sean then introduced the other two to their host. 'Cowboy, Jimmy, this is Jens Larsen, the man you have come to meet.'

'Welcome to my home, gentlemen. Please come inside and meet my wife. She is preparing a small lunch for us. First we eat, then we talk. Okay?' He continued smiling as he shook hands with the other two, then led the way into the narrow hallway that opened directly into the kitchen. Here they met his wife, Ane. She smiled and stood to one side so they could all enter the 'L'-shaped living room, with the dining table set for lunch.

Cold meats and sliced sausages were laid out on plates in the centre of the table, along with several bottles of local beer and mineral water. In an ice-cooler stood another bottle with a skin of melting ice. This one Cowboy and Jimmy knew only too well. They had been introduced to ice-cold snaps back in Århus by Sean.

The next forty minutes were spent eating and chatting. The meal had started with 'Sil', which Jimmy described as tasting 'wonderful, almost on par with the local Danish hot dogs'. The look on his face when told by Jens that it was raw, marinated herring, made the others laugh. But, having tried it and liked it, Jimmy carried on eating. After the Sil on rye bread came the warm liver-pâté, covered with crispy fried bacon and champignons. After that the choice was from the centre of the table. The snaps was drunk with the fish and beer with the remainder. As a dessert Ane had prepared a fresh-fruit cocktail, served in whipped cream and eaten on white, French bread. The three guests thanked their host and hostess for a truly wonderful meal. While Ane went to the kitchen to prepare coffee, the men moved across to the nest of sofas surrounding a large, glass-topped coffee table. Cigarettes and cigars were lit and

Sean began to explain to the others why he had brought them there.

'Do you remember the first night we met, and were getting sloshed in the bar? You, Cowboy, told a story of a murderer who had returned to the scene of the crime shortly after it had been committed, and denied all knowledge of it. And you, Jimmy, knew of a similar case in London. Something bothered me. I knew somebody had told me about something like this before. Years ago. It took me a couple of days to recall who it was. It was Jens. First I will tell you a little about him, and then he can tell you the rest of the story. Is that okay with you, Jens?' Sean looked across the coffee table at the other man, who nodded his head in agreement.

'Jens Larsen is not his name. He was born Alexander Havel, in Czechoslovakia. In 1979 he fled to the West, getting out via East Germany. He tried to sail across the Baltic in a small row-boat and was picked up by a Danish ferry, right under the noses of several East German patrol boats. I was stationed at Gedser, on the island of Falster at the time, where the ferry docked, and I took him into custody when he landed. Everybody had assumed he was East German. Although he spoke good German, I could tell from his accent that he wasn't. When he told me where he came from and found out I could speak Czech, he opened up more.

'He had to be taken to Copenhagen for a complete debrief and, for a short while, because of the relationship that had formed, and because I spoke Czech, I was seconded to our Intelligence Services and took part in the debrief. Before I could bring you two here today I had to get clearance. I spoke to a contact in the IS who okayed it, and then I phoned Jens, who said he was prepared to meet you and tell you what he told me all those years ago. Now you know the background, I'll let Jens carry on.'

'Thank you, Nils. I changed my name, gentlemen, after I got permission to stay in Denmark. I was afraid that somebody might come after me. Not that I had any great secrets to trade you understand. But sometimes they came after refugees just for spite, and to deter others from trying to cross over. You were an enemy of the State and they could get you if they wanted. So, I changed my name as a precaution.

'Ah, Ane, thank you, my dear. Coffee, gentlemen?'

Ane arrived bearing coffee, cups and saucers, cream, sugar and a plate of 'småkager' – homemade biscuits. Jens helped her pass out the cups and saucers, poured the coffee, then Ane left the men to their business.

'You will help me if I get stuck for words, yes, Nils? Thank you. Before I left Czechoslovakia I was a State employee in the Police Department. The Administration Branch and not, like you gentlemen, a, what would you say, "active" policeman? My colleagues and I did all the charge sheets, filing, all the mundane tasks that are part of police work. There was nothing unusual in my job. Everybody worked for the State in one way or the other. After the fall of Dubcek, things were pretty bad for a while. Our so-called Soviet "assistants" showed themselves to be our real bosses. Many arrests were made and many people simply "moved" to somewhere else – but were never seen nor heard of again. The way to survive was to keep your eyes, ears and mouth shut. We were like those three little monkeys – what is it they are called? "See no Evil, Hear no Evil, Speak no Evil". The whole nation was like that. But, like most things, as the dust settles, things relax a little, and we went back to our old pretence that we ourselves made the decisions that affected our country. The Soviets stepped back a

43

little into the shadows and the whole thing was pretty much like it was before Dubcek.

'About 1976 we once again tried for a little more freedom. A man tried to start a . . . what is *"fagforening"* in English, Nils?'

'Trade union,' Sean prompted.

'Ah yes, of course, a trade union – I only remember the word in Czech or Danish. Sorry. But to go on. This man started a trade union. Nothing very big or great to start with, but, oak trees begin as tiny acorns, no? This man, Vaclav Tomanek, was a lot like Lech Walesa in Poland. Very popular, and his small union went from strength to strength. But slowly, you understand. We all remembered what had happened to Mr Dubcek. Before the authorities really knew what had happened there was a national movement, with Tomanek at the head. His Number Two was his best friend, Leonid Husak. They said that Husak was the only man that Tomanek really trusted.

'Although they were harassed several times and in several ways, these were really only minor problems. The trade union was growing – had grown – and Tomanek was so popular that had the authorities arrested him, riots would have broken out, and the country would have been in chaos once again.'

Before continuing he refilled the coffee cups.

'It was in late '78, around September I think, that the whole thing exploded. Husak walked into the small building that was used as the Union headquarters, and in front of many witnesses, shot his friend and leader, Vaclav Tomanek. While everybody was still in shock, he walked out again. The police arrived very quickly and tried to establish what had happened. Even they were shocked when told that it was Husak who had murdered his friend. They couldn't believe it. But the witnesses all knew Husak, they had worked with him for months. Many were his friends. There was no mistake. He was the one.

'Then, while the police were still at the scene taking statements, in walks Husak! Seeing the crowds and the police he knew something had happened, he later claimed, and thought the police had come to arrest his friend. He was of course immediately arrested for the murder. He roared it was a lie, that the State Police must have shot Tomanek and were now trying to frame him. Witnesses said he looked physically shocked to be accused by people he had worked with, his friends and colleagues. He couldn't believe it, couldn't understand it. There never was a trial. According to the police, Husak was shot trying to escape custody. The pistol used in the shooting was found in his home, along with a large quantity of American dollars. Nobody could really explain any of it, but the general belief was that the two men had argued – although nobody witnessed any such argument – over the leadership of the movement. The entire country – even abroad – was shocked over the murder, and over the person who did it. The only man who was capable of taking over the leadership of the movement in the event of the death of Tomanek, was Husak – and he was now dead, shot trying to escape punishment for *killing* Tomanek. And so, the movement just laid down and died. It was all over, once again.'

Both Cowboy and Jimmy had listened, amazed at what they had heard. What the hell was going on, Cowboy wondered. There was the case in Ireland of the murderer returning to the scene almost immediately, Jimmy knew of one in London – and here they were listening to yet a third! He turned to Sean, to ask him a question, only to be stopped before he could ask.

'Just hang on a sec, Cowboy. The best bit is yet to

come. Carry on, Jens. Tell them about the Christmas party.'

Jens nodded, and continued.

'Although Christmas, as we know it here in the West, is not a holiday – or at least wasn't – behind the Curtain, in my country we always remembered our very own "Good King Wenceslas". Why should we have forgotten him when he is remembered all over the world? So, we held parties. Even the Russian "advisors" liked parties.

'It was the Christmas after the death of Tomanek. As usual, everybody was drunk, everybody was enjoying themselves, even the Russians. They tried to be everybody's friend, but the conversation seemed to just dry up whenever they came near one group or another. So, in the end, they went and sat in the corner with a couple of bottles of vodka. They were sitting on one side of a filing cabinet and I, on the way to being drunk myself, was lying on the other side. I don't think they knew or cared that I was there. Perhaps they were too drunk to notice.

'It was a requirement in all the East Bloc countries that we learn Russian in school, I suppose based on the principle that it was easier for all of us to learn that one language, than have the poor Russians have to learn several. So I speak Russian. They talked of many things. Of home, of their families, of food – everybody talks about food, especially when there is not all that much of it – and this and that. I ignored them. Who was interested in listening to that sort of thing? But then I heard them mention Tomanek and Husak. So I listened.

'They talked about how clever they had been – the authorities I mean, not the two drunks. About how clever they had been in . . . in killing two birds with one rock, I believe is the expression to use. In one swoop they had got rid of both of these men. Tomanek was killed, and

Husak was blamed. Because it was Husak that had done the killing there were no riots in the streets accusing the government of collusion with the Russians. Nobody cared either that Husak was killed trying to escape. There had been too many non-governmental witnesses, people who could not have been bribed to tell lies about what they saw, for it all to have been a Russian plot. The two drunks laughed over how cleverly it had been done. Of course it could have been done the other way too. Tomanek could have killed Husak – but they had a better "motive" for Husak to want to kill the other – to take over and get control of the Union.

'Tomanek had *not* been killed by his friend. He had been killed by a professional killer who had impersonated Husak. In the aftermath of confusion he was able to walk away. Everybody was too stunned to move and this gave the killer just enough time to get out of the building. And then, shortly afterwards, the real Husak walked in, into the trap that had been laid for him. The money and the murder weapon were then found in Husak's apartment. Put there, I suppose, while he was being held by the police. Two birds, one rock. The best part of it all was that the killer was an American. Had things gone wrong, well, he could have been arrested for the killing and the blame could have been laid to rest at the feet of American Imperialism. The plan was foolproof. The Russians paid this American one million dollars for his work. In comparison to the damage that would have been done by strikers and riots, with the resulting loss of production, had the Russians themselves done the killings, the amount was a mere drop in the ocean. My two drunken Russian "friends" even mentioned that the code name for the killer was "The Chameleon".'

Both Sean and Jens stared at the other two men as Jens finished his tale. Bewilderment was plain to see on their faces. Cowboy blinked rapidly as his brain went into overdrive trying to absorb the implications of what he had just heard. Three cases, each in a different country. The prime suspect returning to the scene within the hour, witnesses identifying and accusing him, and the suspect denying everything. Weapons and motives found within a short space of time. Three identical murders, three different countries, committed over a period of years – and, from the lips of two drunken Russians, third hand, the name of a professional killer! It was almost too much to accept. But the MO for each was the same. If the one in Czechoslovakia was the work of a hit man, then so were the other two. Which meant that the man serving a life sentence in Port Laoise jail was innocent, as was the man in England.

'Jens, I'm sorry to question your story – but are you seriously trying to tell us that there is a professional killer, an American, code named The Chameleon, who not only makes the hit, but provides a patsy for the job as well?'

Jens looked across to Sean. 'What is this "patsy", Nils?'

'Somebody to take the blame for another's action,' Sean replied.

'Then the answer to your question, Cowboy, is yes. Husak was this "patsy" you mention, and he died shortly afterwards. He would have been shot in any case, what with all the evidence against him. But being shot while he tried to escape meant there was no trial, no asking of unwanted questions. Yes, this professional killer does exist. Or did.'

CHAPTER SIX

Dublin, July 1994

ON THE MORNING AFTER HIS RETURN from Denmark, Cowboy asked for a confidential meeting with his superior, Commander Frank Mooney of the Criminal Investigation Branch.

The relationship between the two men was special, like father and son. For Cowboy, Mooney had come to represent the father he had lost, and for Mooney and his wife Marjory, Cowboy was the child they never had. Neither of them discussed this bond with each other or with anyone else.

Cowboy's recent promotion to Sergeant had been a problem for Frank. He knew that Cowboy deserved his promotion, but also that others knew of the special relationship between the two men. He did not wish to appear to be offering favours. It was Marj, his wife, who had spelled it out for him. 'If he doesn't deserve it, don't give it to him, Frank. If he does, then promote him, and to hell with anybody else.' Cowboy got his promotion, and not one word was spoken against it – at least not that Mooney knew of.

'Hi, Chief. Thanks for seeing me,' Cowboy said as he closed the door to Frank's office behind him. Frank had given up long ago trying to get Johnson to stop calling him 'Chief', as though he wore a feathered war-bonnet. He was used to it by now. 'Here, can you take these home to Marj. I'm sure she'll like them.' He handed over a tin of Danish Butter Cookies. 'These are the real thing, tell her. All the way from the land of the Danes. Here, I got you something too.' From his inside pocket he produced a small packet of Danish cigars, and dropped them on the desk. Frank mumbled a thank you and the cigars disappeared into his top drawer. For years now he had been a secret smoker. He had promised his wife he had given up, but was unable to completely forgo the habit. As an Inspector he had been known to haunt the corridors of CIB headquarters in Dublin Castle looking for unsuspecting smokers he could cadge one off. He never could understand why some people – all of them smokers – seemed to disappear on sighting him.

'So. How was the trip? Anything good come of it?'

Cowboy gave him a brief run-down on everything the IPF had covered during the conference, mentioning a few contacts that had been made, plus a few of the lighter moments of the three-day event. 'But that's not the reason I wanted to speak to you. Something happened while I was there.' He proceeded to tell Frank of the trip he and Jimmy had made, with the Danish policeman, to visit Jens Larsen. Story finished, he asked Frank if it reminded him of anyone, or any particular case, in Ireland.

'The O'Brien case,' Frank replied without hesitation. His brow furrowed in thought as he leaned back in his chair, staring at the ceiling. Going through his mind, like data on a flickering computer screen, were all the events of the case.

'You know, Cowboy, Colloney was the only man I ever arrested for murder that I personally believed didn't do it. It was one of those gut feelings. I was elated by how easily we found the weapon and motive – photographs of his young daughter taken in pornographic poses – but, even with all the evidence stacked against him, even with my own brain telling me he *had* to have done it, my heart was telling me he didn't. But there was nothing I could do. Now this.'

Cowboy sat silently, allowing the other man to relive the case, waiting for him to speak again.

'If this Chameleon exists, what can we do to prove it?'

'I've been thinking of nothing else since I heard the story myself, Frank, and the conclusion I have come to is that if it *was* a professional hit, then something has to have been rigged, to set Colloney up. We can't dispute the gun. Forensic proved it was the murder weapon, and it was found, if I remember correctly, where Colloney could have left it. That only leaves the photographs. Was any check made on them?'

'Why should there have been? Colloney denied ever seeing them, as did his wife. In fact both of them cried when they saw them. That was one of the things I remember most about Colloney. When we showed them to him, the look on his face was one of total disbelief. It was as if we had just kicked him in the stomach. My own instinct at that time was that this was the first time he had ever seen them. His wife threw up when she saw them. Could they have been doctored in some way?'

'Well, I'm no photographer, Frank, but Marlane has told me how photographers can touch up negatives, hiding blemishes and lines, cutting out unsightly bulges. One of the things she always says is that the expression "The camera never lies" is a load of bull. In the professional world they can easily be made to show whatever you want. So yes, I think they could have been doctored. And there's only one way to find out – have them checked.'

'Are you saying what I think you're saying, Cowboy?'

51

'Yea. I want to retrieve the evidence and have the photos checked, and if they *have* been tampered with, I want to take this further. This Danish copper, Sean White, is getting this guy Jens Larsen to make an affidavit over what he knows. It will be in Danish, but Sean will provide a sworn translation of it. He is also trying to contact an old CIA contact from his time with the Danish Intelligence Unit. The reasoning being that if this Chameleon is an American, and the Russians used him, then it's odds on that the CIA might know about him.'

'If they knew about him, maybe he doesn't exist anymore.'

'I'll bet that if they knew about him they used him themselves. Part of the problem is going to be in getting them to admit that he exists – or existed – in the first place.'

Frank got to his feet and paced up and down his small office. He was doing something that he had taught Cowboy to do; to forget emotions and personalities and try to think like the opposition, using cold logic. 'Make your lists,' he always said. 'For and Against, and tick each one off, balancing and counter-balancing each one as best you can. Eventually you will come to the core problems that have to be solved one way or the other, then from that point onwards you have a priority and a direction to move in.'

He continued, 'We have a case that is now . . . what? Seven, eight years old. Not only that, but it is a case that has been solved. One man, Colloney, kills another man, O'Brien, because O'Brien had dirty pictures of his daughter. In his mind's eye Colloney sees more than the photos. He imagines them being taken and everything that might have happened afterwards. It sends him over the top. So he gets a gun and kills O'Brien. Does it in front of a dozen witnesses, each one positive in their ID of the killer. Not one was hesitant about identifying him. As prosecutor I have motive, opportunity, weapon, and unbreakable witnesses. What have you got?' Cowboy made to answer, but Mooney raised a hand indicating he should be silent.

'For the defence we have a story told by a refugee from the East. The man himself admits that when he heard the story he was drunk, and was listening to two other drunks. The story comes from two Russians, a nation this refugee has every reason to hate. Maybe the guy felt he had to come up with *something* to be allowed to stay in the West, and not be handed back to his own authorities. If he was debriefed by the Danes, then you can bet your last dollar that he was also interviewed by the Americans, which means the CIA. An American citizen, a professional hit-man, carrying out a job for the Russians! That should interest the Yanks, don't you think? And yet, a couple of years later a murder is committed in London with the same sort of trade mark as our man? And a few years later, yet another one, in Dublin!

'If the Americans knew about him – which we can only assume they did – and investigated him, and he managed to pull off at least two more jobs that we can say carry his very own brand *after* the investigation, then we can only assume that the Americans have been or are using him themselves. So nothing will come from that quarter. We are back to our refugee. No grounds to reopen a closed case. Right?'

'Correct,' Cowboy agreed, 'unless . . .'

'Unless we can disprove some of the evidence against one of the convicted men. But even that is not enough. If Colloney didn't do it, and the Chameleon did, then who paid him to, and why?'

'We have to know first if the photographs were faked.'

Frank nodded. 'Agreed. Do it, Cowboy. Find them, and get them to forensic and see what they can tell us.'

'I don't want them checked by the Lab boys, Frank. I want to get them done privately, and I know just the people who can help me there. If I take them to the Lab, the very nature of them will get them talked about, and the more they are talked about, the more the word spreads. Which means that some nosy newspaper reporter is going to get wind of it. *If* the photos have been tampered with, and *if* we can reopen the case, then we don't want the Chameleon's paymaster knowing about it until we have more to go on. Do you agree?'

'Point taken, Cowboy. Get 'em done privately.'

Cowboy got to his feet. 'Thanks, Frank.'

'Don't thank me, Cowboy. If Colloney is innocent, I'm the man who sent him down. Somebody set *me* up as well.'

Powerscourt Townhouse Centre is a small, elegant Georgian mall situated on South William Street, on the south side of the city centre, nestling between two of Dublin's busiest shopping streets, Grafton Street and George Street.

Cowboy was sitting with Martyn Wright in the back room of Stringer and Wright, Photographers, drinking coffee, while Martyn studied the photographs Cowboy had brought. Each picture showed a pretty child of about twelve years of age, naked, and in various explicit and pornographic poses. Martyn whistled through his teeth as he looked at them.

'Christ, Cowboy, where the hell did you get these from? I didn't think this was your sort of scene.'

'It's not, dickhead. I want you to check these photos very carefully. I think they were tampered with, and I want you to find out. I also want you to keep your mouth shut tight on this one, Martyn. It's business, and I need to keep it very, very quiet. I'll owe you the best dinner money can buy for this. Will you check 'em for me?'

'Sure, no problem. When do you want them?'

'Yesterday,' Cowboy replied.

Martyn made a face, but did not decline. 'In that case, it'll cost you a dinner for two. Leave them with me for a few hours. Tell you what. Call me here, tonight, around six. I'll be able to tell you then if they're real or not.'

'If they are, I'll need an affidavit. Will you give one?'

'You are pushing your luck, aren't you? Dinner for two, *plus* wine?' He smiled wickedly at the detective.

'You're on. Just remember. Keep this to yourself, Okay?' They shook hands and Cowboy left.

Since his promotion several months before, Cowboy had been a 'floater'. Not yet attached to any particular team, he filled in on odd jobs here and there for other investigators as and when needed, which was why he had ended up in Denmark for the Conference. This situation had begun to bore him, but now he was relieved to have the flexibility. If there *was* a Chameleon, then he wanted the task of hunting him.

Back at the office, which he shared with several other detectives at CIB headquarters, he phoned Jimmy Douglas in London.

'How'd you get on, Jimmy?' Cowboy asked after the initial greetings were over.

'Well, I think I might have had an easier task if I had told my Governor that I had JC outside the "Nick", with three nails in his hand, asking to be put up for the night. You should have heard him. "Let me see if I understand you correctly, Inspector Douglas. You would like to work on a *solved* case, right? One that I personally solved. Are our *unsolved* ones a bit too taxing for you, Inspector?" Then he got mad at me, Cowboy. "Listen," he said, "I'm up to my balls and beyond in new crimes, and you want to fart around with a case that is years old. What are you trying to do? Take the piss? Get the fuck outa here."

'I calmed him down after a bit and gave him the full story. To say he is sceptical would be putting it mildly. But I did get him to agree to reconsider if, *if* you or Sean can come up with something concrete. Can you?'

'I won't know until six tonight. I'll call you at home later. If I do have something to go on, I have something else up my sleeve that you might like. Tell you about it later. Take care.' He hung up before the other man could question him further. At two minutes after six Martyn Wright had confirmed that the evidential photographs were fakes.

Cowboy waited the extra days that Martyn asked for, before going to see Mooney a second time. This time he was armed with the technical evidence explaining exactly how the photos had been created, in the form of an affidavit signed by Wright. In simple terms the 'head' of Sheilagh Colloney had been superimposed on to the body of, not one, but two other children. Martyn had made blow-ups to demonstrate this. He had concentrated on the chest area in all seven photos. On three of them there was a tiny scar on the pubescent left breast. There was no scar on the other four photos, nor was the scar any fault in the photography. Through Jimmy Douglas, Cowboy managed to get a copy of the autopsy report on Sheilagh Colloney, carried out on her body after her death from a drug overdose in London. There was no mention of any scar in the breast area, although the report did mention the tiny needle-marks on the arms of the dead sixteen-year-old. To double-check this, Cowboy found out who the family doctor had been. The

56

Colloney family had had the same private doctor as O'Brien. He confirmed in writing, and was willing to make an affidavit to the same, that he knew of no accident nor operation that would have left such a scar on the girl, and he had treated her from birth until she left home at sixteen. Shown all of this, Commander Mooney was only too willing to seek an appointment with the State Attorney, with a view to having the case re-opened, and a new investigation made into the murder of the financier.

'Come in, gentlemen, come in.' Henry Williams, State Attorney for the Republic of Ireland, rose from behind his desk as the two detectives were led into his office. At forty-five he was Ireland's top lawman, and the youngest ever to hold that position. Top of his class on graduation, he could have been a highly successful lawyer in the private sector, but had instead chosen to work for the State. As a prosecution lawyer he had been extremely successful. Criminals and defence lawyers alike were known to groan out loud on hearing that Williams would be prosecuting their cases. Now he was the head of the law enforcement agencies in the country.

'Please, take a seat, and I'll get us some tea or coffee. What will it be?' Both men gave their preference and he pressed a button on his desk, asking for a pot of tea for two and coffee for one to be sent in. 'Right, gentlemen. To business. How can I help?' He smiled across the desk to where Cowboy and Frank sat in leather chairs. Mooney looked at Cowboy and nodded for him to tell his story from the beginning. At the end of the tale, Cowboy opened his leather briefcase and laid the various affidavits and the photographs on the desk. Williams picked them up one at a time and commenced to read them. As he did so the other two remained silent, drinking their tea and coffee.

'The reopening of the case rests on the photographs, Commander Mooney, agreed?'

'Yes, sir, but backed up with what Sergeant Johnson was told in Denmark.'

'For the moment, that's just hearsay. What makes you so certain that O'Brien didn't fake the photos himself? He might have thought that the risk in trying to get the girl to pose for him was too great. He may have had the work done himself.'

'That is always a possibility, sir, but I don't think so. I was the Inspector in charge of the case. When we found the photographs we searched for others of a similar nature. Books, films, magazines. Anything that a pornographer and paedophile would be expected to have. Nothing was found. No magazines, films, or photos.

'He did a lot of travelling abroad and could quite easily have bought pornography in other countries, and slipped it back into Ireland. The only magazines he took were things like *Time* and *Fortune*. His newspapers were the *Financial Times*, the *Irish Times* and the *Independent*.

'He was a very meticulous man in everything he did, and that included his bank accounts. As you know, sir, bank statements merely quote a cheque number and the amount involved. O'Brien filled in details beside each entry on his statements showing who the payments were to, and for what. He kept them in files, by year and by bank. Nothing showed him making any kind of payment to any organization linked with that sort of stuff. The only thing found, of any sort of sexual nature, were those photographs.'

'Point taken, Commander. Even without the photographs, there is still a very damaging case against Colloney with the witnesses and the gun. Assuming that a professional killer carried out the murder, how did he manage to keep Colloney away from the station at the appointed time, and then have him *arrive* just when he wanted him to?'

'I'm not sure, sir. According to the witnesses, Colloney arrived twice that evening. First time when he killed O'Brien, then the second time, when he was arrested. Yet Colloney claimed he only arrived once! Time plays a very important part in this murder, sir. Time to carry it out, time to get away, and time for the "patsy" to get there. This Chameleon is very very time-conscious. So were both O'Brien and Colloney. O'Brien had a sort of phobia about punctuality. Something he learned in the British Army. Five minutes early was "On Time", one minute late was "Too Late". Colloney had the same sort of training and knew the rules. According to the CIE station-master, you could set your watch by Colloney's arrival time. The train got in at 19:07. If O'Brien was on the train, then Colloney arrived bang on 7.00 p.m. Didn't matter what the weather was like, it was the same. If Colloney didn't arrive at seven, then the CIE man knew O'Brien wasn't going to be on the train.

'To make sure that Colloney was always on time, O'Brien bought him a Rolex Chronometer years before. Both men had the same kind of wrist-watch. According to Sergeant Johnson here, who also owns such a watch, they are considered one of the best timepieces you can buy; very expensive, and very reliable. When we brought Colloney here after the murder I remember that the Desk Sergeant was very impressed with the watch, but mentioned that it was one hour slow. Colloney didn't believe him, insisting that it was a perfect time-keeper. Yet it was exactly, to the minute, one hour slow. The only person who considered the time lapse of any importance was Colloney. Just like the photos, sir – which

59

incidentally both Colloney and his wife believed were of their daughter, there seemed to be no reason to check the time element any further. Why should we? The entire case was wrapped up so quickly.

'Colloney denied three things; killing his employer, ever having seen the photographs before, and being at the station one hour earlier. Part of the set-up must have been fixing his watch. How it was done? I haven't the faintest idea, but somehow or other this Chameleon managed to fix it.'

'You believe this theory about the professional killer, Commander?'

'I do, sir. The photos convinced me. As I told Sergeant Johnson, when he spoke to me about it first, Colloney is the only man I ever had sent down that I wasn't happy about. My gut reaction at the time was that he hadn't done it, but common sense, and all the evidence, told me he had.'

'The whole thing is remarkable, Commander. It sounds like the plot of a good novel.'

'I believe that is precisely the reaction this killer wanted us all to have. It's his MO, sir his trade-mark. And that's where he's made his mistake. We have knowledge of three murders – and time was a key element in all three. It's like a signature. Take each case individually and you have nothing. Put them together . . .'

'And the gun?'

'No prints were found on the gun, and the gloves that Colloney wore that day had no powder marks on them, nor did his hands. Why didn't he throw the weapon away? According to him, because he never had it in the first place! It was made all too easy for us, sir.'

'Okay, Commander. I think you've given me cause to doubt the conviction. What's your next move?'

'I'll let Sergeant Johnson tell you his idea on that, sir.'

Both men turned now to look at Cowboy.

'Well, sir, if Colloney didn't kill O'Brien, and this Chameleon did, then somebody paid him to do it, and paid him a lot. At least one million dollars. To pay somebody that amount of money must mean that a lot more was at stake. Somebody must have expected to recover the fee, with interest.

'O'Brien had no family. His wife had died quite a number of years earlier and they had no children. According to his will, the house and the grounds, plus the cottage the Colloneys lived in, went to them after his death. All the furniture and fittings, with the exception of his art collection, went with the house. The Rolls was left to Colloney himself. Because he was convicted of the murder, Colloney got nothing from the will, but his wife, who was not implicated in any way, was able to inherit. As well as the house and grounds, a trust fund had been set up by O'Brien to ensure that the house could be kept in order, and an index-linked income would be paid to the couple. All of this, as I understand it, was considered to be part of the motive for killing O'Brien – but they had all these things beforehand! All the living expenses for the family were paid for by O'Brien. His art collection, which at the time was valued at being in excess of five million pounds, went to the State.

'We are left with only one direction to look, and that is at JB Finance International. His will stated that his shares in the company were first to be offered to the existing directors, at a preferential price, before being put on the open market. I have it on good advice that no shares in the company ever went on the open market.'

'You think the board of directors had him killed?' Williams asked.

'Maybe not the entire board, sir, but that is the only place where the kind of money to pay the Chameleon

61

could come from. And it was also one of the reasons why it was necessary to frame somebody for the murder.'

'Why?'

'Well, sir, why did he have to be killed by somebody who specializes in providing a patsy? Why wasn't he just a victim of a hit and run accident? A mugging gone wrong? Because if we did not have a strong enough case to go to trial, then our attention would have turned towards JB Finance. As it was, Commander Mooney had no need to look in that direction. He had everything he needed for a conviction. He had motive, weapon, opportunity, and witnesses.'

'And that's where you're going to start looking, I assume. Won't that be somewhat obvious, if the person you *are* looking for is still with the company?'

'Yes, sir. That's why I would like the entire operation to be kept between ourselves at the moment. Reopening the case publicly would show our hand. What I would like is for you to have a word in the ear of somebody at the Inland Revenue, and have them undertake a complete check on JB Finance going back, say, five years. Give Commander Mooney permission for a member of the City Fraud Squad to go in undercover with the IRS people, and we'll brief him on what to look for, going back all the way to the year of the murder. Then we'll have to sit back and keep our fingers crossed that he'll find something.'

Swinging his chair round to face Mooney, Williams asked what he thought of the idea.

'I was amazed when Sergeant Johnson first came to me with the whole thing – especially as it was one of my own cases. But I go along with his plan. It's his ball game and I'm more than willing to allow him to have the case and for it to be confidential, with him reporting to me on a regular basis.'

'Okay, I'll agree. But if we are going to reopen the case, you are going to have to interview Colloney and his wife – which means that he has to be told. The problem is that he has to remain where he is. If we let him out on bail, it will blow your case open, Sergeant. Do you think he'll agree to keeping his mouth shut?'

'I believe he will, sir, once we explain everything to him.'

'Let's hope so. Okay, gentlemen. I'll get on to the IRS and you can pick your man from the Fraud Squad, Commander. Just let his superior know what he's doing.'

All three men rose together and the State Attorney shook hands with the two policemen, showing them out of his office. 'A word of warning to you, Commander Mooney. Watch your back. I think this young Sergeant here might be after your job.'

'Oh, I wouldn't worry too much, sir. Everything he knows he learnt from me, he doesn't really have an original thought in his head.'

Williams laughed out loud, while the other two smiled.

That same week Commander Frank Mooney withdrew Detective Sergeant Johnson from all other duties and gave him a special assignment. The Inland Revenue informed JB Finance International that they were about to commence a complete audit of company records. Inspector Liam Gallagher of the City Fraud Squad was covertly sent in with the IRS people, having been briefed on what to look for. Used to keeping things close to his chest, Gallagher understood that his work was to be confidential. He had worked with the IRS in the past, and would, most likely, do so again in the future. Cowboy had one further request to make of Mooney.

Raising his eyes in mock despair, Mooney agreed and put in a phone call to Chief Superintendent Wilcox of New Scotland Yard. At the end of their lengthy conversation Wilcox granted the request, and Detective Inspector Jimmy Douglas was seconded to the Criminal Investigation Branch of the Garda Síochána for a six-month period to work under the personal command of Mooney. He was to be assigned to work with Sergeant Johnson. Any assistance that Scotland Yard could provide in the operation would be made available. It was further agreed that Mooney would forward the confidential reports on the case direct to Wilcox with a view to building up a report to reopen the suspected Chameleon murder in London. By the end of July Operation Chameleon had officially started.

CHAPTER SEVEN

Dublin, August–September 1994

ON THE SECOND OF AUGUST Jimmy Douglas arrived at
Dublin International Airport to be met by Cowboy.
From there they drove to an inexpensive hotel, The Belview, on the south side of the city, a ten-minute walk
from Cowboy's apartment. It was a small, neat hotel, ca-
tering mainly to the sales profession. It was renowned
for its fair prices and good, wholesome, food. Cowboy
had made arrangements for an unmarked car from the
pool to be lent to Jimmy for the length of the investigation. Despite his seniority in rank, Douglas maintained
that as it was Cowboy's city, he would be the boss. However, should Cowboy ever be seconded to London for
any reason, then any shitty job given to Douglas on this
assignment would be remembered, with interest. It was
agreed on that first night that their first port of call
would be to visit Colloney in Port Laoise maximum security jail. It was possible that he held information that
had not been declared previously. In particular, Cowboy
wanted to know about the missing hour on the day of
the murder.

Port Laoise Maximum Security Prison is one of the
two top security prisons in the Republic, the other being
Mountjoy Jail in Dublin. In both prisons, the majority
of inmates are members of terrorist groups, but they
also house those serving long sentences for criminal

offences. Mooney had made the necessary arrangements with the prison Governor, and two days later the two detectives were facing John Colloney across a table in an interview room. On the table between them were three foam cups of almost undrinkable tea and a carton of 200 cigarettes. Colloney looked suspiciously at Cowboy as he pushed the 200 cigarettes across to him. To Colloney the tobacco was better than money. It was the only currency of any value – apart from drugs – in any prison. Shrugging his shoulders, he accepted the carton.

'Mr Colloney,' Cowboy began, 'I am Detective Sergeant Johnson of the CIB, and this here is Detective Inspector Douglas of Scotland Yard. What we have to say to you is strictly confidential, but I can assure you that, if you answer our questions and keep the entire thing to yourself, there is every possibility that your incarceration here could shortly be over.'

Seven years in prison had changed Colloney. He had been a friendly, easy-going man with a trusting nature, content with life, believing in truth and justice – until the day he was sentenced to life imprisonment for a murder he knew he did not commit. Now he was a man full of suspicion, trusting nobody. A man without any future. Approaching his sixty-eighth birthday, all he had in front of him was another ten years in prison before he would be considered for parole – if he lived that long. Opening one of the packs from the carton he lit a cigarette, inhaling deeply, allowing the smoke to drift slowly from his nostrils.

'I'm listening, Sergeant.'

'We are reopening your case. We now have reason to believe that your employer was assassinated by a professional killer, and that you were framed for his murder. If we are to prove beyond any shadow of a doubt that you are innocent, we need to find new evidence to connect the person who employed the hit man, and that means that you cannot be released for the time being.'

The cigarette fell from the other man's fingers as he stared across the table at the detective. The words 're-opening', 'innocent' and 'new evidence' were vibrating round his skull like the loud clanging of church bells. Jimmy leaned across the table and placed the fallen cigarette in the ashtray. Cowboy gave Colloney a brief run-down on what had started the investigation, how the photographic evidence had been checked and found to be false, and the decision to re-investigate taken. At the mention of the photographs, and how they had been faked, the two detectives watched in embarrassed silence as the man's lips trembled uncontrollably and tears trickled down his cheeks. Reaching into his prison uniform pants he withdrew a soiled handkerchief, wiped his eyes, and blew his nose.

'That, Sergeant – the fact that the photos were faked – is the best news I have heard in over seven years. You have no idea how being shown those photos, and being made to believe that James had taken them, affected my wife and I. I've always known I was innocent, Sergeant, but I also believed that those photos were genuine. It's a very hard thing to try to come to terms with, that some-one you considered to be the best friend a man could have, had been involved with dirty photographs of your only daughter, especially as she was dead.' He reached for the cigarette once again. Taking one or two draws on it rapidly, he stubbed it out, took a swallow of the foul tea, and lit another cigarette.

'I first met James O'Brien in 1943, Sergeant. In the Irish Guards. I was his batman. We went through the rest of the war together and despite our difference in rank, became friends. War does that to men. When you're fighting for your life, and depending on the man beside you, you don't give a shit where he comes from, or what his background is. Men go to war for ideals – but they fight because the bastard on the other side is trying to kill them. I think it was the Yank, General Patton, who said "Nobody ever won a war by dying for his country. He won it by making the other poor bastard die for his." I was a young boy of eighteen when I went to war, Sergeant, and I came out an old man. James was three years older than me.

'After the war, we lost contact. I stayed in England, trying to find work – along with millions of others coming out of uniform. James came back to Dublin and started a financial business. Shortly afterwards he came looking for me. Found me in a food queue in Kilburn. Cold, tired and almost permanently hungry. He took me away from all of that, brought me back to Ireland and gave me a job and my dignity back. He was a man of honour and of his word. A true officer and gentleman – and believe me, there were not all that many of them. He had told me that if he could ever help me, he would, and he did.

'He went from success to success, and I went along with him. I didn't have the brains for the kind of stuff he was involved in, but he always had something for me to do – even when there was nothing for me to do! Eventually he became a very wealthy man and, to the outside world, I became his chauffeur. But it was more than that. It's hard to explain it to you, Sergeant, but . . . oh, I don't know. It was a good friend sharing his success with a less capable one, but giving him the dignity of a job to cover his kindness. The friendship endured. I was the first to marry, and he was best man at the wedding. As a present, Mary and I got the Roller for a month, plus an all-expenses-paid holiday touring Europe. At his wedding, Mary and I were at the head table. James's father had died in the war, he was an only child, and his mother died not all that long after. There was some family, but there had been a falling out years before – I think it was something to do with his father's marriage. James's mother had been married before, and divorced. He never went into any great detail about it, it was just something I came to understand as the years went by.

'Life went on, we were both married, and his career was on the up and up. Then our daughter Sheilagh was born. James and Gloria were her godparents. Two years later, Gloria was dead. Cancer. For a while James was a broken man. Mary and I did what we could under the circumstances and he pulled through the tragedy. He doted on Sheilagh. Nothing was too good for her. He paid for private education for her and always talked about her coming to work in the company. I think he began to see Sheilagh as his own daughter and I always suspected that she would inherit everything from him. Oh, she was a right one, Sergeant.' A smile appeared on Colloney's face as he remembered his daughter. 'She could twist James round her little finger like nobody could. But not in a nasty way, you understand. He knew she was conning him, and she knew that he knew. It was like a game with the pair of them.

'At sixteen she wanted to take a train journey round Europe with a couple of other girls from her school. It was what all the kids were doing then. She got James to back her up in getting her mother and I to agree to it. Off she went, and that was the last we saw of her.' He fell silent as he was remembering the fun-loving, happy young girl his daughter had been. 'Somewhere along the line she got herself mixed up with drugs and died of an overdose in London. A lovely girl, with a bright future, and she got herself involved in that shit. We never knew why – it just happened.

69

'Mary and I were devastated, as you can well imagine, but it also tore poor James apart. He blamed himself for talking us into letting her go, said that if he hadn't taken her side we wouldn't have allowed it and she would still be alive. But Mary and I had to face the fact that it was nobody's fault. She could just as easily have got mixed up with the drug culture here in Dublin. It was sad, very sad, but now a fact of life. We all came to terms with it together. We were close before Sheilagh's death, but we were closer after it.

'James took to eating with Mary and I in the cottage, unless he had guests for dinner, or staying over. I'd pick him up at the station, and by the time we got home Mary had the dinner ready. Sometimes he'd watch some telly with us, sometimes he'd go back to his den in the house and do some work. Then came the murder.

'When I turned up at the railway station that night, and found out who had been shot, I was shocked. At that moment I thought it might have been an IRA hit. James was pretty much against them and there had been one or two approaches to him for contributions. He had always ignored them. I was shocked by his murder, but even more shocked when everybody started pointing their fingers and shouting that I was the one who had killed him. Me! I would have killed *for* him – and they were saying I'd done it. I was taken to the Castle and some Inspector, Mooney I think his name was, came in later with the gun and the photographs. Believe me, Sergeant. When I saw those photographs I *would* have killed him. I was sick. Thoroughly and utterly sick. I puked up everything I had eaten that day. My mind was clouded with visions of James and Sheilagh, of what went on besides the photos. She used to go off with him at times, during her summer holidays, when he went on short business trips. Sometimes people thought she was his daughter. I had terrible images of the pair of them, she, not more than eleven or twelve, and him, old enough, older, in fact, than her own father. I was in a daze all the way through the trial, couldn't, still can't, remember the half of it.

'And now you tell me I'm innocent and that the photographs were faked. Sergeant, I'll stay in here for the rest of my life if necessary – but get the bastard who did this. Get him for James, for Mary and me, but most of all, get him for Sheilagh. For dirtying her memory in the minds of her mother and father.' He began to sob, his head lowered, shoulders shaking. Cowboy and Jimmy let him cry it out of his system, because they both knew that the tears were for the damage done to the memory of an innocent girl. Eventually Colloney once again withdrew his handkerchief and blew his nose, wiping his eyes with the back of his hands. 'I'm okay now, Sergeant. I'm okay.'

'Have you any idea, Mr Colloney, how anybody could have tampered with your wrist-watch?'

'How did you know about that, Sergeant?' he asked incredulously.

'I know, because the uniformed Sergeant who signed in your possessions at the Castle remarked that it was slow, and, for a successful murder, for which you were to be blamed, you had to be kept out of the way for at least one hour. Do you know what *modus operandi* means?'

'In here! It's part of the language.'

'Well, timing is this man's MO. In addition to the murder of O'Brien, we know of at least two others carried out in the same manner. First the killing, with the killer being recognized. Then the killer leaves the scene while everybody is still in shock, and the patsy – you, in this case, – turns up at the scene shortly after. No need for the overworked police to look anywhere else for the

71

murderer. They have him. So somehow or other your watch was tampered with, and it is vital that we find out how this was done. Can you remember the events of that particular day? Was there anything unusual about it? Did you, some time before that day, notice anybody watching the house, watching you? Anything like that, Mr Colloney?'

Colloney lit another cigarette, this time offering the pack across the table. Both detectives took one, knowing full well that what was being offered was not just a cigarette, but the man's trust. He now trusted them, and would tell them all he could.

'Believe me, Sergeant Johnson, I can remember every single event of that day as if it had only happened yesterday. I don't remember the days after so well, or the trial, but that day! I have lived it and re-lived it a million times.

'An old war-wound makes me an irregular sleeper. I usually manage only about four or five hours a night, sometimes it's less. I have got used to it over the years, and I always remembered the words that my training Corporal gave to me. "Never stand when you can sit, never sit when you can lie, and always sleep and eat whenever you get the chance, as you never know where the next one is coming from." So I used to cat-nap during the day.

'I would drive James to the station to catch the 08:10 each morning. He liked the train-ride into Dublin. The only times I would actually drive him all the way in was if he had business meetings that would take him outside the Dublin area. Maybe once or twice a month, something like that. But normally my routine was drive him to the station, then back home again until the evening. After that, I would do odd jobs around the main house, especially if he had guests staying. There was a cleaning woman who came in three days a week to help Mary, but with guests we liked to keep the place extra spick and span. I'd do the shopping for the missus, and she and I'd have lunch. If I hadn't heard from James by 3.30 in the afternoon, then I knew he would be arriving on the 19:07. I can't remember a single time that he didn't call, if he wasn't on the train. However, to be on the safe side, I used to cat-nap on the sofa in his den, so he knew I could be reached there if anything out of the ordinary was to happen. I used to sleep from 4.00 until 6.15. Then I'd go and get him.'

'The journey only takes fifteen minutes,' Cowboy said. 'I timed it, and the CIE guard said he could always set his watch by your arrival. If you hadn't arrived at seven precisely, then he knew that Mr O'Brien would not be on the train. So what did you do between 6.15 and 6.45?'

Colloney smiled at the reference to the CIE guard. He knew that his precise punctuality was known. It was also one of the things that had confused him that day. He had arrived at his usual time – or so he had thought – only to find that everything had gone hay-wire. Somehow he had lost an hour, and he had never been able to explain it. To himself, nor to anybody else.

'I used to freshen up in the downstairs loo, and check on the weather. If it was snowing, or foggy, then it took a little longer than the fifteen minutes to get to the station. I'd leave a little earlier if that was the case. I can tell you precisely how long it takes to make that drive, Sergeant, in all sorts of weather, from a slight snowfall to a blizzard.'

Cowboy nodded, acknowledging that he accepted that as being the truth.

'What about medicine – for your sleeping problem?

Did you take any on a regular basis, at any specific time during the day or night? Or a drink, perhaps?'

'No medicine, but I did take a glass of brandy before my nap. Not a large one, mind you. I was never one to believe in drinking and driving, even before it became such an issue. But yes, I'd have a small tot. It helped. There was a decanter on James's desk. He knew I took it.'

'Would this be well-known? I mean to others, outside of Mrs Colloney and Mr O'Brien?'

'Possibly. I can't say for sure. Is it important?'

'It might very well be. Did you use an alarm to wake you, or did you wake automatically?'

'Both. I always set the alarm, just in case, but I woke before it went off. But now that you mention it, on that day it was the alarm that woke me. Strange, I had forgotten about that. But I don't understand where this is leading, Sergeant.'

'The most important part of this killer's plan was to keep you out of the way, for at least one hour, but not very much longer. You were required to turn up while the witnesses, police, and everybody else, were still at the scene. To me, the most logical way was to confuse you over the time. So how could that be done? A person such as yourself, so precise in your timing? I would suggest that the brandy was drugged with something. What, I don't know. I don't even know if it's possible to put somebody to sleep for a specific length of time. Did you wear your wrist-watch while you slept? Were there any other clocks, apart from the alarm clock, that you would see?'

'I always took my wrist-watch off and laid it on the small coffee table, along with the car keys. There was a clock in the hall, near the main door. But I'd have noticed if it was wrong – or I suppose, in my case, if it was actually right, and my watch was wrong. You only notice these things when they are wrong.'

'How do you mean?'

'What does your watch tell you, Sergeant?'

'The time!'

'No. It tells you how late or how early you are for an appointment. It tells you how long it is to lunch. It tells you how long you have to wait for the bus or the train. The only occasion it actually *does* tell you the time, is if I ask you what the time is. So you see, if my watch, the alarm clock and the clock in the hall all told me I had fifteen minutes to get to the station, then as far as I was concerned, they were showing the correct time. But if one of them had been wrong, then I would have double-checked the others.'

'So somebody changed all three of them – and managed to change two of them back, when you had left the house, and after Mr O'Brien was dead. The only one he couldn't get at was your wrist-watch. You were wearing it, and you were in police custody. And you didn't notice anybody suspicious that day, or over the days – perhaps weeks – prior to the murder?'

'No. I'd have remembered something like that. I'm sure I would.'

'Did nothing out of the ordinary occur, say, a few weeks before the murder?'

'No. No, hang on a minute.' He paused for a moment, thinking. 'There was a reporter, from a magazine. An American one, I think. They were doing an article on the relationship between long-term chauffeurs and their bosses. James told me about how this reporter had contacted him and asked if he would be willing to contribute towards the article. He saw nothing wrong with that – he could be quite generous with his time to journalists. He said that it helped to generate business. He asked me if I'd mind giving my side of the story and I said no. A day or so later a reporter – an English guy, I remember, turned up. Said he was freelance and took care of business "this side of the pond" as he expressed it, for the American magazine. We talked for about an hour, and that was it.'

'Can you remember the journalist's name, and the name of the magazine?'

'I remember the guy's surname – Gordon. I remember it because I instantly thought of "Flash Gordon". It was just something that went through my mind at the time. But I can't remember what the magazine was called.'

'*Time-Life? Newsweek? Fortune?*'

'Nah, none of them, or I'd have remembered. James had those on subscription, and I'd have looked for the interview. This guy, Gordon, promised he'd send a couple of copies of the magazine, but only if the article got published. He said that some interviews got edited or cut out altogether. Nothing ever arrived.'

'What about the house, the main house. O'Brien had a lot of art work. It must have been alarmed, surely?'

'It was. Every window and outside door was fitted with an alarm.'

'What was the access? A key, or a code?'

'A key. James had one, I had one, and Mary had one.'

'It would seem that our murderer is a very versatile man, and very, very, good at what he does. Is there anything else you can tell us that might help us, Mr Colloney?'

'Not that I can think of for the moment, but you can be sure, Sergeant Johnson, that I shall be doing a lot of thinking, and if I come up with something, I'll let you know. That, you can bet on as a certainty. Have you spoken to my wife yet? Does she know what's going on?'

'Not yet. We wanted to speak to you first. We intend paying your wife a visit tomorrow.'

'Be ready for more tears, Sergeant, once she knows that those photographs were fakes. Mary found it very very difficult to come to terms with them. Give her my love and tell her that she is to tell you everything she possibly can about that day. I've always suspected that there was something she knew that she never told me about.'

'Oh? Why?'

'Because, Sergeant, Mary has always believed that I *did* kill James O'Brien, and I think she knows something that she believed would have harmed me in court. I've asked her about it and she has always denied it – but I know my wife. She saw something, and from what you have told me here today, it must tie in with the "time" element.'

Cowboy nodded and rose to his feet. Jimmy and Colloney also rose. As all three shook hands, Cowboy promised Colloney that he would have him out as quickly as he could. He did, however, stress again that it was vital that Colloney kept this information to himself. Colloney agreed.

'Let me see if I've got this straight. You want a drug that can put somebody to sleep for a specific period of time, right?' Jim Morrison, Toxicologist, was sitting in his small cubicle, which passed as his office, in the Forensic Science laboratory, back at Dublin Castle. He was looking sceptically at the two detectives, wondering if this was a joke Cowboy was pulling.

'That's right, Jim,' Cowboy confirmed, 'a predetermined period of time – like an hour, for example.'

'That's a pretty tall order, Cowboy. I can name you numerous sleeping potions – Mogadon, Valmid,

Doriden, Restoril and such. Or barbiturates, like Veronal, Luminal – Goof Balls or Purple Hearts to the kind of client *you're* more likely to meet. Or . . .'

'But don't they all have an increased effect if taken with alcohol?' Jimmy asked.

'That's what kills most users. They take a couple a night for so long that they begin to lose their effect. So they increase the dosage, until that begins to lose effect. So they begin to add a glass of something, whiskey for example, to go with the pills, and before you know it, they have a permanent sleep problem. They don't wake up.'

'Are there any drugs where the effect is *decreased* by alcohol?' Cowboy asked.

'Only one springs to mind immediately,' Morrison replied. 'Diphenylhydantoin – or Dilantin to you ignorant masses. Its effect is decreased with alcohol.'

'What form does it come in?'

'Tablet or liquid. The liquid is colourless and pretty much tasteless. You can take it orally or inject it – but I'd hate to try and be precise about how a specific dosage could be reduced by booze. It would take a lot of experimentation, and even then you'd have to practise on a particular patient, to work out his or her tolerance level. Each person can react differently, tolerance-wise, to *any* drug. What knocks you out in a couple of minutes, might take a shorter or longer time to knock Jimmy here out.

'That's the only one that springs to mind without going through my journals, but that's not to say that there aren't drugs available that could do what you want, including some stuff we don't really know all that much about.'

'What does that mean?'

'Exactly what I said, Jimmy. The Indians in the South

American jungles *live* in the world's biggest bloody chemist shop. Any jungle is a local Boots to those who live in and around it. We, highly educated, westernized yobs have only managed to root round the lower shelves, so to speak. We haven't managed to reach the top shelves yet.

'In a nutshell, the answer to your question, Cowboy, is yes. What you are looking for more than likely exists, but I don't know what it is and probably no one else in my field does either. All I can speculate is that, from what little we know about plant extracts, it is more than likely. Sorry I can't be more helpful, fellahs.'

'Never mind, Jim, you've solved part of the problem – it is possible that such a drug exists. Thanks.'

The following day, the two men drove to the manor house on the outskirts of Dún Laoghaire where James O'Brien had lived. The main house was built several hundred yards back from the main road, fronted by a well-kept lawn with scattered flower beds. To the rear of the house was the cottage that was home to Mrs Mary Colloney. Parking his black Porsche, one of the few luxuries he allowed himself, Cowboy led the way to the front door of the cottage.

The woman who confronted them was of medium build, with grey hair. In her late fifties, she still showed signs of her earlier beauty. Introducing themselves, they told her that they had spoken with her husband the day before. She invited them in to the small tidy living room.

Once again Cowboy explained about their visit to Denmark, told her that her husband had been informed of what they knew – but could not prove – and hoped that she would help in the re-investigation of O'Brien's murder. As predicted by her husband, Mary Colloney

79

burst into tears on being told about the photographs. Allowing her time to compose herself once again, they waited until she restarted the conversation. She dabbed the corners of her eyes with a tissue. 'I'm okay now.' She sniffled slightly. 'Go ahead and ask your questions.'

'Mrs Colloney,' Jimmy began, 'yesterday, your husband hinted that there was something, something from the day of the murder, that you withheld during the original murder investigation. Can you recall what it was, and why you didn't mention it then?'

'Oh, I can recall it easy enough, and the reason I never mentioned it at the time was because I knew – believed – that my husband had committed the murder. I knew it for a fact. Or at least thought I did.'

'Why was that, Mrs Colloney?'

'Because John swore he had only driven to the station once, that evening – yet I had seen him set off at the usual time, return alone and go back into the main house. He was in there for about half an hour, then set off a second time.'

'Could you be more specific about it. Mrs Colloney?' Cowboy asked.

'I was in the kitchen – which looks out towards the main house – preparing dinner. John was taking his usual nap in the study – in case James rang – and I saw him set off for the station. I always put the potatoes on to boil when I saw him leave. I knew they would both be back shortly and then we would eat.

'At about twenty past seven I saw the Rolls arrive back and park as normal. But instead of the two of them getting out of the car, only my husband got out, and furthermore, he went straight into the house. I was a bit annoyed – dinner spoiling and that, you know, but I assumed something had gone wrong with the train, and John was going to phone James.'

'Wouldn't he have come here and told you? Used the phone here?' Cowboy asked.

'Yes, but I assumed John had gone in to check the answer-machine, just in case James had called while he was at the station. He always set the answer-machine when he left.

'Anyway, I set about doing bits and pieces, turning the oven down on the roast, checking on this and that. At about a quarter to eight I heard the car engine start, and John set off again for the station. The only thing that really surprised me at the time was that John had not come and told me what had happened. As you both know, John never came back. He was arrested that night for killing James.

'The reason I never told this to anyone was because I believed my husband *had* killed him. I'm afraid I was not prepared to add even more evidence for my husband's conviction. So there you have it, gentlemen. I've never told anyone, including John. I didn't tell him because I didn't want him to know that I knew he was lying. Or so I thought – have thought – until now.'

'May we see the kitchen, Mrs Colloney?' Jimmy asked.

'Of course. This way.' She led them both into a country-style kitchen. It was large enough to be used for eating in, as was evident by the table and four chairs just inside the door. Both men walked across to the window above the stainless steel sink unit. Through the net curtains they had an unrestricted view of the side of the main house and the slightly curved drive down to the road. They had noted the side door to the house as they had driven past it.

'Is that where your husband usually parked, Mrs Colloney?' Jimmy indicated the side of the house.

'Yes. He parked the car there and both of them always

81

used that door. I think it would have been a tradesman's entrance or such like at one time, but we all used it. The main door hasn't been opened in, I can't remember how many years.'

'So you saw Mr Colloney come out that door, go back in about half an hour later, and come out a second time.'

'Yes.'

'Never had any doubts when he went *in*, coming back alone from the station, that it was your husband?'

'No. I had no reason to think it was anybody else.'

'But it was, Mrs Colloney. The man you saw coming out the first time and going back in half an hour later, was not your husband. Your husband was still asleep at the time, lying on the sofa in the den. Can we get into the main house at all? Just to familiarize ourselves with the layout?'

'Yes, just let me get the keys.' They followed her back to the main door of the cottage. Hanging on the wall was a small set of key-hooks with several sets of keys. Selecting a bunch, she led them towards the main house.

'Mrs Colloney,' Jimmy asked, 'do you always leave the keys there?'

'Oh, yes. That way I always know where they are.' Walking in front of the two detectives she did not see the look that passed between them. Now they knew how the Chameleon would have got the keys to the house and the alarm.

At the main house she unlocked the door, then hurried in to turn the key in the alarm, and turn off the warning, 'buzzing' sound.

'Can you show us where the study is, please?' Cowboy requested. Mary Colloney led the way to a room just off the ground-floor corridor, not far from the door they had entered.

The room felt bare, empty and unused. The furniture, including the desk, was covered with white dust sheets. The book shelves which lined one wall were bare and light patches on the wall showed where paintings had once hung before being donated to the State. The room had a stale, musty smell, with an undertone of tobacco. Cowboy walked slowly round the room, his mind waiting for the information he knew would come to him, by merely touching the contents. Very few people knew that he was a psychic. He had been born with the gift, but it had been suppressed at a very early age, mainly because his elders told him not to be stupid whenever he mentioned things that came to him from the ether. Some of the things he had foreseen had frightened him, especially the death of a school friend, and this too had added to his willingness to suppress his gift. It had come back to him several years before when working on the case of the Java Man. Accepting it then, he had tried to develop it further, but kept it as a secret shared with very few.

As he walked about the room, he began to get images of how it had looked. They came to him like instant photographs, illuminated with flashes of light, like sitting in a darkened room lit occasionally by strobe lighting. He could see the shelves on the far wall lined with books. Saw the military plaques, photographs, certificates, awards and other memorabilia that had belonged to James O'Brien. He saw the desk as it was, with a leather-bound blotting pad in the centre, the desk light, the neat pen holder, the gilt-edged framed photograph of a laughing young girl, eight or nine years old, sitting on a pony. He saw the leather sofa that John Colloney napped on, and the small table beside it. Then he saw Colloney sleeping on the sofa, his Rolex watch lying on the small table. Through the 'strobe flashes' he watched the man rise from the sofa, reach out and touch a button on the travel alarm clock, then place the wrist-watch on his left hand.

In silence, Cowboy walked back to the door and looked along the corridor. Staring at each closed door in turn his eyes were drawn back to a specific one. As the images in his mind showed John Colloney leave the house to start his final journey to the station, the other door opened and a 'twin' of John Colloney emerged. Moving swiftly the 'second' Colloney went to the hall clock and adjusted it. He then moved towards the study. Cowboy walked back in and watched as the man re-set the alarm clock and moved to the desk. The figure opened the centre drawer, reached inside and pressed something. Then he reached inside his jacket pocket, produced a hand gun and a small package, then put both in the drawer. The package seemed to be placed further into the drawer than the hand gun. Cowboy re-membered from the file that the gun had been found on the day of the murder, but the photographs had not been found for a further two days. They were in a secret compartment in the drawer. The man then closed the drawer and moved silently from the room.

Walking to the desk Cowboy whipped back the dust sheet. Opening the drawer in the centre he slid his fingers along the inside until he felt a small indent in the wood. Pressing it, the back of the drawer fell forwards, and there was the hidden recess.

'How did you know it was there, Sergeant?' Mrs Col-loney asked, astonished.

'My father had a desk like this,' he lied. 'He used to keep Liquorice Allsorts in it. He was an "addict",' he smiled. 'So was I, and it was some time before he figured out where his sweets were disappearing to.' Mrs Col-loney smiled at him, accepting the explanation. 'May we look at the other rooms on the ground floor?' he asked.

'Of course.' Leading them back out into the corridor she walked with them as Cowboy, leading the way, opened each door in turn, and merely looked into the rooms beyond. At the room he knew the killer had hid in he smelt exotic food, a mixture of herbs and spices, as if he were walking into a Chinese restaurant.

'Do you smell anything, Jimmy?'

Jimmy stepped into the small reception room, walls bare of frames and the furniture covered with the same kind of dust sheets as the study. He sniffed once or twice. 'Dust and stale air. Is that what you mean, Cowboy?'

Cowboy shook his head. 'Nah. For a minute I thought I smelt something else. Like . . . ah, it doesn't matter.' He turned round to Mrs Colloney.

'Thanks, Mrs Colloney, for showing us the house and talking with us. Please don't talk about the purpose of our visit to anybody. It is imperative for your husband, that it is kept quiet.'

'Thank you, Sergeant, you too, Inspector. I really, really appreciate what you are both doing for my husband. Rest assured I shall say nothing.'

After thanking her once more, the two detectives drove back to the Castle.

Later that night, lying on the sofa in his apartment with Marlane in his arms, Cowboy told her of what had happened in the study.

'It's like watching it all in a kind of series of slides. Like a drum of them, and I'm sitting in a darkened room and every so often a new slide comes up on the screen. It's amazing really.'

'What brings it on for you?' she asked. She had known of his extra-sensory perception ever since it had re-occurred on the case of the Java Man.

85

'I think it was the room, the house. Nobody has lived in it since O'Brien died. The memories I was picking up were some of the last events that occurred there.

'In a way, I think the house was acting like a tape recorder, with the walls absorbing scenes that occurred there. Me walking into the study acted like a sort of "play" button, and those memories were played back to me. I could see Colloney lying on the sofa, his watch on the table, him reaching to switch off the alarm. As he left the house – an hour later than he thought it was – his "twin" emerged from that reception room and set the clocks to the right time. Jeeez, the guy is good. Very, very, good.'

Lying silently, still thinking back over the experience, he suddenly became aware that his shirt was being opened. The hairs on his forearms and the back of his neck began to rise as Marlane gently raked her nails across his chest, making small marks which she kissed, moving her soft lips to his left nipple. Her sharp teeth began to worry at it and he could feel himself becoming instantly aroused.

'Do you think that everything that happens in a house is recorded into the walls?' she whispered, her fingers now working at the opening to his belt.

'I don't know,' he replied, his voice hoarse with excitement. 'I suppose so.'

'Hmmm,' she murmured as she opened his pants wide, her nails tracing his rigid cock, from his testicles to the tip, trapped inside his shorts. 'Just imagine,' she continued, her voice still low and husky now as her own excitement began to build up. 'In years to come, somebody's going to be in this room, and see some of the greatest pornographic scenes of their life, just by standing still. Ohhhh, and who have we got here?' Easing the elastic on his shorts away from his stomach her small

86

hand reached inside and closed round his hardness. 'And who's a big boy then? Come here to Mama,' she whispered, lowering her mouth over the tip, her tongue flicking at the angry red head as her fingers rolled back his foreskin.

'I wish *I* was watching this,' he mumbled as his hips began to rise from the sofa, gently pushing himself further and further into the warm, wet cavern of her mouth. Her only answer was to rasp her teeth along his rigid cock. To hell with the future, this was now, and they were both going to enjoy it. Of that she was totally sure.

CHAPTER EIGHT

Dublin, August–September 1994

KNOWING THAT THE IRS INVESTIGATION into JB Finance would take some time, Cowboy and Jimmy devoted the waiting period to research. They compiled a list of contract killers. The member countries of the International Police Federation were contacted and names supplied. They broke the list down into two parts; Known and Suspect. Most of those on the suspect list were people who were known to be within fifty kilometres of at least three suspicious deaths, but could not be proved to be involved in them. Carlos, the most famous of them all, also known as the Jackal and famed for his kidnapping of the OPEC ministers, was no longer on the list as he languished in a French jail awaiting trial. Others were on the list by virtue of the fact that informants had passed on information about them. Only three females appeared among all the names they collated. One in West Germany, one in Holland and, surprisingly enough, one in Ireland. The Irish girl – believed to be no more than twenty-five years old – Marie Cassidy, was linked with ten murders. A member of the Provisional Irish Republican Army since she was fourteen she was their main 'contract killer for hire'. Her services were provided by the PIRA and they received her fee.

None of the names or records they compiled pointed

them in the direction of the killer they sought. Neither man considered any of the three women to be likely suspects and they were placed in a 'Last Resort' file. Including a list sent to them by the Federal Bureau of Investigation in Washington, they had a total of 117 male contenders – but none of them matched their profile of the Chameleon. Each name on the list was an expert, but none could touch the master of the game.

Towards the end of August, Sean phoned them from Denmark. When Cowboy and Jimmy had started their official investigation they had told Sean, asking him to get in touch with his old CIA contact. The man had been hard to track down, but once found had been happy to co-operate. Although recently retired, 'Buffalo' Bill Owen asked round among his old contacts – and the answer he received each time was 'stop asking questions on this subject'. One of these blocks came from within the CIA complex at Langley, in Virginia. While not providing them with any more information, this reaction did confirm that Chameleon existed and most likely had been used by the CIA themselves. They fed the name into the Interpol computer, but it revealed nothing either. Apart from reinforcing their conviction that the killer did actually exist, they were no further along than the day they had started!

In the time since his arrival Jimmy had proved popular with other members of the CIB. His sense of humour enabled him to accept the teasing and jokes levied at him by the other detectives and he delivered as good as he got in return. On a couple of occasions he had accepted invitations from them to go drinking. Although asked several times what he was really 'doing' in Dublin, he stuck to the cover story of being there to learn about Irish police tactics. One of the invitations he received was to the stag night of a young detective constable from County Kerry, arranged in one of the night clubs in Leeson Street. 'The Strip' as it is better known is the city's nightclub area. These mainly small clubs occupy the basements of some of the city's most elegant Georgian houses in the up-market business district. They are open until the early hours of the morning, charge exorbitant prices for their liquid refreshments, and their customers are a mixture of cops, gangsters, lovers cheating on spouses and prostitutes. On this particular night, Cowboy had a prior engagement and stayed only long enough to give the young copper his best wishes – both on his forthcoming marriage and on surviving the stag night. His appointment was with another woman. A dark-haired, middle-aged, attractive woman – one whom Marlane knew all about. Parking his black Porsche in St Ita's Road, a cul-de-sac on the north side of the city, he walked back round the corner on to Botanic Road to the end terraced house, on the corner of St Mobhi Road, the home of Joan Blackmore.

Joan Blackmore, his psychic mentor, had moved from Ballyfermot two years before and Cowboy was one of a small group she occasionally invited to her home to help them to advance their psychic abilities. As Cowboy knew, being psychic was not a 'gift' as such. It was within the capability of every person – but very very few would accept this fact. Those who openly talked of their ability were at best ridiculed, or at worst condemned as devil worshippers. As a Detective Sergeant in the CIB – and as the most newsworthy cop in the country because of his lifestyle – Cowboy knew that it was best he keep his ability secret. Tonight they were going to attempt to contact the world beyond, the etheric world of those who had died, by means of table-tapping. Cowboy knew the other three members of the 'circle' and each preferred to keep their gifts quiet for one reason or another.

After half an hour of social chat and cups of tea and coffee, it was time to make the attempt. While Joan cleared the low, circular, four-legged wooden coffee table of cups and saucers, taking them to the kitchen, Cowboy moved the table into the centre of the room. Val Beacham, a small, attractive housewife from Drumconda, volunteered to write any messages they might receive. She remained sitting on the sofa while Cowboy, Joan, Paddy O'Connor and Tessie O'Shea all knelt on the carpeted floor around the small table.

'Right, friends, all I want you to do is to gently lay your hands on the surface of the table. I then want you to open your minds to Spirit and hopefully one of them will be able to come through.' As they did as she instructed, Joan closed her eyes, tilted her head backwards, and began to breathe deeply. The other three went through the ritual of concentrating the power of their minds, each of them imagining a door which they slowly opened. They persevered for ten minutes before they received an indication that it was going to work. While Joan, as the most 'senior' and most advanced psychic amongst them remained in deep concentration, the others watched as the phenomena began. The coffee table appeared to move as though it were a living breathing thing. As though the wood had turned to pliable putty or plastic, the centre began to undulate slowly, like a chest breathing. Barely discernible at first, as they all watched the movement became clearer and clearer. Suddenly the table shot to the right of Cowboy, as though pulled by invisible strings.

'Settle down now, settle down,' Joan instructed the invisible power. 'Have you communicated in this manner before?' she asked. 'Answer with one tap for "Yes" and two taps for "No".'

The table tilted slightly, three of the four legs leaving

91

the ground, and gently returned to its original position. The answer was 'Yes'.

'Good,' Joan answered the response, 'then you know how we will work together tonight. Each tap will represent a letter of the alphabet as you spell out any message. Will you now please return the table to its original position.' After a slight pause the table moved back to the centre of the kneeling group, their hands still in contact with the wooden surface. The breathing effect had ceased and the group were ready for whichever entity it was that wished to communicate.

'Do you have a specific message for one of the circle?' Joan asked. Once again the table rose on three legs and gently landed back again. 'Yes.'

'Who is it for?' Joan asked.

Tap, tap, tap. Again the table rose, this time tapping three times before stopping, On the sofa Val wrote the letter 'C' on the note pad resting on her knees. Tap, tap, tap, the table went again, this time raising and lowering 15 times. On the pad Val wrote the letter 'O'. Again the table moved, this time twenty-three times, giving the letter 'W'.

'Is the message for Cowboy?' Joan asked.

The table tapped once in response. 'Yes', the message was for him.

Although a sometimes long and laborious method of communication, table-tapping was quite simple to operate and made it easier for those in spirit to make contact. As the table continued to tap out its message, Val wrote each letter of the alphabet on her pad until the table ceased to make any movement. The message read 'Talk to the one-legged priest that was'. To the question 'Who is sending the message?' from Joan, the reply received was 'Blue Water'. Blue Water was Cowboy's spirit guide, his 'guardian angel' who watched over him as best he could. Since first accepting his psychic powers Cowboy had received several messages from his guide and had on one memorable occasion actually 'seen' him. Although he did not understand the message Cowboy did not doubt its sincerity. But who was the one-legged priest that was? He had no idea. And what should he speak to him about? A name popped into his mind as though in answer to his unspoken question – Chameleon.

'Should I talk of the Chameleon?' he asked, out loud. The table tapped once in response – 'Yes'.

'Who is the one-legged priest that was? I don't understand the message, Blue Water.' Once again Cowboy spoke out loud as though in normal conversation. None present found it extraordinary in any way.

'Think.' came the response.

With that Blue Water faded and another spirit came through with a message for Paddy O'Connor. The message came from his son who had died in a car accident several years back. It was the persistent messages from his son, shortly after his death, telling his father that he was safe, in good hands and that there was no such thing as death that had led Paddy to the awakening of his own psychic ability.

Knowing that the power generated both by those present in the circle and those in the etheric world would not last for very much longer, Joan had a special request.

'Will you allow me to take photographs of the table, balanced on one leg?' The response was a single tap. Leaving the room for a few moments she returned with her camera, already mounted on a tripod. She had loaded the camera earlier with a fresh roll of film. Placing it at one end of the small living room she focused it on the table, and waited. The other three moved away from it. Slowly but surely, the table began to move. With one table leg still on the carpet, the other three moved upwards, inches at a time, until eventually the table was balanced at an unbelievable angle. An angle that was almost perpendicular and would not be possible without some means of support. Joan pressed the shutter-button on the camera time after time as the table rose on its slow journey. As the table lowered itself back down she was about to stop taking photographs when suddenly the table moved once again. This time it hovered horizontally, a good twelve inches off the carpet, all four legs completely out of touch with the ground. Cowboy heard a voice in his mind tell him to sit on the table. Without hesitation he rose from the sofa and eased his muscular twelve-stone body on to it. The table did not budge. As Joan took several more photographs the table eased itself down gently back on to the carpet. With that, it was all over.

The sheer boredom and inactivity of waiting for information, for anything to take the case just one step further, had caused Jimmy to start reading some of the books lying in an open bookcase in the corner of the small office they shared. As Cowboy arrived the following morning and spied the title of the book Jimmy was engrossed in, he clicked his fingers.

'Of course,' he said. 'Paddy Scanlon.'

Jimmy looked up, surprised, expecting to see somebody coming into the office.

'Paddy-fucking-who?' he asked.

'Paddy Scanlon. The book you're reading.'

Jimmy turned the book over to read the title. It was *Mercenary*, by Lieutenant Colonel Mike Hoar, the legendary mercenary who had made a name for himself in what had then been known as the Belgian Congo, back in the '60s.

'What about the book?' Jimmy asked.

'I know just the man who can give us a bit of information on how to go about getting ourselves a contract killer. The book reminded me of him. This guy Scanlon is an ex-priest, ex-mercenary, going back to the Congo days. His final job took him to Biafra, where he left one of his legs. He'll have something to tell us. Nowadays he runs a small hotel in Boyle.' Paddy Scanlon was 'the one-legged priest who was' in the message from Blue Water.

On the journey to Boyle, Cowboy explained Scanlon's background to Jimmy, who found it amazing that he was actually going to meet one of those named in the book he had been reading. Cowboy also explained how the pair of them had met. As a wealthy young man about town, Cowboy Johnson was an essential name on most society guest-lists. Being a 'copper' made him even more alluring and exciting to hostesses. The same had happened to Paddy Scanlon, though his 'events' had been prior to Cowboy's time, and somewhere along the line the two men had met. There had been an instant rapport between them and, although they met infrequently, they enjoyed each other's company, always dispatching large quantities of lager, Guinness and whiskey while enlarging upon stories, telling outrageous jokes and exchanging experiences. They had not seen each other now for several months.

Despite the heavy summer-season bookings, Paddy insisted they both stay the night. There was always room at the inn for Cowboy, he explained. After a large dinner of what the menu proclaimed to be 'Surf 'n' Turf' – fillet steak and grilled salmon – the three men adjourned to Paddy's private living room and drinks were sent for. Social chat over, each man having been brought up to date on the other's activities, Cowboy broached the reason for their visit. In answer to the question about how he would go about hiring a professional killer, Paddy replied 'Take out an ad in the London *Times*.'

'Come on, Paddy, I'm serious,' Cowboy replied.

'So am I, Cowboy, so am I. Don't tell me that an Inspector from Scotland Yard doesn't know that one?'

'I must admit that I've never been involved in actually seeking to *hire* one before, Paddy,' Jimmy replied.

'Ever read the personal columns in *The Times*? You should. Make very interesting reading at times, if you know what to look for. Where do you think I got some of my old jobs from? It's not all "DC. Love you always, MJ." or some such shit. But when I say put an ad in, I don't mean for you to put something like "Professional killer wanted. Good terms, pensionable. Contact Detective Sergeant Johnson, Dublin". Paper wouldn't print that anyway. You don't ask straight out, you have to word it in such a way that the person you are looking for gets the message while to others it doesn't make any sense. Believe me, many people read that paper for just such messages. The code doesn't have to be complicated. Something simple would do. You'll get your answer, one way or the other.

'Got any special kind of killer in mind, or will any old murderer do?' Paddy was still smiling, not fully believing that his friend was serious.

'The one I'm after is very special, Paddy. Very special. We've got a list of the top 100 contract killers in the world back at the office in Dublin – and this guy's so special he's not on it. None of them match up to his skills. He is *the* best there is. His price is the highest also. He was charging $1,000,000 a hit a few years back. For that, he does the job, *and* supplies a patsy. Cases get solved, and nobody looks under the bed. Calls himself, or is known by the name Chameleon. And by the way,

Paddy, all of this is for your ears only. Keep it under your hat, okay?'

Paddy whistled at the price, and nodded his head about keeping quiet.

'For a million dollars I could get you a fuckin' army, Cowboy. For that price he *must* be the best. But for all of that he has to have a soft underbelly – and that's where you'll have to strike.'

'Explain.'

'Well, if he's that good, and his name is not on the top 100, he has to have some sort of an organization. Contact people. Most likely even *they* won't know who he is or where he is. Only how to get in contact with him. He has to have a base somewhere, and will never accept, or have accepted, a contract in his country of residence. The money will be sifted through several bank accounts, in several countries, with pay-offs made along the line, before it arrives where he wants it. His fee will be that big because he has overheads. Overheads to protect his own identity.'

'What about the contact people? What would they do?' Jimmy asked.

'Well, I suppose you could say they do the leg work. The "uniformed branch" as opposed to the "plain clothes branch" – if you get my drift. They will be told to check out the contract. Who's hiring, maybe even why? Who's the hit? Would he or she be expecting a hit? They'd get as much background on both parties as they could, without raising any suspicions, and pass the information on to this geezer. He'd assess what he's been given and make the decision whether to go ahead or not with the job. If he decides to go ahead, then he'd move in, do the hit, and disappear again. If, on the other hand, it was a trap – like I think you are proposing – then I think he might be tempted to do a freebie – on you! Be very, very careful about how you handle this, Cowboy.

'But let's assume the contract is okay, and he carries it out, then the "buyer" is open to blackmail for the rest of their lives. He knows who they are, but they don't know who he is! And of course, if the fee is not paid in full, well, there again, he would be carrying out a second hit, for free. You still sure you want this guy, Cowboy?'

'I'm sure, Paddy,' Cowboy replied without hesitation. 'We have somebody doing life for one of this guy's jobs. It's not so much him I want – although I do want him – but more importantly, I want the buyer, the guy who did the hiring. I want him inside doing the time, instead of the sucker who's doing it for him.' Paddy nodded, knowing that Cowboy was going to proceed with the investigation, with or without his help.

'Okay. So you're going to go on with it. Let's see if we can come up with some sort of message you could use. It has to be slightly obscure but must also be acceptable for insertion. It must appear quite innocent when being read by others, yet, at the same time, be understood by the person you want to reach.' He was silent for a few moments as he thought. 'Something like this: "Some things change permanently. Others are like the Chameleon". That would be chameleon with a capital "C" so our man would know it's his name you are calling, not making one of these "The world ends next Tuesday" statements. You then have to give some sort of reply contact. Something like, for me, "All Ways Paddy".' He reached for the whiskey bottle and poured a generous measure into all three glasses. 'That advert would tell one of his contact people that somebody calling themselves All Ways Paddy wanted to get in touch with Chameleon. I'd watch the personal column for the next few weeks, looking for my reply. That might be something like "Every way and All Ways Paddy. Ring soonest", followed by a telephone number and signed by whatever name I was to ask for when calling. Like "Love, John". I'd phone the number, identify myself as All Ways Paddy and ask to speak with John. Then I would have to say who I really was, and allow a check to be made on me before any further contact. Then I'd be up Shit Creek without a paddle if I was having somebody on!

'If this guy is as good as you maintain he is, then he would not be interested in any forty-eight hour job. He would take his time, and make double sure of everything. He sounds like a real Picasso. Very rare, very expensive, and very, very careful. If you want to get to him, then put an ad in *The Times* – but if you want to take an old friend's advice, Cowboy, forget it. You're not in the same class as this man, and you never will be. This is not some ejit you can get for a few hundred quid. He's the cream. Play with fire and you'll get burnt. Fuck with this guy and you'll get dead – quickly!'

It was late morning when the two detectives took their leave of their host to return to Dublin. As they parted, Paddy gave them one more warning about trying to take this man on. 'You're a big boy, Cowboy, and you make your own decisions. I'd say forget it, but I know you won't, so I'll just say be very, very, cautious. I've met men like him before. Maybe not as good if what you say of him is true, but I know the type. In their world only the stupid and the dead take chances. The stakes are too high. Get yourself a gun, keep your back to the wall, and stay out of dark places. Remember Wild Bill Hickock, Cowboy? The first time he sat without having his back to the wall he got dead – and, incidentally, lost a good hand of poker! Once you start this, there can only be one of two endings – yours or his. Take care of yourself, son. If you make it, come back and tell me all about it, and bring that gorgeous woman with you. I could spend an evening just looking at her.' He laughed and slapped his hand on the other's shoulder. 'Take care of him, Jimmy, he'll get himself into trouble if he's not watched.' With that they parted, Paddy limping away, back into his hotel, the others into Cowboy's car and back to the city.

Taking Paddy's advice, they decided to start checking back issues of *The Times*. At the newspaper's Dublin office they were given free access to all the microfiche files and left to get on with it. They began their search by going back two months from the date of the O'Brien murder, but found nothing. They then went back a further two months, and again nothing. The entry they were looking for, found by Jimmy, was dated four months and two days prior to the murder. It was small and innocuous, just as Paddy had predicted it would be.

Change in the Weather. Change in Time. Change in Style. Like an ever changing Chameleon. How? Where?

D'ARGENT

Convinced that this was the original request for a contact with the killer, and that 'D'Argent' was the code for the person trying to make contact, they slowly and carefully went forward towards the date of the murder, looking for the reply. They found it dated three weeks after the initial insert.

D'Argent. All things come to pass for those who try. Sun. Lon. 385 4111. Cha. Maileon

Progress was being made, albeit slow progress.

Inviting Frank Mooney and Jimmy over to his apartment that evening, Cowboy held a meeting to discuss what the next step was. Still nothing had come in from their undercover Fraud Squad man on JB Finance.

'Are you two sure that you are not paying too much attention to one tree, and missing the forest?' Mooney wondered. 'What happens if we get a clean bill of health on everybody at JB Finance? What then?'

'Frank, it *has* to be JB Finance. We've said it before – nobody pays the kind of money this guy is asking, merely to have somebody killed. There has to be money involved, and a lot of it. Yes, Colloney and his wife gained from O'Brien's death, but the friggin' government gained much much more than them, with the art collection! We know the evidence against Colloney was faked – we've proved it. You can't seriously put the Irish Government down as suspect – so we are back to the one place somebody might just possibly make the kind of return on a million-dollar-investment, and that is the company. Tell him about that phone number in the advert, Jimmy.'

'I asked my Governor to check it out. It is a very discreet telephone answering service. You book their services for a set period – minimum of one month – paying in advance and preferably by cash. It's in your own interest to pay by cash as there is no trace on you personally. You register the name you wish to be known by and a code word and, for the period of time you've paid for, they will accept all messages for that name. You can phone in any time you like, give your name and the code word and they will read back your messages to you. Once passed on, each message is destroyed. No files are kept. This is just the sort of thing that Paddy Scanlon told us about. The Chameleon's contacts – maybe even himself – read the notice in *The Times* and placed a reply using that phone number.

'Our unknown friend, D'Argent, phones and gets asked to leave his name and a phone number where *he* can be contacted – and this gets passed on to

Chameleon. Contact can now be made direct between the Chameleon and D'Argent and the only one at risk is D'Argent. The Chameleon still has the upper hand and is still invisible. Simple.'

'Well, let's hope our fraud man comes up with a lead for you two in the near future. I can't keep the lid on this thing indefinitely unless we progress.'

'And where will that leave Colloney, Frank?'

'Where he is, I'm afraid, Cowboy. We simply don't have enough hard evidence to even go for a re-trial. We have to have another suspect.'

Three days later they had one.

When Frank got word from Liam Gallagher that he had enough information to make a report, he asked him to attend a meeting with Cowboy and Jimmy in his office the following morning. All three of them were waiting when Gallagher arrived. Tall and thin, in his early forties and wearing black, horn-rimmed glasses, Liam Gallagher was considered a whizz kid with figures, and had an infallible nose for sniffing out financial irregularities. He read financial reports like others read novels. He could take in a column of figures, 100 entries in all, quicker than they could be entered into a calculator, and could pin-point a reversed entry like a radar. It had been rumoured that the first lap-top computer was in fact the result of Liam having sexual intercourse with a main frame! For all of this, his personal bank account was the biggest joke of the Squad. It was his wife who ran the home finances.

'Right, gentlemen,' Liam began, 'first a few brief words on the current financial situation of JB Finance. In short, it's not looking too good. They won't go broke for a few years yet, but I suspect that at the end of this fiscal year, for the first time ever, there will be little, if any, dividend payable to shareholders. Up until the beginning of the year everything looked good, but one of their leasing contractors, an American company, has gone bust. A lot of money has gone down the tube on that particular deal – or I should say, deals. JB Finance seemed to like lending them money for lease-back operations. Now the main company has gone bust and all the subsidiary companies are going to collapse with it. Good money is disappearing after bad!

'Following the briefing Cowboy gave me before I went in, I left the IRS boys to get on with their job while I snooped round a bit, going back to the last year that James O'Brien was in the Chair. What the mood of the company was like, who was who, so to speak, and where the money was going. Then I took a look at the year *after* his death, looked at the same things, and almost immediately I came up with a promising target. Then I carried on up until now, just to be sure of all the facts. But let me put it to you like this. If we are looking for another suspect for the murder of James O'Brien, one who stood to make a very large financial gain on his death, then I've got your man.' Enjoying the suspense he had created as the other three waited for him to continue, Liam leaned forward and refilled his tea cup.

'Besides being a very clever man – a financial genius in fact – James O'Brien was also very proud to be Irish. And he wanted his success to be Irish. The parent company, JB Finance, was and is, the headquarters of all the subsidiary companies, all combined under the name of JB Finance (International). There are offices in London, Bern, Düsseldorf and New York, and all are registered here in Ireland as offspring of the mother company. They pay taxes in their respective countries, but the balance sheet is compiled here in Dublin. So, I was able to get my hands on the whole shebang. If he had been a clever bastard, instead of the honest gentleman he was, proud of his heritage, then JB Finance (International) would have been the parent company, with its HQ in Switzerland or Liechtenstein.

'Originally it was a private company, owned totally by O'Brien, and he made all the decisions. But, as things progressed, especially the start of the leasing boom, and the many diversifications it allowed, he needed to take on more experts in different fields. It was also necessary to get more capital, if JB Finance was to take advantage of the opportunities. So he went semi-public. The decision-makers of JB Finance were to be the shareholders. He himself owned 25%, and none of the other nine directors individually owned more than 9%. They could have ganged up on him I suppose, but it seems he picked his people very, very, carefully. He never got gang-banged and he still retained control of his company.

'So, each director was an expert in his own field. Construction – there were three of them; oil – exploration, rigs and tankers; commercial ship-building; plant machinery; and the leisure industry. But the big business was in leasing. You see, with loopholes in the leasing laws, companies were looking to sell their machinery to finance companies, and then lease back the same machinery – without the stuff physically going anywhere – and take advantage of the tax concessions. The *original* idea behind the thinking was that companies could raise the capital to invest in new machinery and to expand – meaning taking on more employees – without the massive overdrafts and bank loans. Let me assure you that that rarely happened. Companies just made more money, paid less tax and higher dividends.

'O'Brien vetoed several large deals that his experts came up with. Although everything looked above board, O'Brien had a nose for a funny deal, and most of the time the man was correct. He made a few mistakes, sometimes missing opportunities where the company could have made more money, but, on the whole, it was all good, solid business. On several occasions he even arranged special rates for certain firms. If they were going through a rough patch but still had a good future, he lowered the leasing rates – without penalty – until things got better. Such favours were seldom forgotten. Those firms went back to JB for future financing even when they might have been able to shave point something of a per cent with another finance company. Most of the stuff that JB got was cream and very little sour milk. Are you all with me so far?'

All three men nodded silently.

'Good. Then came the big one, about nine, almost ten years ago. It was going to bring in over 150 million dollars, but O'Brien was against it – and the majority of the board took his advice. His reason? He didn't like the smell of it. The American company, Sheldon Incorporated of New York were offering to pay over the odds for their services. To O'Brien, it just didn't line up as being a goodie.

'One of the board members was very much in favour of the deal. He tried everything he could to get the majority vote he needed to go against O'Brien, but he failed. When O'Brien died, the deal went through. You already know the terms of the will – his 25% was offered to the board first. If they didn't pick up the options, then the shares went public. That never happened.

'William Jeffery Clark, current Chairman of the Board and Managing Director, at the time of O'Brien's death owned 9% of the company. After his death, Clark bought another 10% and got the proxy vote of another 5% when one of the board retired to the golf course. So William J. Clark has control of the company with a total of 24% of the shares to play with. He was the one who tried hard to get the deal with Sheldon to go through, and did get it through after O'Brien died.

'It was good business – or seemed to be. Initial loans were repaid early, to be replaced by bigger ones, which again were repaid early, to be replaced by bigger ones and then BANG. Classic sting. Sheldon is broke, most of its assets that were used as collateral for the loans have disappeared, and JB Finance is set to lose a bomb.

'At the time of his murder, if Colloney had not been such a prime target, then the CIB would have turned their attention to the company, we would have been called in, and the finger, several of them in fact, might just have pointed at William J Clark the turd.' Liam smiled at his three colleagues.

None smiled back, especially not Mooney. He was questioning his own handling of the original investigation. Had he done his job properly? Was it his fault that an innocent man was in prison? Ruthlessly he pushed these thoughts out of his mind. After all, he had been set up as part of a very elaborate plan which sent Colloney to jail. At the time of the murder, any other detective in charge of the case would have done exactly the same as he had; concentrate on the obvious. The plan had worked, and would have remained watertight, had it not been for a night of drinking and story-telling in Denmark. Here was a chance to put things right, and this time there would be no mistakes.

'Where did Clark get the money to buy the shares, Liam?'

'I don't know, Frank. that was not part of my brief, nor would the information necessarily be in the company's accounts. But he bought them all right, and I would also suspect that he had to pay a large lump sum, cash, and on the quiet, for the proxy shares. He didn't actually need to own the shares, just the voting power. If he had had to buy them, then I'd say he would have had to come up with several million. His way was a good deal for both him and the "seller". The "seller" gets a tax-free lump sum paid into a little overseas bank account – *and* gets to keep the dividends. And they zoomed up a hell of a lot in value over the years. Bugger-all this year mind you. A lot of money has gone down the tube with this Sheldon business.'

'Any idea how much he paid for the 10% he bought?' Cowboy asked.

'Close to ten million pounds.'

Jimmy whistled. 'That's one hell of a lot of money to carry round in your wallet, eh?'

'Small change to some in this line of business, Jimmy,' Liam replied.

'If ten million pounds is small change, what's one million dollars then?' Jimmy asked, looking at Mooney and Cowboy. All three were thinking the same thing. Pin-money to have somebody killed.

'Okay Liam, thanks very much for all your help.'

Liam rose to his feet and placed the thick folder containing his report on Frank's desk. 'Any chance of being told what all this is about, Frank?'

'Not for the moment, Liam, and what you've learned is for yourself and your boss's eyes only. It's important. I promise you'll be the first to know when we let the cat out of the bag. Okay?'

'Does it make any difference if it is or not? Muggins here does all the work and the CIB will take all the credit, as usual.' The thin smile that creased his face belittled the rebuke. When working on their own cases the Fraud Squad often pulled in experts from other branches without making any kind of explanation. He understood the 'need to know' rule.

CHAPTER NINE

Dublin, August–September 1994

GRANTON HALL, A FOUR-STORIED GEORGIAN HOUSE
in the fashionable Blackrock area of the city, started life
as the town house of a titled English landowner with
large estates in Ireland. Just prior to the Second World
War it had been sold and converted into a small but ex-
clusive hotel. In the early '60s, as JB Finance began to
expand, James O'Brien bought it with a view to turning
it into the company headquarters. The house, with a
vast cellar now used as the company's filing vault, stood
in an acre of landscaped gardens enclosed in high walls.
The car park, at the front of the house, had spaces for fifteen cars, and these were reserved for the directors and
visitors only. Surrounding the rest of the house were
sprawling lawns dotted with oak, birch and elm trees,
shrubberies and flower beds. The only way into the
grounds was via large wrought-iron gates watched over
by a uniformed security guard, a retired soldier sup-
plementing his pension.

The hotel reception area on the ground floor had
been retained and the antique french-polished mahog-
any desk was now manned by three young, attractive receptionists. Several works of art decorated the walls, and
the central ceiling chandelier had been incorporated
into the more modern lighting system that softly illuminated the paintings. On arrival, visitors were wel-

comed at reception, then directed to an alcove near the elevator. Leather sofas and armchairs, spaced round a large glass-topped chrome coffee table, allowed them to wait in comfort until a representative from whichever department they were visiting came down to collect them personally.

The rooms on the first floor had all been converted into offices, each one dealing with a specific area of company interest. The second floor contained the offices of the directors and their secretaries, along with a small directors' dining room. The third and top floor was reserved for William J. Clark, the Chairman of the Board and Managing Director. This contained a small reception area which led to his secretary's office and then on to his own. The boardroom was also on this floor, along with a one-bedroom apartment for the personal use of the Chairman.

William J. Clark was a man who appreciated the very best in life, especially if other people were prepared to pay for it. On the day he took control of the company he hired an interior decorator, gave him specific instructions as to what he wanted done, and had the entire third floor completely redecorated. There was a small drop in dividends that year, but nobody complained.

It was his custom never to arrive at the office before 10.00 a.m. but he seldom left before 7.00 p.m. The mail arrived at 8.00 a.m. and was sorted by the receptionists at the main desk. From there it went to the various offices for re-sorting and in Clark's case was opened by his secretary. Only mail marked 'Personal' was left unopened on his desk. Other mail would have her comments in the margin, with notes about action taken or to be taken, or references to his diary and appointments books which were checked well before his arrival so any changes could be brought to his immediate attention.

On the Monday after the meeting between the four detectives, Clark arrived in his chauffeur-driven dark blue Mercedes Benz, at 10.10 a.m. As the driver held the rear door open for him he collected his morning papers and briefcase and without a word walked briskly through the twin glass doors of the HQ. As he stood by the elevator, one of the receptionists nervously approached him.

'Mr Clark, sir. Oh, Mr Clark.'

He turned. The girl was in her late teens, and, if he remembered correctly, she had not been with the company all that long. He smiled at her.

'Yes, young lady. What is it?'

'Sorry to bother you, sir, but this letter was hand delivered this morning at 8.25. I noted the time on the corner of the envelope just in case it was important, sir. The gentleman who delivered it was most insistent that I hand it to you personally. Nobody else, he said. I held it back from the rest of your mail.' She now began to worry about having made a mistake. Maybe she should have given it to his secretary. 'I . . . I hope I've done the right thing, sir.' Her hand was shaking slightly as she handed him the letter. He gave a hurried smile, took the envelope, and entered the elevator, pressing the button for the top floor. He looked at the envelope. Whoever had sent it had made sure that it could not be tampered with without it being known. The gummed flap and all four sides of the envelope had been taped over. Written on the brown envelope, in red, were the words FOR THE PERSONAL ATTENTION ONLY, followed by his name and the Blackrock address written in blue, bold block capitals. There was no sender's name or address on the back. Stepping from the lift at his office he smiled a good morning to his secretary and asked for a pot of coffee to be brought in.

Once in his office, he balanced his Italian, handmade leather briefcase on the polished bog-oak desk and settled himself into his leather chair. He stared at the envelope, turning it over again to see if he had missed anything. Picking up the slim, solid gold letter-opener from the desk he picked at the tape, slicing the envelope open. It contained a single sheet of typed paper. As he read the contents, the blood drained from his face and his hands began to tremble. At that moment Julie, his secretary, knocked discreetly and entered, bearing a silver serving-tray with a Beleek coffee service. The coffee was freshly percolated to the strength he liked. As she placed the tray on his desk, she noticed his paleness.

'Are you feeling all right, sir?'

He looked up, startled to find her beside him. 'What? Oh yes, yes, I'm fine. Eh, just a bit under the weather, thank you. Just leave the coffee will you, and would you ask that young receptionist to come up immediately. The young girl who handed me a letter on my way in.'

'Certainly, sir – but are you sure you are all right? You wouldn't like me to get you an aspirin, or something?' she asked with concern. Maybe she should get him something anyway. He did not look at all well.

'No, no, thank you, Julie, I'm fine, honestly. Just send the girl up and hold all my calls until I'm finished with her.' She nodded and left the office.

As he waited for the girl he sat staring at the leather-bound blotter on the desk, memories of something he couldn't forget running through his mind. The coffee stayed untouched in the pot. There was another discreet knock and Julie entered, holding the door open for the young girl from the reception area.

'Miss Gormon, Mr Clark.'

Hesitantly the girl entered the 'Holy of Holies'. This was the first time she had come above the second floor. She looked around, amazement at the decor and furniture overcoming her terror at being summoned to come up. She *knew* she should have given the letter to his secretary.

'Thank you, Julie. Could we have another cup please?' He gestured in the direction of the young girl, and Julie nodded. Wonders will never cease, she thought. The newest receptionist taking morning coffee with the MD!

'Come in, Miss Gormon, come in. Please take a seat.' He smiled at her, trying to put her at her ease, indicating a leather chair to the side of the desk. Julie reappeared with a second cup and saucer and laid it on the tray, then departed.

'Now, Miss Gormon, I just want to ask you a few questions about the gentleman you said delivered this letter. Coffee?'

At first she was going to decline, preferring tea, but thought better of it. She didn't want to upset him more than he obviously was already. She would certainly have something to tell the other girls during lunch in the basement staff room.

'Thank you,' she managed to whisper in reply. 'I, eh,' she coughed, clearing her throat, 'I hope I haven't done anything wrong, Mr Clark, but the man was so insistent that I hand it to you personally.'

'No, no, no, no, Miss Gormon, nothing like that at all. Cream, sugar?' She nodded and he spooned in two small spoonfuls of sugar and a portion of cream, handing the now lukewarm coffee across the desk. She took the cup, frightened by how fragile the china was, scared she was going to drop it. 'Nothing like that, I assure you,' he continued. 'You were perfectly correct to act as you did, believe me. I just want to know a little about the man. What did he look like? How old was he? Was he tall, short, medium, slim, fat?'

'Oh, I don't know if I can tell you anything about him, sir. He was just a man.'

Clark smiled, charming her, but wanting to lean over and grab her by the neck and squeeze the information out of her. 'Try, for me, please, Miss Gormon. It's rather important that I find out who he was. Start with his clothing. Did his clothes look expensive, or was he a sort of jeans and trainers man?'

'Well, sir, he had a lightweight overcoat on, and was wearing a collar and tie. A maroon tie, white shirt. He had sort of dark wavy hair, and, oh yes, his ears stuck out a bit. I think something had happened to his nose at some stage as well. Broken, I think. He smelt nice, if you know what I mean, sir. Very nice aftershave. Expensive, I would say.'

'There you are, my dear,' he beamed at her, putting her more at ease. 'You see, you do remember. Now. Was he clean-shaven? Beard? Moustache? What about glasses?'

'Clean-shaven, no glasses,' she continued, warming to the game as she continued her description of Jimmy Douglas.

'What about his voice. Educated? Was he Irish or foreign? Did he speak softly or loudly? How did he behave himself?'

'Oh, he was very nice, sir. Kind of flirtatious, if you know what I mean. But in a teasing way. I have a steady boyfriend, and told him that. Anyway, he was much older than me.' She blushed slightly, remembering the cheeky twinkle in the man's eye. 'He wanted to know where I ate lunch, sir. Oh, I just remembered. About his size. My boyfriend is just over six feet tall and this man was not as tall as Larry, just under the six feet I'd say, but stocky and well-built. He spoke with an English accent. London, I'd say. A bit like that guy who plays in *Minder* on the telly. Nice, but not posh, if you understand what I mean, sir. Very sure of himself he was. He asked me to hand the letter to you, but at the same time it was like he was ordering me to do it. Like he was used to people doing what he told them. I think that's all I can remember about him, sir.'

'All!' he smiled again, making a joke of it. 'I shouldn't think there was much you missed, young lady. Thank you very much for your assistance. Now I would like you to go away and forget you ever saw this man. Forget he was here, and please do not speak about it with any other member of the staff. Will you do that for me, please?'

Blushing again, she nodded, not knowing how she was going to explain to the other girls what she had been up to, being sent for by 'God' himself. He continued smiling, but said nothing more. The interview was over, and she got the message.

'Well, eh, sir, if there's nothing else, I'd better get back to reception.'

He nodded. 'Thank you again, Miss Gormon. I won't forget this favour. Good morning to you.'

Placing her untouched cup of coffee back on the tray she walked quietly out of the room, closing the door behind her.

The smile on his face disappeared the moment the door closed behind her. He pressed a button his desk. 'No calls or visitors or interruptions of any kind, Julie, until I say otherwise.' She confirmed his instructions, wondering how she was going to put off the appointment he had with a client in fifteen minutes, but she knew better than to argue.

He opened the single sheet of paper once more and read the contents.

D'Argent.
As you are in the finance business you will understand when I say that the recession is hitting me at the moment. I have a cash-flow problem. I am forced to ask you for a retainer on my services for a short period. Kindly be at The Gresham Hotel, tomorrow evening, for dinner. A table has been reserved in your name, for two, for 8.00 p.m. A confidant of mine will meet with you.

CHAMELEON.

Picking up the phone on his desk he phoned the Gresham. Yes, they confirmed, a table had been booked in his name. Seven-thirty for eight. For two. Had there been a mistake? Should it be cancelled? No, he informed them. No mistake, no cancellation. Replacing the phone, he got up from the desk and walked to the drinks cabinet. Pouring himself a large brandy he stood by the picture window behind his desk, looking down on to the garden, speculating on what his next move should be.

Eventually he returned to his desk. Taking a small, hand-tooled leather address book from his jacket pocket he flicked through the pages. He found what he was looking for. He stared at the number for a moment or two, then, decision made, he reached once more for the phone.

Cowboy took the phone on the fourth ring, listened to the caller, and his face lit up with a smile. Thanking the caller he replaced the phone, then turned to Jimmy.

'Well, he's taken the bait. He's phoned the Gresham asking about the table. He was asked if he wanted to cancel, but said no. Now, unless he calls the police – who would pass a complaint of blackmail on to the Castle – we've got him.

'You know, you really looked good in my coat. It suited you. We'd better dig into my wardrobe for tomorrow night and see if we can come up with something decent for you. We can't have you turning up at the Gresham in *your* togs, can we? You wouldn't get past the doorman.'

They were sitting in Cowboy's apartment, where they had been waiting for Maurice, the *Maître d'* at the Gresham, to call. Cowboy knew Maurice and had given him a story about a trick he was pulling on Clark. Maurice had agreed to call if Clark phoned.

Neither of them had told Frank Mooney about the letter. Frank had left it to the two detectives to figure out some way of making a link between the *Times* advert and Clark, but had told them to let him know what they came up with, before making a move. Cowboy had decided to ignore this instruction, agreeing with Jimmy that a blackmail letter would be the swiftest way of getting a reaction out of Clark. If he had been innocent, then he would have gone to the police with the letter.

'Okay, Jimmy. Phase Two comes into operation tomorrow night. Remember. Let him arrive first, and leave him sweating for a bit. Play it by ear when you are at the table. Easy, or lean on him, depending on how he reacts to you. Don't hang around once he's fully in the picture, head straight back to your place. Marlane and I will see what he does next, finish our meal, then meet you back at your place.'

'What are we doing for the rest of the day?'

'We're staying out of Frank Mooney's way, that's what we're doing. He would not be too pleased about this. It's not quite "ethical", is it? We'll tell him about it later.'

★

116

The 22:00 shuttle from Heathrow to Dublin that night had a last-minute passenger, a Londoner, Richard Gordon. Once through the Blue section of Customs at Dublin, he made straight for the late-opening Allied Irish Bank Bureau de Change to convert some sterling into Irish punts. Armed with a small stack of coins he made his way to the line of public phone booths and dialled a Dublin number. He spoke briefly, listened and then hung up. Shoving a second twenty-pence coin into the slot he called a second Dublin number, letting it ring five times before hanging up. He immediately redialled the same number, and the phone was picked up.

'You are holding a parcel for me,' Gordon said into the mouthpiece.

The other person confirmed that he was, and gave instructions for a pick-up. Gordon had spoken to the same man earlier that day, from London.

'Be at the GPO, on O'Connell Street, at 10.00 tomorrow morning. Watch for a young girl with blond hair worn in a pony-tail. She'll be wearing faded blue jeans, slashed across the knees. She'll enter one of the phone booths in the GPO. When she leaves go into the booth and you'll find a ticket Blue-Tacked to the shelf. Take the ticket to the left-luggage section at the central bus station. What you require will be waiting for you there. You'll make payment in the usual way?'

'Yes. Your bank will confirm the payment as normal.'

'That'll do nicely and have a nice day, sir.' The sarcastic tone was still ringing in his ear as Gordon replaced the receiver.

CHAPTER TEN

Dublin, August–September 1994

William J. Clark arrived at The Gresham Hotel on O'Connell Street the following evening at 7.20 to be greeted by name by Maurice, the *Maître d'*. After assisting him off with his coat, Maurice showed him to his table, set for two, explaining that his guest had yet to arrive. With a slight movement of his hand Maurice indicated to the waiter, who promptly deposited two leather-bound menus on the table, handing one of them to Clark. Gruffly ordering a large whiskey, Clark ignored the two menus and lit a cigarette with his gold Dunhill lighter.

Fifteen minutes later Maurice was smiling broadly as he welcomed Cowboy and Marlane, two of his favourite diners. Quickly palming and pocketing the folded twenty-punt note that Cowboy slipped him he complimented Marlane on her hair, her clothes, and her beauty. With Cowboy's lightweight overcoat and Marlane's wrap in the safe custody of a young bellboy, Maurice led them to their table, not far from where Clark still sat alone. Every head in the dining room, including Clark's, turned in their direction, as they moved through the restaurant. Seating them both, Maurice made way for the head waiter who placed a menu in front of each, quietly suggesting the Châteaubriand, served with sauté potatoes, mushrooms and a selection of vegetables.

Accepting the suggestion, Cowboy ordered a mineral water for Lane and tonic water for himself, at the same time telling the head water to let the wine waiter choose a wine to accompany the beef.

'That's not like you, Cowboy,' Lane commented. 'It usually takes you ages to pick the food and wine.'

'Yea, I know, but I'm just a little edgy about this thing tonight. I think it's because Mooney would bust a gut if he knew what we were up to, but it's the only bloody way to speed this darn investigation up.'

'Here's Jimmy now,' Lane whispered, spotting the English detective as he stood by the door, looking around the dining room as Maurice approached him. She watched the two men confer for a moment, then Maurice led the way through the tables to where Clark sat. Cowboy watched Jimmy's approach from the corner of his eye as his friend sat, leaving Clark in full view. The wire Jimmy was wearing was attached to a recording device taped to the base of his spine. Cowboy had decided against wearing an ear-piece, afraid that it might just be noticed. He would listen to the recording later that night, back at Jimmy's hotel. It was obvious from the way in which Jimmy's index finger was pointing at Clark that he was putting the message across heavily, stressing his words, making sure that Clark understood the implications of not doing as he was told. The conversation seemed to be mostly one way, with Jimmy doing all the talking. Cowboy was slightly concerned that Clark was not reacting in the way they had expected. Jimmy remained seated only for about five minutes, then rose and abruptly walked out of the restaurant.

Clark made no move to leave and when the waiter approached the table, ordered another large whiskey and a Waldorf salad. Neither Cowboy nor Clark noticed the man on the other side of the restaurant who left his un-finished meal a few moments after Jimmy departed, slid-ing a fifty-punt note on to the table beside his plate.

Cowboy and Marlane enjoyed their food. Cowboy noted Clark's departure but there seemed little point in hurrying the meal just because Clark had left. They ate and chatted and joked for the best part of two hours after Jimmy's departure. Eventually it was time to leave. Cowboy asked her if she wanted to be dropped off at either his or her apartment, or if she wanted to come with him to Jimmy's. Not wanting to miss any detail of the evening's events, she threatened him with dire con-sequences if he even attempted to keep her from hearing Jimmy's story. Paying the bill and leaving a generous tip, he thanked Maurice again for his help.

It was just after 10.45 p.m. when Cowboy drove the Porsche into the car park at The Belview Hotel. The night porter recognized him as a regular visitor to the English geezer in number 17 and smiled at him as they passed, heading for the stairs. He paid close attention to the rear view of Marlane until they were out of sight, then returned to his newspaper, wondering where he had seen her before. Arriving at Room 17, Cowboy knocked. No answer. He tried the door but it was locked. He thought he could sense a slight aroma of spices emanating from somewhere. Most likely someone having a Chinese take-away, he mused. Looking at his watch he realized there were ten minutes left before the pubs closed. Trust Jimmy, he thought.

'Bugger must be at the pub. I saw his car in the car park, so he can't be far. He shouldn't be long. They close at 11.00.' Lane made no comment as he led her back down the stairs to the lobby. The porter looked up from his paper but said nothing, watching as they went and sat in the far corner on one of the sofas. They sat chatting quietly, until 11.15. Cowboy decided to ask the porter if he knew which pub Jimmy used near by, and what time he had gone out.

'I saw him come in, sir,' the porter explained, 'about 9.00 it was. He went straight up to his room. He had a visitor shortly after, but the gentleman didn't stay long. A couple of minutes at most.'

Slightly puzzled Cowboy asked what time Jimmy had left, after that.

'I didn't see him go out, sir. I've been on the desk since 7.00. I might have been away for a few moments at most, but I didn't see him go by.' Turning, he checked the racks of room keys. 'His key is not on the rack, and it's a hotel rule that residents leave their keys at the desk before they go out. Are you sure he's not in his room, sir?'

Cowboy felt a wave of dread rolling through him. The hairs on the back of his neck began to rise. Opening his wallet he showed the porter his warrant card.

'Bring your pass key and come with me,' he ordered.

'Is something wrong, sir?' the porter asked.

'I don't know. Just do as I say and bring the key.'

While the porter got the key, Cowboy crossed over to Marlane.

'Stay here, kitten. I'll only be a minute.' She started to rise but something in his eyes told her to leave it. Something was wrong. It was not what he had said, nor the way that he said it, but she knew her man, and he wasn't happy with the situation. She sat down again.

Taking the stairs two at a time, Cowboy raced back to Room 17, closely followed by a puffing, panting porter. At the door the porter's hands were shaking as he tried to fit the key into the lock, failing.

'Give the fucking thing here,' Cowboy growled,

almost snatching the key from the other man's hand and opening the door to his friend's room.

In the middle of the floor, arms and legs spread-eagled, lay the body of Detective Inspector James Douglas of Scotland Yard. His eyes were open and staring and the small neat hole in the centre of his forehead gave the appearance of a third eye, also open and staring. His hair lay in a pool of congealing blood, the stain spreading across the worn carpet. The smell of Chinese food became stronger and stronger to Cowboy's nostrils and he suddenly remembered when and where he had smelt a similar odour. It had been the day he and Jimmy had visited the house of James O'Brien, when he had seen the images of the killer moving from one room to the other. He cursed himself for not making the connection when he had knocked on Jimmy's door earlier. Not that it would have made much difference. Jimmy had already been dead by then, but he had wasted half an hour sitting downstairs. In his mind he heard the words of warning they had received from the ex-mercenary, Paddy Scanlon. 'If you want to take a friend's advice, Cowboy, forget it. You're not in the same class as this man, and you never will be. Fuck with this guy and you'll get dead.' Well he *had* fucked with the guy, and he wasn't dead. But Jimmy was. Jimmy the Joker would be telling no more jokes, chatting up no more 'birds' and drinking no more pints of bitter. No more jokes, no more booze, no more Jimmy.

It was only as he closed and locked the door to his friend's room that he saw the porter, stretched flat out on the corridor floor in a dead faint. He hadn't even heard him fall.

By the time his colleagues had arrived from CIB Headquarters at Dublin Castle, Marlane was gone. Cowboy had sent her home in his car, promising to come to her as soon as possible. There was nothing to be gained by her staying and the inevitable press coverage of the murder would not be good for her image. When allowing the night porter to call a contact on one of the tabloid newspapers, Cowboy got him to agree to say nothing about Marlane. The porter would have called the newspaper in any case – all porters throughout the city earned extra money by tipping off contacts about their guests – but this way Cowboy had made it seem like a deal between them. The steely glint in Cowboy's eyes left no doubt as to what might happen should the porter break the agreement. Everybody could be got for something, some time. Soon after his colleagues arrived the newshounds were on the scene *en masse*, other papers tipped off by members of the Garda and by detectives giving favours on account. By the time Commander Frank Mooney had arrived, the crowd outside the small hotel had grown and uniformed Gardai had to ease a path through the throng for his car. He had been called at home by Cowboy and informed of the murder. The duty team of detectives waited outside Jimmy's room for the forensic team to arrive. Jimmy was known to them, as most of them had been at the recent stag night. The cover story that he was on a secondment to learn Irish police tactics was accepted – or, as Jimmy put it to them, he had come 'to teach the thicko Micks how to detect'. His humour and friendliness had made him popular. The death of a fellow policeman in the line of duty always elicits strong emotions in any force, reminding them that there, but for the grace of God, they could all go. Frank Mooney found Cowboy sitting alone in the manager's office.

Cowboy was feeling a deep sadness at the death of his friend, and anger too, but he was also feeling guilty. He had agreed to the blackmail letter idea and had been the one to suggest that Jimmy should play the 'baddie' role. He was also remembering the warnings of his mercenary friend, and how he had ignored the advice. He was angry at himself, and he was overwhelmingly angry with the Chameleon. Frank Mooney knew how Cowboy was feeling, but had no intention of letting him wallow in his misery. There was a job to be done.

'Right, you. Tell me exactly what happened. From the beginning.'

Cowboy told him of the events that had led to Jimmy's death. He saw the angry flash in Mooney's eyes as he explained about the blackmail note, but Mooney said nothing, allowing Cowboy to complete the tale, finishing off by explaining that he had sent Marlane home, to keep her out of the investigation.

'That's about the first feckin' intelligent thing you've done since you started, Cowboy.'

'I know, Frank. I should have come back here immediately after Clark left the Gresham . . .'

'In which case there would be another two bodies lying beside Jimmy's,' Frank interrupted.

'But Clark . . .'

'Clark didn't do this, Cowboy. Use your head. He's involved, most definitely, right up to his pink little ears, but he didn't pull the trigger. He's no hit man. But he contacted somebody, maybe your Chameleon.'

'You going to get a warrant for his arrest?'

'Let's let him sweat a little bit first. Let's give him a shock. As far as he's concerned a nasty little blackmailer has been taken care of and the problem, *his* problem, has gone away. Wait until he sees tomorrow's headlines and reads that the man was a Scotland Yard detective. That'll give him an early bowel movement at the breakfast table, then we'll arrive and see what he has to say.'

There was a knock on the door and Detective Inspector Frank Kennedy popped his head round the door. 'Oh, there you are, Boss.' He entered the room, closing the door behind him, and handed a small flat object to Mooney. 'We found this in Jimmy's room, pushed under the bed. Thought you might like to hear it straight away.' It was the tape recorder, the 'wire' that Jimmy had worn for his meeting with Clark.

'Anything else?' Cowboy asked.

The other man shook his head. 'Nothing yet. Doesn't really look like the place was searched – but there again, if the guy's a professional, then it wouldn't, would it? From the way Jimmy's lying, and from the look on his face, I'd say he got hit the moment he opened the door. Took a pace or two back into the room and *wham!* That was it. Small-calibre pistol from the looks of the wound. Small entry hole, and no great mess in the room.' Kennedy saw Cowboy wince. 'Sorry Cowboy, I just thought you should know. If it's any consolation, he died immediately. Knew no pain.

'As nobody heard anything – none of the other guests nor the night porter – I'd hazard a guess that the pistol was silenced. I'll be back upstairs if you want me, Boss. Okay?'

'Thanks, Frankie, I'll be up shortly,' Mooney replied.

'Frankie.' The detective turned as Cowboy called his name. 'Thanks. I appreciate your telling me.'

'Yea, well . . .' Kennedy shrugged his shoulders and closed the door behind him.

Mooney pressed the 'rewind' button on the small recorder, taking the tape back to the beginning. Pressing the 'play' button, the two of them listened to Jimmy's voice as the tape started rolling.

'Testing, testing, testing. 5–4–3–2–1. This is Detective Inspector James Douglas, seconded to the Irish CIB.'

He read out the date and the time which was followed by a slight click as the recorder went into the 'hold' mode, automatically. Almost immediately his voice came on again.

'Good evening, Mr Clark. Ordered yet?'

'Who the hell are you, and what do you want?' Clark sounded angry but not frightened.

'Relax, Mr Clark. Who I am is not important. But you know who I am from, and what is being asked of you. Our . . . mutual friend . . . asked that I come and see you on his behalf concerning a retainer. For possible future services – or possibly to prevent his future services, if you see what I mean. It's a call for old time's sake.' Jimmy chuckled. Even to the two listening detectives he sounded ominous.

'I don't need your . . . friend's services. Now or ever.'

'Don't be too sure, Mr Clark. Sometimes doing *nothing*, can be a service to some people – if you see what I mean. You've done well for yourself, Mr Clark. You got what you wanted, when you wanted it, with the help of our friend, and things have gotten better and better for you. Now our friend is asking a small favour. He has many overheads and income has dropped. The recession even hits this business, you see, Mr Clark.' Cowboy couldn't help but smile at Jimmy's remark. 'Cash-flow problem, Mr Clark,' Jimmy continued. 'I'm sure it won't last for long. He'll get things straightened out and then no problem. But just now he's having some trouble.

'He's asking for a small retainer, say £20,000 per year, for the next couple of years. That amount won't hurt you in any way. It won't even make a dent in your small change, will it now, Mr Clark?'

'This conversation is ridiculous. I refuse to have anything to do with you, or your so-called friend.'

'In that case, why did you come here, Mr Clark?' Jimmy's tone of voice then changed, and the menace was evident, the threat obvious. 'Listen, Clark. I just told you that doing nothing can be as much a service as doing something. Ever heard the joke "Usually I kill for money, but you're a friend so I'll kill you for nothing"? Don't be stupid, Clark. Pay the money for a year or two and that will be that. You can deduct the amounts should you need our services again.

'You have five days from tomorrow in which to pay half a year's retainer, second half to be ready in three months' time. That gives you plenty of time to get it together. A man like you should have no problem in raising ten grand in five days. The graveyard is full of stupid people, Clark. Don't be a stupid person, okay?'

'I need time to think,' Clark replied.

'Don't think, Clark. Act. You have five days. I'll call you at the office then. Good night, and by the way, *bon appétit*.' And with that the tape went silent. Mooney was just about to rewind it again when Jimmy's voice came on again against a background of traffic noises.

'Cowboy, I've just left the Gresham and am walking towards O'Connell Bridge. I have a gut feeling I'm being followed. It's not Clark, or I'd have spotted him, but somebody's on my tail. I'll lose them, and make my way back to the Belview. See you later.' There was a short pause on the tape then Jimmy's voice yet again, only this time it was a whisper.

'Cowboy, I'm back at the hotel, and it's 8.45. You're still stuffin' your face with food and ogling that luscious bird of yours. I think we may have a nibble on the line. Somebody's at the door and it's too early for you.' There was a slight pause, then Jimmy spoke again. 'Listen, buddy boy, you take care of yourself, y'hear?' There were then sounds of movement which they guessed was Jimmy pushing the tape, still in 'record' mode under the bed. The sounds that followed were too faint to be heard clearly. Mooney rewound the tape several times to the beginning of that section, but the recording was too low for either Cowboy or himself to understand what was happening.

'I'll get this to the Lab first thing. With the equipment they have we should be able to hear if the porter farted when the tape was running.'

Cowboy nodded. He didn't particularly care what they did with the tape. They could turn the tape back, but they couldn't turn time back, couldn't reverse it all so that the ending would be different. He knew, as Mooney did, that the last words they could hear plainly on the tape were words of farewell. Jimmy knew they had hit the jackpot, but was unable to avoid what was coming to him. His last words were a warning that his friend should watch out. Cowboy sat crouched in the chair, his head in his hands.

'Go on home, Cowboy. Go to Lane. She probably needs you now, after the shock of this happening. Go out via the fire-escape. Stay well clear of the newspapers. None of the lads will say you've been here, I'll see to that. Go on. Off with you. I'll see you in my office at eight. I'll have everything sorted by then and we'll both go and pay Mr Clark a morning visit.'

Cowboy nodded his head in agreement. He had no desire to face a bundle of screaming newspaper journalists in search of a morning headline. Lane would be needing him, just as he needed her. 'Thanks, Frank. I'll be okay in the morning, I promise.'

'I know you will, son, I know you will. And stuffin' it to Mr Clark is going to be your pleasure. I'll see you at eight.'

*

Frank walked down the stairs from the manager's office behind the stretcher carrying the body. As the swing doors to the hotel opened flash bulbs popped, photographers jostling each other to get a better angle, a better shot. The stretcher was loaded into the ambulance and it drove away, siren blaring.

'Hey, Commander. What's the story?'

'What's happened, Frank?'

'Who's the corpse?'

The badgering pressmen gathered round him with their questions, some, the older ones, with pencils poised over notepads, the younger ones thrusting hand-held dictaphones towards him. Over his head towered the large boom microphone of a television crew.

'Okay, gents. Just a quick one for the moment. You'll get more tomorrow: The dead man is Detective Inspector James Douglas of New Scotland Yard. I'll arrange for his photograph to be distributed to you, back at the Castle.' Frank wanted to get a photograph of Jimmy in the early morning editions if possible. That would make Clark choke on his breakfast.

'What's a Scotland Yard man doing in Dublin, Frank?' Unable to see who had asked the question because of the glaring television lights, Frank turned in the general direction of the speaker.

'He was here on a six-month secondment to the CIB. Looking to see how the CIB and Scotland Yard could work together.'

'Was he on an active case?' came another call.

'No,' Frank lied. 'He was just here as a visitor.'

'How come he's dead, then?'

'If we knew that . . .' Frank was getting irritated. 'I don't know why he's dead. *Yet!* But we will. Rest assured, we will.'

'Could it be something he was involved in back in

England?' yet another journalist asked. 'A revenge killing, perhaps?'

'I don't wish to speculate at this point in time. When we have more details, I'll let you know. That's it for now, gents. Good night.' Ignoring further questions, Frank got into his car and ordered his driver to take him to the Castle. His first priority would be to get an APB – All Points Bulletin – to all ports and airports. Special attention to be paid to all departures. Anyone acting suspiciously was to be detained for questioning. Any known criminals leaving the country, for whatever reason, were also to be detained and questioned. A description of the wanted man would follow a.s.a.p. Kennedy had made it his priority to get the night porter down to the Castle so that a photo-kit expert could work with him to get a likeness of the visitor he had seen going up to Jimmy's room. The computer could 'draw' the picture from the description and once a good likeness was made, it would then search all the files on record to try and match the description with somebody who already had some form. Once the APB was out, Frank then had the very unpleasant duty of calling Chief Superintendent Wilcox of Scotland Yard to break the news to him that one of his men had been murdered.

Although his key opened the lock, he couldn't open the door. Marlane had the safety chain on. He knocked and called her name.

'Lane. Lane, it's me. Cowboy. Open the door.'

She had fallen asleep on the sofa. A troubled sleep, with bad dreams, in which she was standing by an open doorway looking down on the dead body of Cowboy Johnson. In her mind she heard her own name being called. Now it was her turn to die. Suddenly she woke, startled, and sat up straight. She heard him call her name again. She ran to the door, pushed it closed, struggling to get the chain off, then threw it open and fell into his arms, sobbing. He squeezed her tight, his left arm holding the small of her back, his right hand holding her head tightly to his chest. As her body jerked with her sobs he whispered sweet words of comfort to her, kissing her hair over and over again. Pushing her forward slightly into the room he gently kicked the door closed with his foot.

'There, there, there, it's all right, kitten. I'm here, you're here, and we're both safe.' He caressed her hair, rocking her gently in his arms. She broke away from the embrace, sniffling, and went to the kitchen for a piece of paper towelling. Blowing her nose she sat crouched on the sofa, feet and knees together, her hands resting in her lap, staring at the carpet. Cowboy took his coat off and laid it on the armchair, then joined her.

'Why?' she asked, her tear-stained face looking up at him. 'Why was Jimmy killed?'

'Because we didn't take enough care, sweetheart. Because we didn't know enough, and somebody thought we knew too much. It was a mistake, kitten. If they had known he was a policeman, he wouldn't be dead.'

'Great. That's great. Tell that to Jimmy. Tell that to his family. Is that what you want me to think when I look down on *your* body? "They didn't know he was a policeman." Is that it, Cowboy? Is that it?' She was getting angry.

'Take it easy, darling,' he pleaded with her. 'Hey, remember who you're talking to. This is the Cowboy, the fastest gun in Dublin. Nobody's going to get me, you know that. The goodies always win in the end.' He was trying to make her smile, to take her mind off the sadness, but most especially to stop her thinking of *his* body lying on a morgue slab in front of her eyes.

'Will you *shut up* with all that stupid cowboy shite. For God's sake, this is not the Wild West, and you don't carry a gun, and the dead man *was* one of the goodies. He's dead, and the fuckin' baddies got away.' Her anger at him drained away with her outburst and she threw her arms around him, holding him close. 'Please, darling, don't you understand, they – whoever "they" are – could kill you just as easily as they did Jimmy! Then what would I do? I couldn't bear that, I couldn't bear to be without you in my life.' Once again she started to sob, her face pushed close to his shirt front, smelling him, wanting to unzip his skin and crawl inside his body, to be a part of him.

'Shush, it's okay, sweetheart. I'm sorry about the stupid talk, and I swear to you I'll be careful. I swear it. Listen to me now.' He gripped her head gently between his hands and held it so he could look directly into her wet eyes. 'Jimmy didn't die in vain. Because he died we now know at least *why* he died, and we know the man who caused his death. From him we'll get further information that will eventually lead us to the killer. But it's late now, sweetheart, and I want you to go to bed and try and get some sleep. It will all seem different in the morning, I promise. Come on now. Dry your eyes, there's a good girl.' He handed her a clean handkerchief from his pocket and she used it to dab at her eyes, blowing her nose once again. 'Come on. Off to bed with you.' He stood up, taking her by the hand, raising her to her feet.

'You're not leaving!' She looked up at him, her eyes full of fear that he was going to leave her on her own. 'Don't go, Cowboy. Please don't. I'll never fall asleep unless I know that you are lying there beside me.'

He leaned forward slightly and kissed her very gently. First on each eye, then each cheek, the tip of her nose, and finally her trembling lips. 'I'm not going anywhere,

132

sweetheart. I just have a few things to think over, but I'm coming in to lie beside you. I swear. Now go on in and brush your teeth.' He turned her in the direction of bathroom and gave her a gentle smack on her bottom. He watched the sway of her hips as she did as he told her.

Cowboy went into the kitchen to make her favourite night-time drink, thick chocolate with a liberal dash of cognac. He could hear her moving about in the bathroom and eventually heard the toilet flushed and she came back into the living room. His breath caught in his throat as he looked at her. Her hair was loose and brushed back, hanging below her shoulders. Face freshly scrubbed, she looked so young and defenceless. She was wearing one of his shirts as a nightgown. It was so big on her that the shoulders were near to her elbows and it fell below her knees. She looked like a child wearing Daddy's shirt.

'Cowboy, will you hold me while I fall asleep?' Her large, dark blue eyes, almost black they were so deep, pleaded with him, and there was a catch to her voice. He opened his arms to her as he sat on the sofa and she folded her body round him, sitting on his lap. 'Here, drink this. It'll help you to sleep. When you're finished I'll carry you to bed and I promise I'll stay with you.' She held the mug with both hands taking deep swallows of the lukewarm chocolate, content to be where she was. When she had finished he took the mug from her hands, placed it on the coffee table and carried her into the bedroom.

He turned back the large, goose-feather duvet and she climbed into bed. He took his jacket, shoes and tie off and slid in beside her, holding her close to him, tucking the quilt all round her, making sure she would not be cold. 'You old fuddy-duddy,' she yawned on to his chest, opening the buttons of his shirt so she could rest her cheek on his bare skin. He smiled, agreeing with her. Where she was concerned, yes he was 'an old fuddy-duddy', and would, he hoped, always be like that. He felt her lips gently kiss his chest and her tongue licking his skin, tasting him, then she began to fall asleep. 'I love to hear your heart beat,' she whispered, 'even if, at times, you are such a heartless bastard. Promise you won't leave me when I'm asleep.'

'I promise, woman,' he smiled in reply. 'Now shut up and go to sleep.' He leant forward and kissed the top of her head. She moved about a couple of times, trying to get closer to him, and eventually she fell into the deep sleep of shocked exhaustion. The hand that clutched his shirt front relaxed.

He lay in the darkness, thinking. He could not sleep and knew it was useless to try. He held her for the best part of an hour, then gently disengaged himself and eased himself out of the bed. She felt him move and, in her sleep, tried to prevent him. He whispered to her that he wasn't leaving her, only going to the toilet. She whimpered in reply and fell back into her deep sleep once more.

In the tiny kitchen he made a pot of coffee, adding a large splosh of brandy to it. In her handbag he found an unopened packet of cigarettes. Like him, she was an occasional smoker. Taking the coffee and cigarettes he went and sat in the armchair by the living room window with the curtains drawn back, and looked out into the night.

Closing his eyes he willed himself to relax, inhaling and exhaling slowly. It was something he had learned from Joan Blackmore, who had been the one to explain his gifts to him. As he began to relax he mentally ordered his mind to 'open'. In his mind's eye all he could see was a darkness deeper than pitch. It was as if he were looking out into deep deep space. Nothing distracted him. Very faintly he began to notice an odour. As it grew stronger, he recognized it as the same one he had smelt in James O'Brien's house and in Jimmy's hotel room. He had associated it with Chinese food, but it was not so much the food as the exotic spices, blending together, that gave off the aroma. Images, more like colour slides, began to drift past. Jungle scenes of vegetation, colours so vivid they seemed unreal. Giant flowers with glowing colours were everywhere and in the background the sounds of birds, twittering in the trees and the occasional cough of an animal not far away. The smell grew in intensity and the deep, rich scent of the spices surrounded him. It didn't last long, perhaps only seconds, then it all disappeared and he was once again sitting in the armchair by the window. He could make no sense of what had occurred but that did not matter. He knew that, given time, it would all fall into place. He went back into the bedroom and looked at the sleeping figure, more girl than woman. The love he felt for her was like a physical blow to his heart and it brought a smile to his lips. Very gently he lay down on the bed beside her, careful not to wake her. Sensing he was there she turned over, fighting the duvet that surrounded her, eventually managing to place her head on his chest and sighing contentedly. The next thing he knew, it was morning.

At 8.45 that morning, the last passenger on the 09:00 flight to London was checking through the boarding gate at Dublin Airport. Richard Gordon was on his way home after a successful business trip to the Irish capital. He had been to Ireland before, several times, but only once before on behalf of his 'boss', and that had been as a supposed 'hack' for an American magazine. This time however, his fee had been considerably larger. He had no complaints.

As he went through the gate leading to the plane he paid no attention to the small camera fitted above the doorway. Even if he had noticed it it wouldn't have bothered him. Airport security world-wide had tightened up over the past few years. What did he have to be scared of? There was no police file on him in Ireland.

CHAPTER ELEVEN

Denmark and Dublin
September 1994

VIBY, A SUBURB OF THE CITY OF ÅRHUS in north Jutland, lies a fifteen-minute bus ride from the city centre.
The main road of what was once a provincial village is
now a dual-lane motorway. Just round the corner from
Viby lies the European highway artery, the E45. The
main road through Viby is Skanderborgvej – the road to
Skanderborg – which lies on the 170 south of the city.
Most remnants of the provincial town it used to be have
long been replaced by multi-storied buildings consisting
of several banks, a shopping mall, a Superbrugsen
supermarket and the Mercur hotel. Skanderborgvej 24
houses a branch of Den Danske Bank, situated beside
the Viby Centret shopping mall.

On this hot afternoon, two months after the international police conference in the city, the glass doors of
the bank swung inwards and Arne Fries walked in carrying a leather briefcase. The time was exactly five minutes to two, and Fries informed the girl at the counter
that he had a 2.00 p.m. appointment with the bank's
'Prokurist', Peter Schantz. The Prokurist was the bank's
number two man, after the manager, authorized to make
and sign deals on the bank's behalf. He was also authorized to foreclose on questionable loans and accounts.

Arne Fries's face was well-known to employees of the
bank. In recent weeks they had begun steps to cancel

Fries's overdraft facility and were also calling in the loans he had with them. It had been a necessary step, as far as the bank was concerned, as the interest on the loans, plus his overdraft, was exceeding the income of his business. There was the strongest of possibilities that the bank would be filing bankruptcy proceedings against him. Fries and Schantz had held several meetings over the past few weeks, trying to resolve the situation. On the last few occasions Fries's voice had become so loud in the heat of the arguments, that it had carried out into the banking hall. As far as the bank was concerned it had to protect its loans. It was pointless to throw good money after bad. From Fries's point of view the bank was bleeding his one-man business to death. He was positive that an extension of his credit would save the firm. Schantz was not so sure. He had reluctantly agreed to one more meeting with the angry businessman before an absolute decision was made.

At two minutes past two, three gunshots were heard in the banking hall coming from conference room number one. The door opened and Arne Fries hurried away, still grasping his briefcase. Nobody made any effort to stop him. Customers and staff alike were struck dumb and immobile for the few seconds it took Fries to hurry out of the bank. Once through the swing doors he turned left and left again, into the small car park. From the sound of the gunshots to his disappearance took twenty seconds.

As the glass door swung shut behind Fries, one of the stunned staff stood on the alarm button beneath his feet, shouting at a colleague to lock the main doors, barring exit and entrance until the arrival of the police. One of the female members of staff began to scream. Another colleague pulled her tightly to him, holding her as she screamed her fear into his shoulder. Jørgen, the man who had moved first, ran to the conference room door and jerked it open. Lying face down on his desk was Peter Schantz. Jørgen went to him and tried to find a pulse in his neck. He hadn't expected to find one and his fears were confirmed. Correctly assuming that Schantz was dead, he left the room immediately, locking the door behind him.

Kriminalassistent Nils Sean White arrived on the scene at 2.29 p.m. accompanied by Kriminalbetjent – Constable – Andersen. A patrol car of the city's uniformed civil police had arrived moments after the alarm had gone off. A policeman now stood guard at the entrance to the bank while his colleague stood by the conference room door. They had both gone to see if they could assist Schantz, but all they could do was confirm that he was dead. It was a simple enough case. Arne Fries, angry that the bank was foreclosing on him, with the result that he would lose everything he had worked to achieve, had blown a gasket and shot the man he felt was personally responsible for his troubles, Peter Schantz. The bank staff explained to the detectives about the angry scenes, the loud shouting, that had occurred on previous visits.

As he walked round the banking hall asking questions of the witnesses, Sean began to get a feeling of dread. The hairs on the backs of his hands rose and felt itchy. For Sean that meant something funny was going on. It was sheer intuition, but intuition was something all good cops paid attention to. There was something not right about this. At 2.55 p.m. when he turned in response to the screaming of one of the bank staff, the hairs on the back of his neck also stood up. The screaming woman was pointing to the glass doors.

A crowd had gathered outside the bank after the alarm had gone off and there were now fifty or sixty people standing gaping at the activity inside. Standing, arguing with one of the uniformed policemen was – according to the screaming woman – Arne Fries.

Sean issued a command for the man to be brought inside the bank. The two uniformed men rushed to the doors, opened them and much to the surprise of everybody on the street, dragged the accused man into the bank. He struggled, demanding to know what the hell was going on, at the same time telling the policemen to get their hands off him. Telling him to shut up, Sean grabbed the surprised man's left wrist, pushing the sleeve cuff up out of the way, baring the wrist-watch. Arne Fries's digital watch showed the time to be 13:58. He had, he explained to Sean, come for an appointment with Peter Schantz at 2.00 p.m. Sean let the man's wrist go and turned away, checking, just to be sure, his own watch. The minute hand was just coming on to the 12. It was exactly 3.00 p.m. Fries's watch was precisely one hour slow. Kriminalbetjent Andersen could not understand Sean's remark as he heard him mutter 'Shit! The bastard's been here. The Chameleon.'

Frank Mooney had spent the night at his office in Dublin Castle, sleeping on the couch. It was not the first time he had done it, nor did he feel it would be the last. The system had changed considerably since he took command of the Criminal Investigation Branch. His ways were not the ways of his predecessor, who had spent more of his time placating politicians than he did backing his undermanned and overworked staff. Even now he was off the streets, Frank still felt and thought like a street cop and understood the pressures his men were under. He had explained how he intended to operate to his wife, Marjory, prior to accepting the promotion, and asked for her advice. Her answer was that she had been a policeman's wife for almost thirty years now and saw no reason for anything to change in the way he worked. Whatever he decided, she would back him.

Leaving the shower room in the basement he walked along the corridor to his office dressed in his old striped dressing gown. Taking a button-down-collared white shirt from the selection he kept at the office, along with fresh underwear and socks, he sipped tea made for him by the desk sergeant. Beside the tray with the tea lay the early-morning editions of the newspapers. Running his electric razor over his face he glanced at the headlines on the top one.

SCOTLAND YARD DETECTIVE MURDERED IN DUBLIN HOTEL

The article went on to give details of the finding of the body, making reference to the officer's secondment to the CIB. It then went on to ask speculative questions as to why the Yard man had been murdered and asked where Detective Sergeant 'Cowboy' Johnson was and what the two detectives had been working on. Despite the denial of Commander Mooney of the Dublin CIB, the report had it on good authority that the famous Johnson and the dead detective were in fact working together on a 'hush-hush' case. The reporter hoped to be able to provide readers with the answer to these, and other questions, in a later edition.

Ignoring the remainder of the papers Mooney dug out a bottle of Old Spice and splashed a handful over his face and torso. It had not been a good night for him. He had rung Chief Superintendent Wilcox to tell him of the murder and to offer his condolences. Asking the Chief Superintendent to keep the case under wraps a little longer, he informed him that an arrest would be made that morning. It was a heavy price to pay, but the death of Douglas confirmed, without any doubt, the existence of the Chameleon. He apologized as best he could for the death of the Yard detective on 'his patch'. He could not help but feel in some way responsible. Wilcox had understood this feeling quite well. He would have felt the same way if it had been an Irish copper killed in London. Promising Wilcox that he would send him a copy of all reports on the murder, including the autopsy, he concluded the conversation by saying that all necessary arrangements would be made to fly Douglas's body back to London, as soon as possible. After that he had fallen into a troubled sleep.

When Cowboy arrived at 7.50 a.m. he offered him tea, which was declined, then both men made their way along to the Forensic Science laboratories on the second floor. Billy Cleary had been called out during the night to work on the tape recording made by Douglas, with instructions that the last part was to be 'cleaned' so the final conversation could be heard. The tape was ready on their arrival. Setting the tape recorder in the 'play' mode, Cleary cued the tape fast-forward to the point where Douglas had warned Cowboy to be careful. They listened to the sound of the knock on the door and the soft sound of Jimmy's footsteps as he crossed the room, after sliding the recorder under the bed. They heard the door open, then Jimmy speak.

'What the fuck . . .'
'You're sticking your nose in where it is not wanted. Good bye.'

The second voice was male and also spoke with an English accent. It was definitely not William Clark. There followed a sound like a champagne cork popping, followed by a thump. The door was closed and they listened to breathing. The door was opened and closed once more, followed by a 'click' as the key was turned in the lock. Leaving instructions for voice prints to be made of the three voices on the tape, Clark, Douglas and the unknown killer, Mooney led the way back to his office. Billy Cleary promised Mooney the best contour voiceprint he could make on the spectrograph and returned to his lab. If they managed to catch the unknown killer, the voiceprint would play an important part in the prosecution's evidence.

Lying on Mooney's desk were several telephone messages, two of which had been put on top for his immediate attention. One was from the State Attorney's office 'requesting' Mooney to phone as soon as possible. The second was from a young woman named Gormon, employed as a receptionist by JB Finance. She had rung the Castle that morning after reading of the murder in the papers. She was sure, from the published photograph, that the dead man was the same one who had visited JB Finance two days before. Mooney handed the note to Cowboy to read and picked up the phone. 'Margaret, will you get me the SA's office, please.' As he waited for the connection to be made he gave Cowboy his instructions.

'Send a car to pick that girl up. I don't want her blabbing to too many people about this, especially the papers. Her statement will tie the rope round Clark's neck that little bit tighter. I also want a statement from your *Maître d'* friend at the Gresham. I want the connection between Clark and Douglas as tight as a duck's . . . Hello, Mr Williams? Good morning, sir. Yes, sir, I've read them too.' He waved a hand to Cowboy who left the office to execute his orders.

Malahide lies to the north of the city. Situated on the coast, the property prices are the kind that do not get mentioned on estate agents' brochures. 'Price available on application' or some such phrase was the usual way of saying, 'If you need to know the price, then you can't really afford it'. It was a very fashionable place to live. Many of the properties were large, with grounds extensive enough to require the attention of professional gardening staff. One of the larger ones was owned by William J. Clark.

The house itself was in many ways similar to the headquarters of JB Finance. It was a well-preserved Georgian building with four double bedrooms with en suite bathrooms, two elegant reception rooms, a stately dining room and a study. The kitchen was immense and ran the width of the house, at the rear. The house had its own tennis court, swimming pool, and a private section of beach which lay at the back of the grounds.

At 8.30 Clark sat at the dining table ready to enjoy his breakfast. Juice was already poured into the Waterford crystal glass by his plate and as he sat, Marie, the maid, was on her way in from the kitchen with a pot of freshly brewed coffee. His toast and scrambled eggs were being prepared. Beside his plate lay the morning editions of the London *Times*, the *Financial Times*, the *Guardian*, the *International Herald Tribune* and the *Irish Independent*. Bidding a good morning to his wife Dorothy, who sat opposite reading *Hello* magazine, he poured his first cup of coffee and reached for the papers.

As he raised his coffee cup to his lips with his right hand he flicked open the folded *Independent* with his left. The headlines and the photograph of the dead man hit him like a physical blow. It was not so much the murder but the words 'SCOTLAND YARD DETECTIVE' that caused him to drop his coffee cup, staining the Irish linen tablecloth and his trousers with warm coffee. The crash almost made Dorothy drop her own coffee cup.

'What *is* it, William?' she asked, annoyed that their

polite morning ritual had been interrupted. Marie rushed in from the kitchen to see what was happening. Clark pushed his chair back from the table. To his wife he curtly replied 'Nothing!' and ordered Marie to clean up the mess. He left the dining room and went straight to his study. Dorothy knew better than to follow him in there, but reached across the table and picked up the paper. Apart from the report of the murder of the English policeman there were reports on the peace-keeping force in Bosnia, an article on Hilary Clinton, another on John Major and another one about the Irish farmers bleating on again about the GAP talks. What on earth had caused him to drop his coffee, she wondered. None of the articles seemed to be the kind that would affect JB Finance!

In his study, Clark went straight to the phone and dialled the home number of his lawyer, Eamon Dalton. The annual retainer he paid Dalton gave him the right to cause Dalton *coitus interruptus* if Clark felt it was urgent. When he finally got connected to Dalton he ordered him over to Malahide immediately. 'Don't bother to finish your breakfast. You can have another one here. Just get over here as quickly as possible.'

'Of course, William, whatever you want. But wouldn't you like to explain to me what's going on first?' The nasal drawl of the other man, which irritated so many of his opponents and friends – the few he had – now irritated Clark.

'Just get the fuck over here *now*! I am expecting a visit from the police very shortly and I want you here.' With that he slammed down the receiver. The crystal stopper on the Waterford decanter was flung to the floor as he poured a large brandy into a crystal glass.

They arrived at 10.30 in an unmarked police car. Mooney informed Marie who they were and that they wished to see Clark. Although she had received instructions that he would see no visitors, apart from Dalton, that he would not take any phone calls, nor was he to be interrupted for any reason, she had a feeling that those instructions did not include the police. Asking Mooney and Cowboy to wait in the hall she announced their arrival and a moment later showed both men into the study.

Clark and Dalton were sitting in the chairs by the fire, which, despite the warmth of the day, Marie had lit earlier on Clark's instructions. Dalton claimed to be a 'super-lawyer', by which he meant he was one of the highest-paid barristers in the Republic. A person's wealth was the only criteria for being accepted by Dalton as a client. Legal Aid and Eamon Dalton had yet to be introduced to each other, and most likely never would be. He was a master of the technicalities and had more cases dropped on the grounds of legal loopholes, than on evidence of the innocence of his clients. Dalton stood up, arm resting on the high mantelpiece, his face beaming with a smug, professional, smile.

'Ah, Commander Mooney, CIB and the famous Detective Sergeant Cowboy Johnson. Good day to you both. How is your dear mother, by the way, Johnson? Please give her my regards next time you see her, there's a good lad.' Switching his radiant smile to Mooney, he continued. 'Now, Mooney, what can we do for you on this fine morning, eh?' The nasal twang was very prominent, and the smile a discreet sneer. Cowboy and Mooney nodded in his direction by way of greeting, but gave their full attention to the seated Clark.

The man who was always so proud of his bearing and appearance seemed to have vanished. He had not changed his trousers since the accident with the coffee cup and now looked more like an old man who had wet his pants than the managing director of one of the most successful companies in the country. He was a stark contrast to Dalton.

'It's your case, Detective Sergeant. Carry on.' Mooney instructed Cowboy. From his inside pocket Cowboy produced a small laminated card. Without referring to it he began to caution Clark.

'Now listen here, Mooney,' Dalton interrupted. 'That's enough. Take your ridiculous charge, and get out of this house. My client will agree to forget this interruption and will not press any charges of police harassment or attempted false arrest provided you leave immediately. Do you hear me, Mooney?' Dalton had taken his hand off the mantelpiece and was speaking directly to Mooney, shaking his finger, like a headmaster to a naughty pupil, for emphasis.

Mooney, who had been watching Clark while Cowboy read out the charge, now turned his attention to Dalton.

'Mr Dalton. For a start off, you will address me as Commander Mooney, or Sir, whichever you like. You will further address Detective Sergeant Johnson as such, and not as a "good lad". If you interrupt Detective Sergeant Johnson once more in the execution of his duty, I, personally, will arrest you for obstructing a police officer in the course of his duty. Am I making myself clear to you, *Mister* Dalton?'

About to answer back, Dalton saw the look in the other man's eyes. Mooney actually wanted him to interfere. Damn the man, Dalton thought, but he could wait. And when the time came Mooney would regret the day he had crossed him. With a sneering smile he made a mock bow of acceptance of the rebuke.

Still looking at Dalton, Mooney ordered Cowboy to start all over again. 'We have no wish to see the course of justice perverted by a technicality, such as not reading

147

the accused his rights, now do we, Mr Dalton?' The flash of anger in Dalton's eyes told Mooney that he had read the interruption correctly. Later Dalton would have claimed that his client had not been cautioned properly and would have attempted to use that to have the case thrown out of court.

Cowboy began again, repeating the first charge which related to the murder of Inspector Douglas, then adding; 'You are further charged with causing, and being an accessory to, the murder of James O'Brien. You are not obliged to say anything if you so wish, but anything you do say will be taken down in writing and may be used in evidence against you. Do you understand the charges against you, Mr Clark, and your rights as I have just read them to you?'

Expecting, from the moment he had read of the murder in the newspaper, to be charged in some connection with the murder of the Scotland Yard detective, the actual reading of the charge shocked Clark. At the charge of being an accessory to O'Brien's murder, he crumpled even further. All he could do was nod his head in answer to the question.

'Please answer the question verbally, Mr Clark. Do you understand the charges and your rights in this matter?'

Clark looked up into Cowboy's eyes, expecting . . . what? He didn't know. Understanding maybe. All he saw was determination in the other man's eyes. 'Yes, Sergeant Johnson I understand both the charges and my rights.'

'Now William, that's it. Not another word out of you until I instruct you otherwise. As your lawyer I will take over from here.' Turning his attention now to Mooney, and ignoring Cowboy, Dalton continued. 'I trust, *Commander*, that you have some reason for bringing these ridiculous charges against my client. It is my client's contention that he neither knew, nor has he ever met, nor had any dealings whatsoever with this Detective ... whatever his name was.'

'Detective Inspector James Douglas.' Cowboy informed him through gritted teeth, longing to sink his fist into Dalton's face. 'The *late*, Detective Inspector.'

'Yes, well, I sympathize over his unfortunate death, of course, but one must state the case on behalf of one's client. And as for the murder of James O'Brien! We all know that the murderer was sentenced to life imprisonment for it. He was the man's driver, and the reason was something to do with pornographic pictures, I believe, of the driver's young daughter. My client never even *knew* the driver. Perhaps you'll be kind enough to explain these charges, Commander Mooney.'

Mooney nodded. 'We can prove that not only did your client know Detective Inspector Douglas, but met with him shortly before the murder. The witnesses to that meeting are Detective Sergeant Johnson here, plus a few others, among them the *Maître d'* at The Gresham Hotel.

'As for your client's involvement in the murder of James O'Brien, perhaps your client would like to tell us who D'Argent is, and more importantly, who the Chameleon is?'

Clark made an audible gasp at the mention of the two names. It was as if he had heard the final nail being driven into his coffin.

'I would, ah,' he cleared his throat and tried again. 'I would like to make a statement, Commander Mooney, if I may?' He looked up at Mooney, silently pleading for a chance to clear his conscience. Mooney nodded.

'Now listen to me, William. Not a word. Do you understand. Not one word.'

'Shut up, Dalton,' Clark instructed his lawyer. 'I know what I am doing and, in a way, I always knew it would eventually happen. Just do as I instruct you. Do I make myself clear?'

A slight flush appeared on Dalton's face. 'Have it your way, William,' he replied, 'have it your way.'

'May I tell my wife where I'm going, Commander?'

'Of course, Mr Clark. Please ask her to come in here.'

Clark nodded and turned to the button set into the fire surround. When Marie answered the call she was asked to invite Mrs Clark to come to the study. The four men were silent as they waited.

When she arrived, he explained to her that he was going with the two policemen to Dublin Castle to help them with a case they were working on. He would phone her later. They looked at each other intensely for a few moments, her eyes begging him to tell her what was going on, his pleading with her to help him. Silently she took a step forward and put her arms around the man whose name she had carried for nearly thirty years. She kissed him on each cheek, then looked him straight in the eye.

'I'll be here when you need me, William. I am only a phone call away. Please remember that.'

Clark could not answer. There was a catch in his throat as he nodded his head, and blinked his eyes. Collecting his panama hat from the hall stand he went with Cowboy and Mooney in the police car, while Dalton followed in his own. Dorothy was still standing by the door to the study as they all drove away. She looked round the room. Lying on the floor, by the chair where her husband had sat, lay the morning newspaper, front page open, showing the headlines. She glanced at it, then closed the door to the study behind her and went to cancel all appointments until further notice.

CHAPTER TWELVE

Dublin, September 1994

'MY NAME IS WILLIAM JEFFERY CLARK. I have been read my rights by Detective Sergeant Johnson of the Criminal Investigation Branch and understand them fully. I am making this statement voluntarily and of my own free will. My solicitor, Mr Eamon Dalton, is present with me.'

They had reassembled in Mooney's office on their arrival at Dublin Castle. An interview recorder was sent for and set up on Mooney's desk. Two brand-new, sealed cassettes were opened and inserted into the recorder, one for the CIB and one for Dalton. The 'record' button would activate both recordings to ensure exact copies of what was said. Behind the desk sat Mooney and by his side, Cowboy. Facing them across the desk, the machine between both parties, sat Clark and Dalton. The date, time and the names of all present were first spoken into the machine by Cowboy, then Clark commenced to make his statement.

'About ten years ago, I can't quite be precise about the dates, I was invited to join the board of JB Finance by James O'Brien, the then Managing Director. I was also offered shares in the company at a preferential price. In order to avail myself of this offer I used all my cash reserves and mortgaged my home in Malahide to the hilt. My wife and I have a taste for expensive things and we enjoy the luxuries and good life that money can bring. Within a few years, despite an ever-increasing salary and dividends from JB Finance, my expenditure was beginning to exceed my income. I am not a person who likes to make cutbacks, and so I was looking for a way, or ways, to increase my income.

'Around about this time JB Finance was approached by an American company, Sheldon Incorporated, through our New York office, to arrange the financing of a large hotel and casino complex in Atlantic City. The deal was considerably larger than any JB Finance had been involved with before but over a period of fifteen years the income on that deal alone was going to be worth in excess of 150 million US dollars. It fell within my division and, after studying the portfolio, I recommended the deal to O'Brien. Later, at a board meeting, the board was split on accepting or rejecting the deal. The Chairman, O'Brien, cast the deciding vote. At that stage the answer was no, but the idea was not rejected outright. A further investigation was to be made and a second vote would be taken when that investigation was completed.

'This was not the first time that O'Brien had turned down a lucrative deal. Usually he had very sound reasons for these decisions. It was generally accepted within the company that he had a "nose" for what might appear to be a good deal, but which in reality was quite the reverse. To a large extent his "nose" was correct, but he had made a few mistakes. I was convinced that he was making a mistake on this one and, without his knowledge, I carried on dealing with Sheldon Inc. I explained to them that O'Brien was against the deal, but that I and several others on the Board were in favour of it. I went further by telling them that a more detailed investigation into Sheldon Incorporated was to be undertaken.

'I was invited to the United States to meet with several of the executives of the company, and I went. I was treated most royally during my stay. The best of everything was provided. The best suites in the best hotels; a limo, a driver and an executive assistant at my disposal round the clock; the best seats at the theatre, restaurants: you name it, I got it. The "executive assistant" was a young female and when they said she was at my disposal day and night, that is exactly what they meant. The more I saw of Sheldon's interests in the States, the more convinced I was that O'Brien – by going against the deal – was going to cost, not only the company, but myself as well, a considerable amount of money.

'Now, of course, I realize that O'Brien was correct. Sheldon Incorporated is in the position of having used five times its actual value as collateral over the years. Assets they claimed to have owned were never owned by them. They were operating a very well thought out and prolonged "sting". All of this has only come to light recently. It began with late payments on the loans, then insufficient payments and then nothing. JB Finance was not the only company caught in the "sting" – but that's little consolation when JB Finance will be lucky to survive. A case of putting all one's eggs in the one basket, so to speak. A police investigation is going on in the States into the link between Sheldon Inc. and organized crime. But then, that was all in the future. All I knew was I was being wined and dined for the initial loans, and everything in the garden looked rosy.

'During my stay the question as to how O'Brien could be made to change his mind was raised. In a round about way a suggestion to make a cash payment to the Cayman Islands on his behalf was put forward. I laughed at this, as I knew the man. I said that if anything could *stop* him from changing his mind it was just such an offer. In jest I said the only way at present – that is, at that time – for the deal to go through was over O'Brien's dead body. I *was* only joking! However, while everybody was still laughing over this I was asked what would happen to JB Finance if he *did* actually die! The conditions of O'Brien's will were well known to all the board members. In the event of his death, his shares in the company would first and foremost be offered to the other board members. I told them this, and the current value of his shares and then the matter was dropped.

'It came up again several days later at a dinner party. It was well known by all those involved that I wanted the deal to go through, and I had also expressed an interest in being Chairman of JB Finance, if the possibility ever arose. You must understand, Commander, that Americans have a way of putting you at your ease, making you feel that they are the best friends you ever had, and that they want to assist you in any way that they can. I mentioned things to them that I had not mentioned to anybody else. They had got to know me inside out in a very short space of time. At this dinner party I was asked if I was interested in having my wishes fulfilled, sooner rather than later.

'I had had quite a bit to drink at the time, but I remember replying that for all of that to happen James would have to fall under a bus. "And what if he did die?" I was asked. I felt the change in the atmosphere. I sobered up immediately. This was no "let's suppose" story. This was a direct question about the death of James O'Brien. I tried to laugh the whole thing off. To start with, I said, should anything happen to him I felt sure that one of the first places the police would look would be at the company and at his will. No, thank you, I said. His death was one thing, but my going to prison was an entirely different kettle of fish. Then came the "what if" bit. What if O'Brien was to die, and what if somebody else, somebody else with a very strong motive became the suspect? And what if there were witnesses who could swear that this other person actually committed the crime? What if the finger of suspicion would never, ever, point at me? What then?'

Clark leant forward and poured himself a glass of water from the container on the desk. He drained the glass in one go, then continued. While they listened attentively to Clark's story, Dalton was the only one who seemed to be finding it all difficult to believe.

'I don't know how to explain what was going through my mind at that time, Commander. I was being offered the gold at the end of the rainbow. As it was, if O'Brien had agreed the deal, I stood to make a considerable amount of money, in a one-off commission, plus the increase in dividends that the deal would bring. But if O'Brien was out of the picture completely, then I stood a very good chance of being able to buy most of his shares and of increasing my stake in the company. I knew that O'Connor wished to retire. If I could show him the increases I could get him, then he could go off to his golf and, for a back pocket payment that the taxman would know nothing about, I could get his proxy. I also knew that I would get the position as Chairman. I could have it all. The only obstacle that stood in my way was . . . James O'Brien himself. Not really knowing what they were going to suggest I said that, of course, if O'Brien died, and if their "magician" could ensure that there was no way I could be implicated in the deal, then, well . . . I could possibly go for it.

'Well, of course, things could not be *that* simple. What was to stop me changing my mind after the deed was done, they wanted to know, and implicating everybody else. No. I would have to be implicated on the basis that everybody had to have their finger in the pie. They, Sheldon Inc., would loan me the money to hire this man who would do the job. They would tell me how to get in contact with him. He would want to know who was hiring him as part of his own protection. So I would have to undertake that process myself. However, once O'Brien was out of the way, then Sheldon Inc. would, again, loan me the money to buy shares in JB Finance; a larger portion of O'Brien's shares, plus a pay-off to O'Connor to ensure I would get his proxy. Once I had all that, I had JB Finance. I am deeply ashamed to say that I accepted their offer.

'At this point, Commander, I would like to make it perfectly clear that O'Connor knew, and knows, nothing of the murder of James O'Brien. He was not involved in any way. All he wanted to do was to retire to the golf course with a golden handshake.

'They had explained to me that the man who would undertake the job was a very special man, and I don't just mean that he was a hired killer. Before he would take the . . . the contract, he would make his own investigation into whoever was hiring him. He would also investigate the person he was being employed to kill. Nothing could, or would, be done on a "next week" basis. This was going to take time. Anything up to six months. Once he accepted the contract the first half of his fee, $500,000, was to be paid into a bank account. If he did not hear anything to the contrary within ten days, then he would carry out the job.

'Part of his special talent was that he guaranteed somebody would stand trial for the murder and that no suspicion would fall on the actual "employer" – in this case, myself. Once a suspect was arrested and the police convinced that they had their man – or woman – then the second half of his one million dollar contract was payable. It was explained to me that irrespective of how the "contract" was killed, or how convinced I was personally that somebody else *had* actually committed the murder, the second instalment of the fee was payable. Failure to make the payment within one month would lead to my own death!

'I was given details as to how to contact the man, and advanced all the money I needed, not only to pay for the death of James O'Brien, but also to buy the shares and take control of JB Finance. This included a payment of £100,000 for O'Connor, for his irrevocable proxy. Do you think I could possibly have some tea or coffee, Commander?'

Mooney nodded and Cowboy switched off the recorder then went to arrange for refreshments for them all. Clark took a red silk handkerchief from his breast pocket and wiped the sweat from his brow, then lit a large cigar, puffing swiftly on it. Dalton sat staring at his client in disbelief. He had known William Clark for years and could not take in what he was hearing. Looking at the stern-faced Commander of the CIB he knew that *he* believed it. Not only believed it, but had been actively investigating it for some time. For the first time in his life, Eamon Dalton was speechless. Cowboy returned with the refreshments and passed round cups to each man in turn. Clark gulped his coffee down and, as Cowboy refilled his cup and turned the recorder back on, continued his story.

'I took an advertisement in the personal column of the London *Times*. I used the code word "D'Argent" – money in French – for myself, and "Chameleon" for the man I was to contact. That name had already been given to me to use. I scanned the personal column daily and eventually found my reply. I was to contact a London telephone number on a given day. It was an answering service.

'Again I used the name D'Argent and was instructed to be at a certain restaurant the following Wednesday, in London, where I would be contacted. It was a Chinese restaurant in Soho and I was to use the name D'Argent when I arrived.'

Only Cowboy's eyes gave evidence of his reaction to this mention of the Chinese restaurant. The psychic 'smell' he had perceived had been correct. But he also felt there was more to it than just a restaurant.

'I made arrangements to be in London that week visiting our London offices and, at the appointed time, went to the restaurant. I gave the name D'Argent and was informed that a table had been booked in my name. I was led upstairs to a smallish dining room – used as an overflow from the main one downstairs I would guess. There were four tables in the room, but only one laid out for a meal. Behind the table was a set of Chinese screens. On the table, propped against the flower-vase, was an envelope addressed to me in the name D'Argent.

'The letter instructed me to sit with my back to the screens and under no circumstances to turn around, no matter what I heard. As soon as I was seated a meal was produced for me from the dumb waiter by the Chinese waiter, then he left me alone.

'I am not a great lover of Chinese food, and to be honest, I was not particularly hungry. I was quite nervous, actually. It is not every day that I set out to order a colleague's death. I sat there for about fifteen minutes, picking at the food. Then I heard a door open behind the screens. A man's voice asked how I had come to hear of Chameleon, who I was, and what I wanted. He warned me to tell the truth or, as he put it, "suffer the consequences". I told him what I knew and what he wanted to know. I had been forewarned of the questions I was to be asked by the people at Sheldon Inc. Trust was needed on both sides. I had to trust Chameleon and he had to be able to trust me. After I had answered his questions, giving him details on James O'Brien, I was told I would hear from him shortly. The meeting was over. His parting words were not to try and follow him nor to turn round as he left. He also said that the meal had been paid for.

'Despite not knowing who this Chameleon was I had a very strong suspicion that the man I had met was not him. It had been my understanding that the Chameleon was an American. This man spoke with an English accent. It may have been a phoney one, but I doubt it. Anyway, that was the end of that and it was almost a month before I heard any more. A letter was addressed to my home in Malahide. It was registered and heavily taped, marked for my personal attention. I read it in my study.

'It informed me that the contract I had requested was accepted. I was given the details of a Swiss bank account into which I was to pay the initial half-million dollars. The letter went on to advise me that I had ten days after the deposit of the money to stop the action. If I wanted to cancel the contract I was to put an advert in *The Times* to that effect. There would be no refund, but the second half of the fee would be cancelled. After the ten days had passed, the contract would be carried out and then the second instalment would be due. Should I neglect to pay it then, the letter stated, the "infringement clause" would come into effect. I was in no doubt what that meant. I carried out the instructions I was given, then sat back and waited.

'When Colloney was arrested for the murder of O'Brien I was convinced that I had just wasted five hundred thousand dollars! I had paid a hired killer to do a job that Colloney had done for revenge. However, if my memory serves me well, while the police found the murder weapon on the day of the murder it was a day or so later before the photographs of Colloney's daughter were found. On the day after the murder, and before you had found the photographs, I received a courier letter informing me that the final incriminating evidence required would be found in a day or two. This evidence would be photographs. I was also informed that the second payment was due within fourteen days.

'When the dust settled over O'Brien's death, and his will was read, the shares were offered to the board members. I bought enough, what with the proxy vote I already had, to give me control of JB Finance and got myself voted into the joint positions of Chairman of the Board and Managing Director. Obviously one of the first deals that went through was the one with Sheldon Incorporated.' He lapsed into silence for a few moments, refilling his cup again, this time with cold black coffee, and draining it in one go.

'That takes care of O'Brien,' Cowboy spoke. 'Now tell us what led to the death of Inspector Douglas.'

'When I received the letter at my office the other day you can imagine the shock it gave me. After all these years, this was coming back to haunt me. The letter demanded money and I knew it would not cease there. More would be required and I would be slowly drained, financially, until I couldn't pay. But I knew the letter had not come from the Chameleon.'

'You *did*! How did you know that?' Cowboy asked.

'Blackmail was something the Chameleon had warned me about. He had told me that there were others within his organization. People he employed to carry out investigations on his behalf. They were highly paid and there was little or no risk in their work. He assured me that they did not know who *he* was, but, it wouldn't have taken a great deal of intelligence for anybody to put two and two together in, for example, my own case involving O'Brien. He guaranteed me that I need never be afraid of blackmail. If I should receive such a threat then it would not come from him. Furthermore, if such a threat occurred, and I contacted him immediately, then he would take the necessary action to see that the threat was not carried out. He gave me a telephone number to call should I ever need his services again, of if I should be threatened. I don't know why – maybe I just wanted . . . needed to . . . but I believed him.

'After I received the letter from Detective Inspector Douglas, I made a phone call and left a message on an answering machine. About ten hours later I got a call at home. I was told to go to the Gresham and meet with this man. He would be observed. If I had to make any payment there and then I should make it, or as much as I could. I would be reimbursed at a later date. However, I was to try and bluff my way for a short time. The black-mailer was more interested in receiving money than in going to the police, so I would have some time before any threat was carried out. That would be enough time for the Chameleon to sort the problem out for me. I did as instructed, met with Inspector Douglas at the Gre-sham, and after he had gone I left shortly afterwards. The first I knew of what had happened to him, and who he actually was, was when I read the newspapers this morning. I realized then that the police knew of, or at least suspected, my involvement in the murder of James O'Brien. I knew I would be getting a visit sooner rather than later.

'Although I may have met the Chameleon I am not aware of the fact. I have no idea – other than my suspicion that he is an American – who he is. Neither did I ever get to see the man I met in the Chinese restaurant in London. If either of them stood in front of me now I could not identify them. Can I ask a question, Commander?' Mooney nodded. 'What made you re-open the O'Brien case?'

'You wouldn't believe me if I told you,' Cowboy answered for Mooney.

Clark turned his attention to the younger man. 'But how were you so sure I was involved?'

'We weren't. If you had gone to the police with the letter, like any honest, innocent citizen would have done, you could have bluffed it out and you wouldn't be sitting here now. But you didn't go to the police, did you, Mr Clark?'

Clark merely shook his head.

'There are questions that need to be answered, Mr Clark, beginning with the names of the people involved in Sheldon Incorporated.' Clark nodded. 'The name and address of the Chinese restaurant where you met the Chameleon's contact. The Swiss bank account numbers and any documents relating to the payments you made.' Clark nodded again. 'And lastly the telephone number you rang to inform Chameleon that you were being blackmailed.' Clark reached into his jacket pocket and brought out a small leather-bound notebook. Opening it at the page required he handed it to Cowboy. 'It's a Hong Kong phone number, Sergeant.'

CHAPTER THIRTEEN

Hong Kong, September 1994

THE WOMAN LEAVING THE GROUNDS of the large house in Kowloon was dressed in the black pyjama suit and wide-brimmed black hat of the Hakka people. Shuffling along, Chinese fashion, she kept her head bowed as she walked towards the MTR – Mass Transit Railway – sub-station. Buying her ticket for the Central District, on the Hong Kong side, she stood waiting with hundreds of others for the train to arrive.

Crossing the harbour via the MTR tunnel she arrived at Central ten minutes later. Disembarking at the Gloucester Road sub-station she turned left into O'Brien Road. Taking the first left into Jaffa Road she continued on down to the corner and her destination, the Hong Kong Toy Emporium. As usual the shop was crowded, mostly with tourists, jabbering away to each other and their children in a host of languages. The vast counters displayed hundreds of makes of brand-name toys. It was a child's paradise where fantasy and reality mingled.

Effortlessly avoiding bumping into other customers, she made her way towards the rear of the store, ignoring the staff. There sat the man she had come to see whom she knew only as Li, and who, to the best of her knowledge, was the owner of the store. He was hunched over an instruction booklet on one of a new range of computers which had just been delivered. Looking up as she approached he placed the booklet to one side and stepped out from behind the counter to meet her, bowing at the waist and smiling a greeting. With his left hand he waved her into the store room and from there led the way to a small office. Neither of them spoke one word.

Going straight to the large, old fashioned safe in the corner, he opened it and extracted a parcel from the top shelf, handing it to her. In return she put her hands inside her baggy blouse and extracted a thick envelope which she gave to him. It contained 100,000 Hong Kong dollars, none of which would appear on his sales and receipts ledger for the Inland Revenue. Parcels exchanged, they bowed once more to each other. He led her to the rear exit and, tucking the parcel inside her blouse, she retraced her steps to the house in Kowloon.

Once inside the grounds she relocked the gate behind her. The pathway to the house led her through a miniature Japanese garden, with beds of shrubs and plants with multi-coloured flowers. In the shade of the house itself were a collection of bonsai trees. Looking for all the world like their giant brothers, none of them were larger than 18 inches in height.

The ten-roomed colonial-style mansion was set in landscaped gardens, totally surrounded by a 10-foot-high wall. Built into and along the top of the wall were electronic sensors which triggered alarms if anything heavier than a cat rested its weight there. There were three ways into the grounds: one was via the gate the woman had used; the second gate opened on to a path leading directly to the kitchen and was used by the staff and the delivery boys from the local merchants; and the third and main entrance was by way of a heavy wrought-iron gate, electronically controlled by the security staff. Spread all over the gardens were tiny, disguised, television cameras which showed every detail of the grounds on the banks of screens in the security room. Only one car was parked in the four-car garage built to one side of the main door to the house. The staff consisted of a cook and helper, two gardeners and six security staff, divided into three teams. They manned the security room twenty-four hours a day, all year round. The security men came from Ultrasafe, a Hong Kong based security firm famed for its discretion and reliability. The gardeners had been looking after the grounds during the tenancy of four owners and were both old men now. The cook and her helper were both Vietnamese and had come with the present owner and the woman, when they first arrived in the late '70s.

Once inside the air-conditioned house the woman went straight to the study at the rear. Knocking on the door, she waited until she heard the metallic 'clunk' as the electronic bolts were withdrawn. Opening the door she entered, closing it behind her. Apart from the owner of the house, she was the only other person allowed to enter this room.

The man smiled at her. Behind her she once again heard the 'clunk' as the bolts were shot and the heavy metal door, disguised with wood panels, was once again bolted.

'Good morning, Angel,' the man greeted her as she removed her wide brimmed hat and shook her long, jet-black hair, free. She smiled, nodded, and placed the parcel on the desk.

The man wore a pair of loose fitting shorts, and nothing else. It was difficult to pin an exact age on him. He could have been anything between thirty and fifty. In peak physical condition, he had been doing his hour-long morning session of Tai Chi Chuan, known to westerners as slow-motion kung fu.

He was clean-shaven, his mousy-blond hair cropped short, close to the skull, US Marine style. The thing most people noticed on first meeting him were his eyes. Light blue in colour they seemed cold and penetrating. Most people, when they spoke to him face to face, were unnerved by his stare. Only the woman, Angel, had ever seen a genuine smile from him. Then his face would light up and his eyes seemed to twinkle. Hers was the only company he ever enjoyed.

She watched him as he carefully opened the parcel she had brought. The muscles in his arms moved gracefully as he gently opened the box and withdrew the contents. His body was lean, muscular and slightly tanned, except for the small circular white patches that dotted his chest and the uneven white lines, also on his chest and on his back. Some of these patches were the result of professional attention. The others were, as he once explained to her, 'chop-suey surgery' carried out as best as could be achieved under difficult circumstances. These patches of new skin never tanned. Some of the wounds she knew intimately, having attended to them herself years before. Others were older and had been there when they first met. The lobe of his left ear was missing, eaten by a rat. The scars on his legs were from when he had been tied up and caged like an animal. There was a knife wound just below his shoulder blade. These were the ones she herself had tended to.

Taking the contents of the parcel in his hand he studied it, moving it round and round, stretching it, checking for faults. He couldn't find any, but he was not yet finished. Pressing yet another button on the console on his desk the far wall opened like two swing doors. Behind this false wall was an alcove 18 inches deep. Spacious

166

enough for its purpose, yet not deep enough to arouse any suspicion if the room was broken into.

The backs of each swing portion of the false wall were lined with mirrors. The back of the recess itself was covered with photographs of a man. Taken from numerous angles it showed the man entering and leaving buildings and cars, eating, walking, sitting, standing, heading away from and towards the camera. All the pictures had been taken without the knowledge of the subject. There was also a video cassette lying on a small shelf which had also been shot without his knowledge.

Standing in front of the alcove the man sprinkled talcum powder on his hands, then rubbed it all over his face, head and neck. Next he took the contents of the parcel and, stretching it cautiously, pulled it over his head and down to his shoulders. Adjusting it carefully he spread the loose ends over his shoulders. Opening another box that lay on a shelf, he took out a wig and placed it on his head, then turned and faced the woman.

'Well?' he asked. 'What do you think?'

She moved nearer to him, her expression serious as she adjusted the head mask, looking for faults. With one eye on the photographs she trained the other on the man himself or on the mirrors, which showed the profile. Eventually she nodded. 'As usual,' she replied to his question, 'it's perfect.' The man in the room had become the man in the photographs.

'Good,' he smiled in reply, the lips of the tight-fitting mask moving as he spoke. Very gently he rolled it up over his face and head, turning it inside out in the process. Angel handed him a towel and he wiped the powder off his face and neck.

Two hours later, the same man was sitting in the office of the Hong Kong Director of the Banke de Constantine of Zurich. His eyes were now covered by expensive Porche Carrera shades in a gold frame and a bushy, sun-streaked moustache covered his upper lip. He was dressed in a hand-stitched, made to measure, off-white safari suit and a dark tan, open-necked shirt. His only jewellery was a solid gold Rolex, worn face down on his left wrist. He looked like an extremely wealthy busi-nessman with accounts worth several millions of US dollars, which was what the director of the bank knew him to be. He had politely declined the offer of a glass of sherry, or any other refreshment.

'I think all your instructions are clear, Mr Wainwright. The deposit of half a million has been cleared and the amount, less the normal charges, has been credited to your main account. I've noted your instructions con-cerning the additional $500,000 from the same source. If we have not received it by 2 October, you will be notified.'

'And the Trust Account?' Wainwright asked.

'That now stands at almost five million dollars. That includes the last transfer and accrued interest to 31 August. Oh, just a moment. I have a note here concern-ing your bi-annual instructions. It is almost renewal time. Would you like to renew them for another two-year period, or change them?'

'Renew them. Only this time make them "until ad-vised otherwise". I doubt if I shall be needing to make any changes. I shall leave the bank to administer the account and make the payments as before. There will be no more receipts to that account for the foreseeable future. How long can the account sustain the payments as they are?'

The director made a few calculations on the machine on his desk.

'Assuming an upwards trend in the exchange rates,

168

and allowing a 2% fluctuation in interest rates, up or down, I should suggest that the present payments could be made, without alteration, until the year 2000.'

'That's fine,' Wainwright replied. 'Can we get the paperwork out of the way now?'

'Of course.' The director lifted his phone, asking his secretary to come in. As he replaced the handset the door opened and a tall, attractive Eurasian girl entered, smiling in Wainwright's direction. Her boss handed her a sheet of paper.

'Please amend Mr Wainwright's instructions to "until further notice". All other details to remain the same, except for the bi-annual clause. Delete that, please.'

'Certainly, sir.' The girl took the sheet and departed, closing the door behind her.

'It will only take a few minutes. Sure I can't offer you something? Tea, coffee?'

'No, thank you. I'm fine.' Wainwright smiled politely at the director, his dark glasses hiding the fact that the smile did not reach his eyes.

'While you're here, Mr Wainwright, the bank has been contacted by each of the four beneficiaries. Are you still adamant that you are to remain anonymous?'

'Yes.' It was a final, not for discussion, answer. 'Please inform them – should they again request this information – that any attempt to trace my identity will only lead to a cessation of payments. Don't carry out that threat. Just make it.'

'As you wish, Mr Wainwright.'

They sat in silence as they waited for the assistant to return with the papers. Normally the director would make some small talk about the latest party, or perhaps a reception at the Governor's House. Something that both he, and a customer of Wainwright's standing, would have been invited to. But with this man he could never think of anything to say. Nobody knew his interests, or anything about his business dealings. Apart from his large cash accounts he had an investment portfolio which was worth several million, yet he was not known to attend any AGMs or even send a representative. He lived in the big house in Kowloon with a couple of servants, and the other mystery, the woman. They were well-suited to each other, he thought as they waited, wishing the girl would hurry up. They were both polite, but never talkative. The only thing which the Director knew about, that nobody else in the Colony was aware of, were the donations he made, each quarter, to four organizations. Just then the girl returned. Wainwright signed the original and the copy, with the Director and the girl acting as witnesses to his signature. Both documents were then stamped with the bank's franking stamp and that was the end of their business together. As the girl left the office, Wainwright folded the copy document and placed it in his inside pocket, then shook hands with the director and left, never to return.

Two days later, on 16 September, Charles Wainwright, travelling on an American passport with a Hong Kong residence visa stamped in it, passed through passport control at Kai Tak International. He was booked on a JAL flight to Rome. His luggage consisted of one suitcase and a briefcase which he carried with him on board. Both had been checked, but the mask was not found. It was hidden in a thin compartment in the lid of the briefcase.

In Rome, Charles Wainwright disappeared and another American citizen, Kenneth Dam, was booked on a single ticket from Rome to Frankfurt. On 18 September, James Bishop, yet another American passport-holder flew from Frankfurt to Kastrup, Copenhagen, on an SAS flight. The Chameleon had arrived in Denmark.

On that same day bankdrafts, drawn on the Banke de Constantine of Zurich, were received by four separate children's organizations: St Christopher's Orphanage at Ma-lie Shui, in the New Territories of Hong Kong; the headquarters of the United Nations Children's Fund in Geneva; the International Red Cross office in Bangkok; and a small orphanage for handicapped Gurkha boys in Katmandu, run by an ex-Royal Army Pay Corps Sergeant of the British Army. The accompanying letter informed each beneficiary that the amounts were the normal quarterly payments, as requested by the anonymous donor. The letter stated further that any attempt to trace the donor would only lead to a cessation of payments.

At four minutes past two, on the afternoon of 22 September the man that witnesses claimed was Arne Fries was driving a rented pick-up van from the customer car park at the rear of Den Danske Bank, Viby. Removing the specialist mask as he entered the van he drove off in the direction of Århus city centre. As he drove, he removed the foam-padded belt from beneath his shirt that had added several pounds in weight to his appearance. Heading down towards the harbour he turned on to the A15 for Ronde, by the Atlantic Hotel. Just past Risskov he turned the van into the parking area of a large building which backed on to the sea. Parking, he removed the dark-brown contact lenses from his eyes and placed them in his pocket.

The building was a combination restaurant, lounge bar and discothèque. It was owned and managed by Arne Fries. The man sitting in the van, watching the building, would have been recognized under several different names, including Charles Wainwright. Beside him on the passenger seat was the same briefcase he had carried all the way from Hong Kong. Opening it he slid the slightly damaged mask into the secret compartment and closed the case. In his pocket was the gun he had used to kill Peter Schantz. He looked at the Rolex on his wrist. 14:29. As if on a signal, Arne Fries came out of the building from a side door and walked directly to the Volvo Estate parked near by. Getting in, he drove off towards the city centre. Had he bothered to check the clock on the dashboard it would have read 09:30. For the past two days the clock had been going mad. The day before he had checked the connection from the battery, but could not find any fault. There was none. It had been simple for the man sometimes known as Wainwright to enter the car and set the clock hours ahead. He had changed the time on three separate occasions. As he waited to join the stream of traffic heading for the city centre, Fries looked at his wrist-watch. 13:32. Plenty of time for his appointment with Peter Schantz.

As the Volvo disappeared in the stream of traffic, Wainwright left the van and strolled towards the entrance which led to the private apartment above the restaurant. Using a thin piece of plastic he easily opened the door and quietly ran up to the third floor. He paused at the top of the stairs, listening. There was no sound of any other person in the apartment. In the bedroom he found the bed unmade, the clothing scattered as though the person had woken later than expected and was rushing. He smiled, knowing that was exactly what had happened. Fries, working until five or six each morning, habitually woke at noon, but that morning he had overslept. Moving quietly but surely, Wainwright placed the murder weapon in a drawer containing underwear. Shoving the pistol to the back he covered it with several pairs of underpants.

He then proceeded to change all four clocks in the apartment, putting each one forward exactly one hour, to read the correct time. Arne Fries would never know that the generous American who had insisted on buying him several drinks in his own bar the previous night had doctored one of them with a precise dosage of a slow-acting sleeping potion. The people of the jungles of South-East Asia did not have access to chemists, but they knew the ingredients of the plants and shrubs that grew all round them, and knew how to use them. At 10.00 that morning Wainwright had visited the apartment and adjusted the clocks back one hour, including the alarm clock by Fries's bed, and the wrist-watch on his arm. Fries had slept on, undisturbed, in his drugged sleep.

Quickly checking the apartment once more, Wainwright left the way he had come in, checking that the main door was locked. He then drove the rented vehicle back towards Århus and the harbour, parking in a bay in the public car park by the dock of the Århus–Kalundborg ferry. Dropping two ten-kroner coins in the parking meter he left the van where it was. He had made arrangements for it to be picked up there by the hire company at 4.00 p.m. Taking his suitcase from the back of the van, and the briefcase from the passenger seat, he locked the doors, hiding the keys in the exhaust. Having purchased his ticket the day before he walked on board the ferry that would take him to Kalundborg, where the Copenhagen train would be waiting.

He would be spending the night in Copenhagen, then catching the London flight in the morning. There had been a small problem that needed looking into in Ireland. He had sent one of his European contacts to deal with it and he now wanted to make sure that everything had been sorted out satisfactorily. Making his way to the

cafeteria on board he bought two vienerbrød – Danish
pastries – and a coffee, plus a copy of *Newsweek*. Sitting
by a window he relaxed in his seat for the crossing.

CHAPTER FOURTEEN

Dublin and London
September–October 1994

IT WAS THREE DAYS AFTER THE MURDER of Detective
Inspector Jimmy Douglas, and the day after the shooting
of Peter Schantz in Denmark, that Sean White phoned
Cowboy.

By that time a deal had been made with William J.
Clark. He had signed his confession, relating his personal involvement in the murders of Douglas and
O'Brien, but that got the CIB no nearer to catching the
Chameleon. If an announcement of the arrest of Clark
was made public, then Chameleon would go to ground,
burying himself even deeper than before. There were
leads that could be followed up – the contact phone
numbers and the Swiss banks – and the CIB needed
time. To do that, Clark had to remain out of prison,
while Colloney had to remain inside. Colloney had already agreed to remain in Port Laoise jail and it was
agreed, with the State Attorney's permission, for Clark
to be effectively put under house arrest at his home in
Malahide. Any private calls made to his office were
diverted to the house. As far as his staff were concerned,
he had suffered a minor stroke and was convalescing at
home.

A full report had been passed to Wilcox at New Scotland Yard and a round-the-clock watch was made on the
Chinese restaurant where Clark had met his contact.

The answering service in London had been contacted, but there were no files kept of messages and that particular lead was a dead end. Wilcox had made a private and confidential call to a colleague in the Hong Kong police department for assistance. Due to the reputation the Hong Kong police had achieved in the late '70s and early '80s, when a large number were under investigation by the International Commission Against Corruption – ICAC – Wilcox had picked his man carefully.

A senior official of the Irish Foreign Service was already in contact with the Swiss authorities over the bank account that Clark had made his million-dollar payment to. As the Irish could prove that the money received was the result of a crime, the Swiss were ready to hear the evidence and, if convinced, would be willing to provide information on the account. Miss Gormon, the young receptionist at JB Finance, had received a visit from Cowboy. He had explained to her that it was imperative that she kept what she knew to herself, for the time being at least. She had been shocked to learn that the man who had delivered the letter, and who had tried to chat her up, had been an English policeman. She agreed to say nothing of what she knew until told otherwise.

Cowboy had suggested setting himself up as a target for the Chameleon, using the same route Clark had used – an advertisement in the London *Times*. Mooney vetoed the idea immediately. To start with it would take much longer and there was no way that they could keep the case under wraps for that long. 'Remember,' he reminded Cowboy, 'he doesn't take on quick jobs. He would take the time to investigate you, and if he had the slightest idea that you were a policeman, he would back off immediately. Or, alternatively, he might just succeed beyond our expectations. He might actually get you. It's too dangerous.'

The day after the murder of Jimmy Douglas was announced in the media, an answering machine in Hong Kong recorded message after message for Chameleon to contact London. Angel received the messages hours after they had been left, but she herself was unable to contact the Chameleon to warn him.

Cowboy and Marlane had just finished dinner in his Ballsbridge apartment when the phone rang.

'Yea, Johnson speaking.'

'Cowboy, it's Sean. Sorry to disturb you at play. I rang the Castle and they told me you were "out", so I took a chance on calling you at home. I need your help. Anything that you have that will help me convince my superiors that this Chameleon actually exists.'

'Why, Sean? What's happened?'

'I am convinced that he paid us a visit yesterday.' He went on to explain about the shooting of Schantz. He had told the story to his boss who at first thought Sean was taking the piss, and then thought he was having a nervous breakdown. He would not listen or accept anything to do with a 'hit man' theory. They had the body, the weapon, the motive and the witnesses. The case was clear-cut, open and shut. Fries was guilty and that was that.

'Sean, I'll be on the first flight to Denmark in the morning. You can tell your boss that I'll be bringing enough evidence to show that the Chameleon exists. We have a full confession on our case here, including all the details on how the contact was made. I'll bring photocopies of everything with me. We also received a very personal calling card from the Chameleon.'

'Oh yea? What was that?'

'Jimmy Douglas is dead, Sean. Not, we think, by Chameleon himself, but by a sub-contractor.'

'Oh shit, Cowboy, I'm sorry. I didn't know. When did

177

it happen? How did it happen?' Very briefly Cowboy explained the events that led to Jimmy's murder. He'd give Sean the full details when he saw him the next day. He asked him to make a reservation for him at the Atlantic Hotel for about three days.

Later that same day, the Chameleon was having a meeting with Gordon, his British contact man. This time it was Gordon who sat with his back to the silk screens in the upstairs room in the Chinese restaurant. He had been in the middle of eating his sweet 'n' sour pork with chips, when he heard the slight noise behind him. He felt a chill of fear run through him. It was the same each time he had met this man. An ex-paratrooper, with active service in Ireland and the Falklands, Richard Gordon had not been afraid of any man, until he met the Chameleon.

'It's about time you got here,' Gordon complained. 'I've sent message after message to Hong Kong for the past couple of days, trying to get in touch with you.'

'I was on business, on the Continent. A matter which does not concern you. What went wrong?'

'I don't know, I honestly don't know. But something's gone up the Swannee. The guy in Ireland was a Scotland Yard detective. Somebody must be on to you.'

'Did you question the man before you killed him?'

'No. You said to take care of him, that he was trying a bit of black. How the hell was I to know he was a copper? All I know is, where you find one copper, you find another and another.'

Gordon fell silent, trying to eat some more of his meal, but found he had lost his appetite. Not being able to stand the silence any longer he pushed the plate away from him.

'What are we going to do?' he asked.

For a moment longer Chameleon remained silent, his brain computing various options to overcome this problem. Gordon was correct, somebody had discovered he existed and was trying to trap him. He still remembered, on rare occasions, the last time he had been incarcerated. It would not happen to him again.

' "We", ' he eventually replied, 'are not going to do anything. What I do from now on is no concern of yours. As of yesterday, I retired. For good. No more contracts, so ignore any messages you might find in the papers. I've arranged for some severance pay to be made to your account. I have done the same with all my contacts. 100,000 US dollars. That should keep you going for a while. Forget the Irish problem, I'll look into it myself and deal with it as I see fit. After that I shall disappear. I suggest you do the same, at least for the time being. The phone contact in Hong Kong is terminated. Do not call that number again.

'One final word of warning. Don't think about "doing a bit of black" yourself. Do not make any attempt to contact any of our old customers. If you do, I shall get to hear about it, and that would bring me out of retirement. Do I make myself clear?'

'Sure. Anything you say. You've always paid well, and I've kept most of it for a rainy day. I think it's pissin' down right now, don't you? Don't worry about the clients. I've no need to get in touch with them. You can trust me.'

'Good. Then we part as friends. Take care of yourself and take a holiday for a few months. Now put the menu card over your face, and keep it there until I've gone. Wait for five minutes, then you can leave. Do it now.'

Gordon took the plastic menu holder and held it closer to his face. He heard the screen move and felt rather than heard the other man move past the table and out the door to the stairs leading down into the restaurant. Only then did he remove the menu from his face. It was when he exhaled that he realized he had been holding his breath. He wiped his napkin across his forehead.

So that was it! It was over. But there was a nice payment in lieu of notice. One thing he had learnt early on in his dealings with the Chameleon was that he could be trusted. If he said a hundred grand had been paid into his account, then the hundred grand was already there. It was funny how he had changed his habit, at the end, though. Before, he had always left the way he had come. By the back door. He had never previously used the main, public, exit.

In the first-floor room, above the Import/Export firm on the opposite side of the road from the Chinese restaurant, one of the two Scotland Yard detectives was speaking with Chief Superintendent Wilcox on the hand-held radio.

'Yes, sir. About five minutes ago. We've got some photos, but he moved very carefully, almost as if he knew somebody was watching. No facials. He used the side door in the next street as the way in, like the source in Ireland said he did. There could be another little meeting going on right now. Okay, sir. Roger and out.' Switching the radio set off he reached into his belt and took out the .38 checking the load.

'Okay, Tommy, it's John Wayne time. The Governor's sending the cavalry, but he'd like us to order ten portions of number 26.'

Tommy nodded without speaking. He hated moments like this, when that sudden chill ran down his spine. He was always okay once the action started, but this one was a special case. Jimmy Douglas had been a mate. Detective Sergeants Lorrie Norton and Tommy Curtis had both worked with Jimmy and liked him. Now he was lying on a slab in a morgue in Dublin, and it was odds on that the bloke who just walked into the Chinese restaurant had something to do with it. Tommy checked his .38. Locking the door to the room containing the surveillance equipment behind them, the two detectives made their way down to street level. Crossing the busy road they paused at the corner, looked each other in the eye, nodded, then separated.

Tommy strolled into the restaurant, stopping just inside the door, his eyes scanning the lunch-time customers, looking for a familiar face. There were none. A waiter approached him, smiling, a menu folder in his hand. He waved the waiter aside and moved towards the stairs. A second waiter approached and this time Tommy produced his police card, but kept moving. As he got to the bottom of the staircase the second Chinaman tried to stop him. Pushing him to one side, he withdrew his revolver and began to move up the stairs. The waiter began to shout in Chinese. Tommy moved faster, heading for the door at the top. As he arrived at the door he heard a crash, followed by a shout. 'STOP. POLICE. KEEP YOUR HANDS ON THE TABLE!' Lorrie was inside.

Standing back he kicked the door. Grasping the revolver in both hands, arms stretched out in front of him, he entered the room and dropped to one knee. 'POLICE,' he shouted. Lorrie's eyes never moved from the suspect sitting at the table. Tommy's pistol traversed the room, coming to a stop at the lone diner seated at the table.

Richard Gordon was coughing and spluttering, choking on a chip. Behind him, to his right, was an armed policeman, and kneeling by the door, a second one. In the distance he could hear the wail of police sirens. Recovering from his choking, trying to suck air into his lungs, he

181

stayed as he was, both hands on the table in front of him, just as he had been ordered to do. There was no way that the Chameleon could have known of this pending raid – yet he had left only minutes before, changing his exit route for the first time. No wonder he was the best in the business.

Two blocks away, about to turn into Piccadilly, Chameleon heard the sirens and instinct told him they were heading in the direction of the Chinese restaurant. It was the same instinct that had kept him alive for years in the jungles of South-East Asia. The same instinct that had kept him one step ahead of the law ever since. He just operated in a different jungle now.

He wasn't worried about Gordon. He would not be of much use to the police. They had never met face to face that Gordon knew of, and the only contact he could give them was the answering machine in Hong Kong. The staff at the restaurant would not be of much use to the police either. He had paid enough money into the coffers of the Green Dragon Triad to ensure that. Anything the police got out of the Chinese staff would be misleading rather than helpful. He entered the nearest coffee shop and ordered a *cappuccino*.

So, it was over. Funny how it had turned out though. He had planned for the Danish job to be the last. He had been at the top of his profession for a long time. He knew, without any conceit or false pride, that he was the best there was. Only one small thing niggled him now. How and where did he make a mistake? What put the police on to him in the first place?

Not his contacts. To start with, none of them knew who he actually was. Secondly, he paid them enough money to ensure their loyalty. Oh sure, over the years one or two had tried it on. Two of them had tried to blackmail clients – and he had thought another was trying the same in Ireland. The other two had paid the price for their stupidity, and he had made sure that others knew of the price they paid. He had his reputation to think of, and his word. He was the best, and he gave the best protection to his clients, *that* was why he stayed on top for all these years. But something had gone wrong in Ireland. At first he had thought it was Gordon trying a bit of blackmail. He had been the original contact with the client. But Gordon had assured him that he wasn't and he had believed him. Sending Gordon to sort out the problem had been a mistake. Something along the line had gone wrong – or had it? If he had gone to sort out the job himself, would he still be here, sitting in a coffee shop, while Gordon was being picked up? He did not like loose ends. He could not finally retire until he knew what had happened in Dublin.

A Scotland Yard detective working in the Irish capital meant that the Irish CIB had to be involved. But where had it all started? Maybe Clark knew the answers – but where was Clark? If it was not a set-up, then Clark was in prison. If he wasn't . . . There was only one way to find out. But first he had to call Hong Kong. Leaving his half-drunk *cappuccino* he dropped some coins into the saucer and walked out of the coffee shop.

CHAPTER FIFTEEN

Denmark
September–October 1994

COWBOY'S FLIGHT FROM DUBLIN landed at 13:15 at Kastrup, Copenhagen. Waiting for him on the other side of Customs and Passport Control was Sean. With over an hour to wait for the flight to Tirstrup they sat in the cafeteria, drinking coffee laced with the whiskey Cowboy had brought and eating smørrebrød – Danish 'open' sandwiches with a selection of cheeses and meats. As they ate Sean explained what had happened at Viby.

'The timing was perfect – yet again! Schantz is shot in a room with only one other occupant – Fries – and only one way in. A member of the bank staff had met Fries when he arrived, told Schantz he was there, and led him to the room. After the shots Fries walked out, just like that.'

'If he spoke to somebody, then he must have spoken in Danish,' Cowboy commented.

'He did, but all he said was that he had an appointment with Schantz for 2.00 p.m. That's easy enough to learn. I could teach you half a dozen phrases in an hour or so.

'After the shooting, Fries walks away and we get called. We're at the bank and suddenly one of the women tellers is screaming and pointing to the door. There's Fries, banging on the glass door demanding to be let in! I knew, I fucking *knew*, at that moment, that

184

Chameleon had been. I grabbed Fries's wrist and checked his watch. Exactly one hour early! Fries claimed he had only just arrived, blah, blah, blah. Trouble was, I knew the poor bastard was telling the truth. But I also knew we were going to find the weapon, and that nobody, apart from me, was going to believe him. Sure enough, we found the gun hidden in a drawer in his apartment. No prints. The motive, or the reason rather than motive for the death, was anger and frustration. Schantz, acting on behalf of the bank, was foreclosing on Fries's loans. Fries was going to lose everything he had worked for. He's quite quick-tempered and hot-blooded, sees Schantz as the man, rather than the bank, who's going to cost him, and bang, bang, bang. Everything nicely wrapped up.'

'No way he actually *did* kill the bank man?'

Sean shook his head. 'No. I'm positive of that. You know what it's like, Cowboy. You can tell the innocent ones easy enough. It's in the eyes. Let's face it, if he *was* guilty, why do it in front of witnesses? He could have taken Schantz out any time, any place. No. He's innocent all right – the trouble is proving it. That's why I called you. I also called my ex-CIA friend, Buffalo Bill. He's in Sweden at the moment, visiting his wife's family. He's going to come over and speak with us. Anything he tells us will not be backed up in any way. We won't be able to use it as evidence in court, but it will give *us* a little more background detail.'

'Well, at least we have something here that we can show your boss.' Cowboy indicated his briefcase, then proceeded to tell the Danish policeman the events that had led to the death of Jimmy Douglas and the confession by Clark.

The flight from Kastrup to Tirstrup was uneventful and there they picked up Sean's car. At 4.30 p.m. Sean

was introducing Cowboy to his superior, Kriminalpoli-
timestre – Criminal Police Chief – Christiansen. Sean
had explained on the way that his boss spoke perfect
English. He also reminded Cowboy that he would hear
him being referred to as 'Nils' rather than Sean. After
the introductions, Cowboy produced the photocopies
and handed them to the sceptical police chief. He read
them slowly, not wanting to misunderstand anything,
and only occasionally asking Sean to translate for him,
to make sure he fully understood. Finally, he placed the
documents on his desk top and looked across at the
other two men.

'Unbelievable. Simply unbelievable. If it were not for
these papers I would be throwing Nils here out of my
office. But I must accept the facts you bring with you,
Sergeant Johnson. Sorry I doubted you, Nils, but what
you were suggesting, that what I was convinced was an
open and shut case, was the work of some super
contract-killer . . . well, I just . . .' he shrugged his
shoulders. 'I'm lost for words.

'But it doesn't solve our problem. We have, on the one
hand, a murder, plus suspect, weapon, motive and witnesses. If we were to go to court tomorrow Fries would
go to prison on what we have.

'On the other hand, you now come to me with pretty
strong circumstantial evidence that Fries is *not* the killer.
You have raised doubts, but that's all, so far.' He raised
his hand to stop Sean from interrupting. 'I know, I know
– but where's your *proof*, Nils? If there is a paid killer,
then there is a paymaster. Who would pay one million
dollars to kill this bank man? Where's the connection
between them? What's the motive?'

'May I have your permission to speak with this man
Fries, Chief Christiansen?' Cowboy asked. 'He might be
able to provide us with some sort of a lead, even if he

doesn't know it himself. You have just raised the question – who would pay one million to have the bank man killed. May I suggest that you are also pointing in one direction that should be investigated. Schantz's role at the bank. There has to be, *has* to be, a much greater financial gain behind the bank man's death. Do you agree?'

'Yes, there would have to be something very big involved, Sergeant. You have my permission to speak with Fries, but I cannot make him talk to you if he does not wish to. Also, if he wishes his lawyer to be present, that must happen. Nils knows the rules, he'll keep you on the straight and narrow.' He gave Cowboy a friendly smile across the desk. 'I'll take your tip and have a word with a friend of mine. He is a senior manager at Den Danske Bank here in the city. I'm sure I can get him to look into deals involving both Schantz and Fries. Who knows what might turn up, eh? Okay Nils, take it from there. And thank you for coming to Denmark, Sergeant Johnson. I do not like killings, especially ones that happen in my city.'

Thanking his boss, Sean led Cowboy to his small office. He made a quick phone call and arranged for Fries to be brought to the office from the holding cells, then made a fresh pot of coffee with the stain-spotted machine resting on the office window ledge. Taking a packet of Prince cigarettes from his desk drawer, along with a bottle of 'Gamle Danske' Danish bitters, the two detectives waited for the arrival of Fries.

Fries was still dressed in the same clothing he had been arrested in, two days before. Normally a neat and tidy man, his clothes were now badly in need of a pressing and his shirt collar was sweat-stained and ruffled. His face was haggard, mainly from lack of sleep, and he was unshaven. He couldn't sleep because he could not

187

believe what was happening to him. He looked suspiciously at the two detectives as he entered, sitting himself down uninvited in the moulded plastic chair by the desk. Sean offered him coffee, a cigarette and a glass of Gamle Danske. Looking puzzled he accepted all three without a word, throwing the glass of bitters back in one go. Taking a sip of the strong black, unsweetened coffee he lit the cigarette and looked bemusedly at Cowboy. Cowboy was coughing and spluttering over his glass of bitters, turning tear-filled eyes in the direction of his friend, silently asking what the hell it was he had given him to drink. Sean smiled, then spoke to Fries.

'Herr Fries, do you speak English?' he asked, in Danish. Once again Fries turned to look at Cowboy, then back at Sean, nodding his head. 'A little,' he replied, also in Danish.

'Good.' Sean replied, still speaking Danish. 'This man is a Detective Sergeant from the Criminal Investigation Branch of the Irish Police Force. He has come here because I asked him to, and because he and I are the only two people in Denmark, apart from yourself, who know that you did not kill Peter Schantz.'

'So why am I under arrest, if you believe me?'

'Because we can't prove it. If you were to be put on trial tomorrow everything is against you and you would be found guilty. We have to find the reason why you were set up – which we believe you were. Everything that has happened to you has happened on purpose. You are meant to be found guilty of the murder. Can you carry on a conversation in English? I can assist you with difficult words, but it will be easier all round if we speak in English. Can you do it?'

'Yes, I think so,' Fries replied, switching to English.

'Good. Now before we go any further with this conversation you can, if you wish, insist on having your lawyer present. But the questions that Sergeant Johnson here will ask you are going to be more for background than about the murder. Do you understand?'

Fries nodded. 'Yes. Forget the lawyer. He believes I'm guilty anyway, and all he can "advise" is to plead guilty, to make it easier for myself. I do not intend pleading guilty to a crime I did not commit. So,' he turned and looked directly at Cowboy. 'What do you want to know?'

'First of all, Mr Fries, I would like you to know that I am currently leading an investigation into a similar killing in Ireland, that goes back years. We know we are on the right track, because a detective working with me on the case has been murdered. Peter Schantz was killed by a professional contract killer who is known only by the name of the Chameleon. You know what a chameleon is, Mr Fries?'

Fries looked at Sean for assistance.

'Kamæleon,' Sean said, pronouncing it the Danish way.

'His name derives from that animal's ability to change its appearance – just as he does. This killer, looking remarkably like you, killed Schantz, and you are under arrest for the murder.'

Fries looked from one man to the other. Were they joking? Was this some kind of a sick, stupid game?

'Please understand me, Sergeant, I am thankful for you coming to Denmark to try and help me, but this story is so . . . so . . .' He looked to the ceiling, as though seeking inspiration before continuing, 'so incredible. I don't know what to say?'

'That is precisely where this man Chameleon has so much success. We don't know *how* successful he has been. All we know for certain is that he killed a man in Ireland several years ago by the name of O'Brien. An innocent man is sitting in a jail in Ireland serving a life sentence for that murder. We also know that he was responsible for having a detective killed in Dublin a few days ago. We *know* all of this, but proving it is something else. His success has been built on the total absurdity of his methods.'

Shaking his head, Fries could still not grasp the reality of it all. 'It is difficult, Sergeant. All *I* know is that I did not kill Schantz. Ask me any questions you like. Anything that will help me get out of here, I am prepared to give.'

'Thank you, Mr Fries. Now first of all, for somebody to impersonate you, and to be able to do it so well, you must have been under surveillance for some time. Have you had any idea that anybody was watching you over the last couple of months? Somebody who could study the way you walk, mannerisms, hand movements, head movements, things like that. Maybe you just had a "feeling" about this, but could not understand the feeling?'

Fries shook his head immediately. 'Nothing like that, Sergeant. But it would be easy enough to watch me for a good length of time, if you wanted to. All you would have to do is come to my bar. I am there every night. I like to keep a personal contact with my customers, even if they have been falling off recently.'

'Oh? Why is that?' Cowboy asked.

'Because the police will not give me any protection, nor my customers. There have been fights with what we call "Rockers" here in Denmark. Leather-clothed motor bikers. Hell's Angels, if you like. All the police can do is arrive too late and then threaten to take away my liquor licence and close me down. I do not know what your system is in Ireland, Sergeant, but in Denmark the police find it so much easier to close a place down and put somebody out of business, than to arrest the people who cause the trouble.' The bitterness was evident in his voice as he spoke.

Cowboy looked at Sean, who nodded his head. He knew that what Fries said was right. 'It's true, Cowboy. I know it sounds ridiculous, but that's the way it works. Each licensee is responsible for keeping peace in his own place. It works, unless some others decide to cause a lot of bother. If the civil police get called to a place too often, then when the licence is up for renewal, the police oppose it on the grounds that there is too much violence at the place. All I personally ever could see in this system was that the problem moved from one spot to another and meanwhile somebody, as Mr Fries just pointed out, gets closed down. But I don't make the rules. I only follow them.'

'Have you always had problems with these Hell's Angels, Mr Fries?' Cowboy asked, turning back to Fries.

He shook his head. 'No. Only over the past year. Before that time they never came near me. My place was not exactly the type of place they normally hang out. Let me explain what my place *used* to be like, then perhaps you will understand.' He reached for another cigarette, lit it and inhaled. He paused, trying to get his thoughts into order, then continued.

'There are many places in Århus for the young people. All these clubs and places we used to call discos. Every second street has a hamburger bar or a grill bar filled with kids, with the latest craze in music blaring out all the time. I'm not against them, in fact I think they are a good idea. But there's no real place for the 30–40-year-olds to go and relax, unless it's an expensive nightclub. No place where there is a bit of romance to be found. Good, but inexpensive food, and a pleasant atmosphere. Do you know the kind of place I mean, Sergeant?'

Cowboy nodded. It was the same in Dublin and other cities. The young had the ready money, so they were well catered for. All that was left for the older generation was the pubs or night clubs.

'I have worked in the bar and restaurant business all my life, Sergeant. For many years I worked in a town to the north of here. A place called Randers. I used to have this idea, a "dream" I suppose you could call it, of having a place where people could come and relax, have a good time, some nice food, a few drinks, and not be ripped off. I saved as much as I could, hoping one day that I could have such a place. And then, out of the blue, I came up on the Tips. Almost 750,000 kroner.'

Cowboy glanced over at Sean for an explanation.

'Tips are the Danish version of the football pools. You make your forecast, pretty much the same way as the pools, and if you come up on a good week . . . well, you can win quite a bit.'

'Well, now I had the money to make my dream become reality. I had almost 200,000 kroner of my own money saved. I felt I had enough money which, along with a bank loan, would get me the kind of place I was looking for. But Randers was not the place to do it, I felt. It was too provincial. So I came to the city, to Århus, looking for the place. And I found it, just outside the city. Not *in* the city, but not so far away that people would be put off coming.

'The building itself had been lying empty for a few years, but the structure was solid. It was big, three floors, had a large area outside for parking cars, and it backed on to the sea. It was everything I wanted it to be.

'I found myself a lawyer and made arrangements to buy the place. Without disclosing my intentions about what I wanted to do with the building I managed to get it for a deposit of 50,000 kroner and took over the existing loans on the building. The bank were happy to sell it, as it had been a repossession. The previous owners had gone bust and so the bank had taken the place back.

'Using my own money I hired an architect, told him specifically what I wanted, and we started. My priority was to get the bar open first, and, from the beginning, the only music that was played there was easy on the ear. It was the kind of music I wanted, blending in with the atmosphere I intended to create for the whole place. After I got the bar going, I started on the kitchens. I had a sort-of international cuisine, but it was all straightforward stuff, nothing too fancy.

'For the summer, I fixed up the back of the building and put in a terrace, with tables and chairs and umbrellas. I sold ice-cream, cakes, coffee, liquors, beers, soft drinks. Last of all, I opened a small dancing area. You could call it a disco, but it's not really. I was playing music you could dance to. The kind where you could get close to your girlfriend or wife. Sure I played some rock 'n' roll, but only the good stuff. Not the crap they call music today.

'It all took a while, but soon I was having a full house every Friday and Saturday night, and people were also coming to eat out during the week. In the summer it was necessary to get there early if you wanted a place on the terrace. I was successful.

'The renovations I made after the bar got going were paid for with money I borrowed from Den Danske Bank, in Viby. My accountant introduced me to Schantz, I explained my plans, showed him what I had done and what I intended doing, and that was that.

'That first Christmas I invited the bank to hold their Christmas party at my place, and they came. Schantz was really impressed with what I had done. I told him of my plans to expand even more and he said there would be no problem over more loans. I took him at his word, applied for further funding, got it, and, as I said, everything was going great.

'Towards the end of last year I got the idea of doing something with the rooms on the first floor. Renting them out in the summer months, sort of thing. This is a lovely part of Denmark, Sergeant, and I was in a good position. I had the city next door, the sea at my back, and nature all round me. Then, out of the blue, I got an offer to sell the place. Some American company wanted to buy me out. They offered me two million kroner cash, and they would take over the existing loans, the old ones on the building, plus the new ones I had arranged. It was a good offer and I thought about it. I was tempted, but in the end I said no. I had always worked for somebody else until I bought that place. My instinct about how to make a success of it had been right and I was making a good living. I had a lovely apartment over the place, I had a nice car, and my place was popular. If I might say so myself, *I* was popular. I mixed with my customers, bought them drinks, took an interest in them, occasionally paying for a meal if I discovered that the couple were celebrating something, like a birthday or an anniversary. Things like that. I helped to make them feel important, and they were. Without them, I was nothing. I loved my work, Sergeant, I really did. I was giving a service to my customers that many other places could not be bothered to give. I enjoyed being my own man, so I said no to the offer.

'Schantz thought I was mad. He said I could do the same thing in another place and with less overheads, having all that cash. But Los Palmas – the name I gave the place – was special to me. I wanted to keep it.

'The next offer was a surprise. The same two million cash, the overtaking of the loans and a job offer. They said they intended building a large hotel in the grounds and I was offered the job as General Manager, on a good salary, plus . . . a payment of 100,000 *dollars*, anywhere I wanted in the world. I thought it over again, and once again decided against it. I was actually expecting to receive another offer and was wondering how much this one would be for, when the trouble started.

'As I told you, Los Palmas is not quite the place for Rockers. We did not play their kind of music, nor did we cater for the piss-on-the-floor-puke-on-the-table kind of customer, so they didn't come. But suddenly they were arriving on their bikes, roaring up and down in the car park, frightening the guests on their arrival or departure. It was happening several times a week and, of course, by the time the police arrived, they had always gone. Then damage was done to the cars parked in my car park. Eleven cars had their tyres slashed in one night, my own included. I began to notice the drop in customers. Then the Rockers started to move into the building. They would come in and order food and then refuse to pay for it saying it was bad, or just simply not pay for it and walk out. One of two of my girls – the waitresses – got pushed around a bit.

'I went to the police and asked for assistance. I was advised to hire some bouncers! Here I was, Sergeant, an honest businessman, paying a great deal in taxes, and I am being told by the police that they could not, or would not, do anything to help – except to advise me to hire my own thugs! Well, I did – but when one of them was beaten half to death outside the place one night, the others "retired". I did not blame them. I went to the police again, and that was when I was told that the police "might possibly" lodge a complaint when my liquor licence was due for renewal, if I didn't manage to keep the peace at Los Palmas. Let me ask you a question, Sergeant. What do *you* think was happening to me?'

'Sounds to me like somebody was making a concerted effort to put you out of business by getting rid of your customers.'

'Precisely, Sergeant. That was what I was thinking also. My expenses were increasing week by week – almost daily, in fact. All the damage that was being done, furniture getting broken, glasses smashed, toilets being vandalized. None of it covered by my insurance. I thought about taking up the offer on the place, but I was told that the company had purchased another building instead and were no longer interested. But the bank was very good about it all. Schantz offered to lend me more and more money. He said it was only a temporary phase. The trouble would go away soon, no problem. I wanted to believe that, Sergeant, so I borrowed more to keep going, to keep the place open. In the end most of the customers stayed away and my income dropped, but the overheads were still there and the loans had to be repaid.

'I met some of my customers, on a few occasions, in the city. They got embarrassed when they saw me. They were sad that they did not come to Los Palmas any more, but when they went out for an evening with their wives or girlfriends, they did not want to be involved in fights, or have their cars damaged. I told them I understood. I would be the same myself. They wanted to come, but were afraid to. Los Palmas was dying on me, Sergeant. It would have been cheaper for me to close the doors and sack everybody.

'The bank, from offering me more and more money, were now asking for it all back. Everything I had dreamt about, and to a large extent had succeeded in achieving, was going, slipping right through my fingers. The dream, Sergeant, was turning into a nightmare. And now this!

'My place will be repossessed and sold. All the buyer will have to pay is the extent of the outstanding loans – and maybe not even that. All my money is lost and, if the bank don't recover enough to cover the loans, then I am still responsible for them. I will owe them, have nothing to pay them with, and no chance to be able to start again. Now I shall be put away for this crime that I did not commit and which I do not understand and when I come out there will be the bank, with their hands held open, looking for the money I owe, plus all the interest. Basically, all I can do is declare myself bankrupt. You both say you know I did not commit this murder. *I* know I did not commit this murder – but how are you going to prove it?'

Sean, for the first time, began to see the logic in what had happened to Fries. A pattern was emerging from the story. Businesses went bust every day, but this one seemed like a deliberate attempt to close Fries down. Why? To get the building. He had been offered a good price, and refused. So they 'increased' his overheads and drove him towards bankruptcy. But why kill Schantz? Why hadn't they just killed Fries? Why kill *anybody*?

Cowboy had risen from his chair and was looking out the window, thinking the same thoughts as Sean. Why the killing? There had to be a reason for that.

'What was the name of the American company that put the bid in for your property, Herr Fries?'

Fries tried to cast his mind back to when the offer was made. Thought lines appeared on his forehead and he scratched the back of his head.

'Shelby. Shelby Incorporated, or something like that. I can't remember exactly, but I'm sure I have the name written down somewhere, back in my office.'

Cowboy turned round from the window. 'Could it be a company called Sheldon Incorporated, by any chance?'

Fries's face lit up. 'That's it. Sheldon. Not Shelby. You know them?' He noticed the look that passed between the two policemen. Slowly Cowboy nodded his head.

'Yes, we know them. It is the same company that was involved in the murder in Ireland. The one that I am investigating. We are not certain, but we suspect that the company was a cover for American organized crime. The Mafia.'

'The *Mafia*! What would the Mafia want with my place?' Fries asked, bewildered.

'That's a good question, Herr Fries.' Cowboy thought for a few more minutes. 'Tell me, what would happen to Los Palmas if *you* were to die?'

Fries seemed to be even more perplexed by this, than he was about the Mafia connection.

'I suppose my brother Tage would get it. He is my only relative. I was married, but I've been divorced for about ten years. There are no children, so, yes, Tage would get it.'

'And what would he do with it?' Cowboy continued.

Fries pondered for a few moments. 'Probably run it, or try to run it. A lot of the debts could be paid off from my life insurance policy. I suppose he would get the money on that too. I don't know. Is it important?'

'How much is your life insured for, Herr Fries?'

'Two million kroner,' he replied.

'About two hundred thousand pounds,' Sean informed him.

'And that would be enough to pay off all the debts to the Den Danske Bank?' Cowboy asked.

'Just about. It certainly wouldn't leave all that much owing to them.'

'This Rocker gang,' Sean interrupted. 'Do you know which one it was?'

'The Rattlers. They wear a coiled snake on their jackets. Do you know them?'

'Oh yes, I know them all right.' Turning to Cowboy he continued. 'We have a nice little conspiracy going on here I think, Cowboy. Somebody put The Rattlers up to causing the trouble, which in turn pushed Fries to borrow more money than he can afford, which in turn leads to the place being shut down.' Turning back once more to face Fries he went on. 'But I can't see why they didn't just kill you, instead of putting you in the frame for Schantz.'

'I can,' Cowboy said. 'If Herr Fries were dead, then the insurance money would go to pay off the bank, and ownership of Los Palmas would go to his brother. Perhaps he might try to run it. Even if he sold it, he would be selling a building that was mortgage-free. This way it goes to the bank, and they can sell it to cover their loans. Guess who the buyer would be? No, killing Herr Fries here would have been a mistake. Framing him for a murder makes a lot more sense and, I think you'll find, will also make a lot more money for somebody. I'll give you odds of 100 to 1, Sean, that the late Herr Schantz is involved in this. This is another "two birds with one stone" case. Schantz *has* to be involved, but perhaps he might not have liked being involved in murder – Fries's murder, that is. Maybe he would have told somebody – maybe even the police – that he had some suspicions about the death of Fries. This way, *he* is the murder victim, Fries goes down for it, the building is repossessed, gets sold to cover the debts, and this Sheldon Inc. gets it. Which was what they were after in the first place. The big question is why they wanted it so badly? Can you talk to these Rockers, Sean?'

'Oh yes, oh yes. And they'll talk to me too, that I can guarantee you.

'Well, that has to be the next step.'

'And what about me?' Fries asked.

'I'm sorry, Herr Fries,' Sean replied, 'but you are going to have to stay where you are for the moment. Please bear with us. I know it's a lot to ask, but think about this. If it hadn't been for the fact that another murder was already being investigated, you'd be looking at going to prison for this. As it is, there is a very strong possibility that you will be out of here shortly, even if it's only on bail. Can you stick it out?'

'I'll have to, won't I? But I am grateful for what you are doing. I knew I hadn't killed him, and it's a great relief to know that at least somebody else believes it too. Any chance of getting a change of clothing and washing stuff?'

'I'll make arrangements to have you taken back to Los Palmas and you can collect whatever you need,' Sean said. 'Be patient, Herr Fries, just be patient. We'll have you out of here as quickly as possible. In the meantime I'd like you to make a written statement covering everything you've just told us. We're going to need it.'

It was late evening by the time they left the police station and both men were hungry. Returning to the same restaurant they had eaten the first night they met, Mama Mia's, they sat and discussed the case.

'I want you to go back to your hotel after we have eaten, Cowboy. I'm going to pick up a couple of colleagues, then we're going to pay a visit to The Rattlers. I know their leader. A real, 100%, son-of-a-bitch by the name of Sorensen. I've had dealings with him before. He thinks he's a tough bastard, but I'm a tougher and bigger bastard than he'll ever be. By the time I'm finished having our little talk tonight I'll know for certain if the departed Mr Schantz was mixed up in all of this.

'I don't want you involved in what's going to go down tonight, Cowboy. This is my problem. To be honest, I feel a bit bad about it all. If what Fries has told us is the truth, and if I get confirmation from Sorensen, then, as far as I'm concerned, we, the police, the so-called up-holders of law and order, are by neglect implicated in Schantz's death. I don't like that one little bit. Do you understand?'

Cowboy nodded. 'I felt exactly the same way when I heard that story from Jens Larsen about the Chameleon. We were used. You sure you don't want me along tonight? I don't mind coming, you know that.'

'Yea, and I appreciate the offer. But this is my city, my country. I don't want to get you involved. We'll deal with the problem, don't worry.'

Sean picked Cowboy up at the hotel the following morning shortly after nine, and once more took him to the station. Sean was wearing a tight bandage on his left wrist and there was a bruise on his cheek – but he had a signed statement from Sorensen over The Rattlers' part in the harassment of Fries and Los Palmas. Peter Schantz had paid Sorensen to take his men out and cause as much trouble as possible for Fries. If they were successful, not only was there extra money promised, but a request for a loan to purchase a building that Sorensen wanted would also be looked on favourably. Sorensen wanted to open a motor bike repair shop. They had their tie-in between Schantz and The Rattlers. What they now needed was proof of some sort of collusion between Schantz and Sheldon Inc.

Chief Christiansen listened to what they had to report and read the statement that Fries had made. He also read Sorensen's statement. He looked at the bruise on Sean's face and the bandage on his wrist.

'Voluntary statement?' he asked, holding the document up with his hand.

Sean nodded. 'After I had explained to him that a man's life was at stake, he felt it was his civic duty to make a complete and truthful confession over his own, and the gang's involvement at the request of Peter Schantz.'

'Hmmm, I see. Oh by the way, Nils, did you see the report that came in from the city hospital?'

Sean shook his head. 'No. What was it?'

'Seems somebody worked Herr Sorensen over last night. Gave him a right beating according to the hospital report. Black eyes, fractured jaw, couple of ribs cracked, and a pair of very sore nuts. He told the hospital that he had been worked over by some members of another Rocker group. Must have happened after you had spoken to him, eh?'

'Must have, Chief. We're going to have to do something about the violence that's spreading throughout the city. If not, we'll only get ourselves a bad name. You can imagine what Fries's lawyer will make of his request for help from the police, and his not getting it.'

'And what will the prosecutor make of it, if he can prove that Fries *knew* that Schantz had paid The Rattlers to cause the trouble? Another motive for killing Schantz, wouldn't you say?'

That was something that Sean and Cowboy had discussed together. While proving the link between the bank man and the Rockers, they were also giving the State another reason why Fries would go after Schantz. Not only had he called in the loans, but he had caused the trouble that *led* to him calling in the loans. But it was a risk that had to be taken.

'Under normal circumstances I'd say you were correct, Chief. But we have this Sheldon company involved in one murder already. The one that Sergeant Johnson is investigating. We also have Clark's confession as to how this hired killer works. On its own, what you are saying is bad for Fries, but with what we already have from Ireland, it shows a pre-planned conspiracy.'

Chief Christiansen agreed, nodding several times. 'Point taken, Nils. And now I have some good news for you two. I spoke to my friend, Jorgen Pedersen, of Den Danske Bank yesterday and gave him our suspicions. He sent a team of bank investigators out to the Viby branch yesterday. Damage limitation he called it. He's expecting the pair of you this afternoon at 2.00. He says he thinks he's found something.'

'Thanks, Chief.' Sean winked at Cowboy. Things were moving, and moving in the right direction.

'By the way, Nils, what happened to your wrist and face?' Christiansen asked, his smile barely concealed.

'Fell down the stairs in the apartment.'

'There *are* no stairs in your apartment, Nils.'

'I know, that's how the accident happened. I'd forgotten.'

'Get out, Nils, just get out. I don't want to know any more.'

'See you later, Chief,' and with that Sean ushered an openly smiling Cowboy out of his boss's office.

Identifying themselves at the bank in Viby they were led into the office used by the late Peter Schantz. Jorgen Pedersen rose from behind the desk to greet them, offering seats and asking if they would like coffee. Both accepted and coffee was poured from the percolator in the corner. Settling himself back into the chair behind the desk Pedersen opened a file.

'I have gone through Peter's personal accounts and the business accounts he has been involved in over the

203

past two years, and I have to admit I'm not happy with what I have found. To begin with there is too much money in his accounts. His home loans have been repaid at a rate that I would not really have thought possible on his salary, even taking his wife's earnings into account. That's point one.

'The second point involves an American company by the name of Sheldon Incorporated. Within the framework of that, there are the accounts of Herr Fries, and somebody called Verstralen in Brussels. I have not been able to fathom it all out yet and we are going to have to get a warrant to search Peter's home to see if there are other documents there. It seems there is a secret plan to put up a new EEC building, here in Århus. This Sheldon Inc., through a subsidiary in Naples, seems to be involved and my guess is that the ground that Fries's bar cum restaurant is built on, is the place where this new building is going to be. If that is the case, then Herr Fries is sitting on a gold mine. One, I might add, that Peter Schantz seems to have been aware of. Yet Peter was calling in his loans, pushing Fries towards bankruptcy which would have made the bank look for a buyer as quickly as possible . . . and guess which company is sitting in the wings?'

'It's beginning to fall into place now, Herr Pedersen. Sergeant Johnson here and I had a long talk with Fries over what would have happened to the building if he had been killed, rather than Schantz. Fries's brother would have inherited the place, but all of that would have taken time, what with probate and so on. By that time plans for the EEC building would, most likely, have become common knowledge and Fries's brother would have been the one sitting on the gold mine. This way – with Fries accused of Schantz's murder – the building would be sold to Sheldon Inc., and the link-man, Peter

Schantz, is dead and out of the picture. What is it they say? "Dead men tell no tales!" Jesus, these are clever bastards. You will most likely find that Chief Christiansen will want to send in the Fraud Squad to look into Schantz's dealings.'

'I was expecting that. I am, in any case, legally bound to report the irregularities I have found, so they would have been here eventually. I'm sorry about Peter. I liked him, and he was the last person I would suspect of something like this. Such a shame, such a shame.'

On Cowboy's last day he and Sean took the early flight to Copenhagen to meet Sean's retired CIA friend. They met for lunch in a city restaurant not far from the famous Tivoli Gardens, and Cowboy was introduced to Buffalo Bill.

'I feel like I'm the odd man out here,' Sean said as they seated themselves at the table. 'I've got a Cowboy on one side and a Buffalo Bill on the other. I feel I should be called Geronimo, or something like that.' The three men ordered steaks and salad, with draft Carlsberg to wash it down, and Sean brought Bill up to date on what they were investigating.

'Well, gents, I'm not going to be able to point a finger and say, "that's him", but I can give you what little – and I mean little – I've picked up on your man. Like all good stories there is a beginning, and this one, as far as I can figure, began in Vietnam.

'Most of the 2,000 MIAs – that's "missing in action" – who never came back were air crews shot down over the jungle, but a few of them were Special Services people. These were highly trained assassins, usually sent off to take out certain North Vietnamese officials, and the occasional one from the South for one reason or the other.

'War does strange things to men. Some freeze when the action starts, some run away, some become heroes, and some, the very few, find what they've been looking for all their lives without knowing it. My money is on your Chameleon being ex-Special Services, and while I have no way of knowing or proving it, I did hear a rumour a few years back, of an ex-Special Services guy who took out a number of high-ranking *American* officers, throughout the region. To begin with these jobs were credited to the Commies, but more and more the rumour spread that it was an American. It's one of those tales you hear and shove to the back of your mind. When you phoned me, Sean, and asked if I'd ever heard of a hired killer by the name of Chameleon, I asked around. As you know, the answer came back for me to keep my nose out. That only made me more curious, so I made a few calls to a few more people I knew well, people I could trust, and asked the same question.'

Bill drained his glass and looked round for a waiter, needing a refill. He smiled at the other two, enjoying teasing them with the wait. It was his story and he'd tell it how he liked. Eventually three more glasses of beer were brought to the table and he continued.

'I got some strange answers, which confirmed, but didn't, if you know what I mean, that the firm had used him on a couple of occasions, as did, would you believe, Mr J. Edgar Hoover! Nothing that could be proved, but . . . To say this guy is good is like calling Picasso a dabbler in paint. He is the best there is, and I *mean* the best. Over a period of maybe twenty years he was credited with six hits. And they've just the ones he did on behalf of Uncle Sam! How many more did he do on his "private" account? At a million a go, that's money. Big money.

'Now another thing that ties him in with Nam was his

original contact. A woman, believed to be Vietnamese. The legend is that she was very beautiful, except for a scar on her neck. But he stopped using her after several years and developed a string of international contacts, none of whom knew what the fuck *he* looked like. A very cautious man.'

'What makes you think he is one of these MIAs?' Cowboy asked.

'Because it's easy to find the ones who came back, and nobody's been able to find this one.'

CHAPTER SIXTEEN

London and Dublin
October 1994

COWBOY TOOK HIS LEAVE OF SEAN and Buffalo Bill that same afternoon, and caught a flight to London. There he met with Chief Superintendent Wilcox, at New Scotland Yard. Immediately after his arrest on suspicion of murder, Richard Gordon's photograph had been faxed to Frank Mooney in Dublin. Back came a positive identification from the night porter at Douglas's hotel. Gordon had been the man who had gone to Douglas's room the night of his death. The CIB had also checked the security video recordings taken at Dublin Airport, as well as others in the country. They got lucky quickly. Richard Gordon was instantly recognizable boarding a Dublin to London flight the morning after the murder, although the name did not appear on the passenger flight list. The final nail in his coffin came after Scotland Yard sent a copy of the tape recording made at their initial interview with Gordon to Dublin Castle. The spectrograph voiceprint made of this conversation matched perfectly with that taken from the tape found under Jimmy Douglas's bed on the night of his murder.

Gordon was immediately charged with the murder of the Scotland Yard detective. It was yet to be decided who was going to try him, the Irish, where the murder was committed, or the British, because of Douglas's status. The murder of a British citizen by another British citizen, even in a foreign country, was a chargeable offence. With this hanging over his head, and hoping that any assistance he gave the police would be taken into consideration, Gordon had given as much detail as he knew, concerning his association with the Chameleon. He also gave the contact telephone number in Dublin where he had obtained the murder weapon, and details of how he had returned it, prior to leaving the city. He had parcelled the gun and silencer in their original box and placed it back in a left-luggage locker at the bus terminal in the early morning, then took a taxi to the airport. The key to the locker was picked up there. He had left it in an envelope addressed to a Mr Boyle and placed it on the 'Notice to Arriving Passengers' board, just outside the Customs area.

He was also able to confirm that Colloney had been set up and framed for the murder of O'Brien. Gordon had been the one who had dug up the detail on Colloney's daughter for the Chameleon, and had done the research necessary for the killing. He had followed Colloney for weeks, taking photographs, watching his movements, picking up information. It was Gordon who had impersonated the journalist who claimed to be doing a story on top executives and their drivers. This confession, along with the doctored photographs, was more than enough to get Colloney out of his life sentence.

The O'Brien murder was the only Irish one that Gordon had been involved in, but he was able to give the names of five British people on whom he had carried out similar investigations and the names of those who had employed Chameleon's services in the United Kingdom. But of the Chameleon himself, Gordon had no knowledge.

After his stint in the Paras, Gordon had become a minder. First for a few pop stars and on a couple of occasions, Hollywood actors and actresses. Then he had become the UK minder for a rich Arab, escorting him from one London casino to another, carrying a briefcase stashed full of £50 notes. Through others he was introduced to in the casinos, he met some of London's most influential gangsters and through them was introduced to a 'liaison' man from one of the New York Mafia families. It was through him that the contact with the Chameleon was made. Gordon had received a phone call one day asking him if he was interested in making a lot of money. He was. His first meeting with the man he came to know as Chameleon was made in the Chinese restaurant. They had never, to the best of his knowledge, met face to face.

He occasionally received instructions by mail to a post office box number he kept at a newsagent's. All these letters had been typewritten, were never signed, and he always destroyed them. He was the one who held the accounts with the answering service, opening them when necessary, as he had done when answering the newspaper advert taken by Clark. That was his own way of keeping in the background. He had met Chameleon about five times in all, each time sitting with his back to the silk screens in the restaurant. As he told the detectives, the last meeting was the first time he had known the Chameleon to leave by the public restaurant. Of the five Brits he had researched three had died but the remaining two were still alive. It could only be assumed that those still living had had their contracts cancelled for one reason or the other.

One of those killed related to the story that Jimmy Douglas had told on the night that he and Cowboy had first met Sean in Denmark. It meant that three more men were serving life sentences for murders they did not commit. The Home Secretary was going to be busy reviewing their cases, Wilcox had commented to Cowboy.

Nothing could be proved about the Chinese restaurant. Yes they rented the room out for private functions. Would Scotland Yard like to rent it, for one of their parties? They'd get a discount! Chameleon? No, they didn't serve that on the menu. A *man* named Chameleon? So sorry, but they could not help, but please call again. As Wilcox explained they were more than likely members of one of the Triads, acting under instructions from Hong Kong or Holland.

Wilcox had also received information back from Hong Kong about the telephone number there. The phone was in a locked room of a small drapery shop on the Kowloon side. It was connected to an answering machine. The 'bell' on the phone was connected to the door and whenever the phone rang, the owner explained, he went in to change the tape. He was paid 500 Hong Kong dollars each month to post the tapes in padded envelopes, on the day the calls were made, to a post office box number. The PO Box was in the main Kowloon Post Office, but access to the boxes was available twenty-four hours a day from outside the building by way of an exterior lid with a security lock. The name and address to which the box was rented was fictitious. The old man who owned the drapery shop knew nothing about the person who rented the room from him. The arrangement had been going on for many years and the money arrived at the beginning of each month, in cash, in the post.

Wilcox also revealed to Cowboy what the Chameleon had told Gordon – that he had retired and that the phone number in Hong Kong was no longer to be used.

And that seemed to be that. Cowboy caught the last flight from Heathrow to Dublin.

The following morning, Frank Mooney brought Cowboy up to date on what had happened in the three days he had been gone. Pressure had been exerted on the Irish Foreign Office, who in turn had requested urgent assistance from the Swiss authorities regarding the bank account used by the Chameleon. The Swiss had been co-operative. Usually within three days of receipt of funds, they told the Irish, the account was virtually cleared, leaving only a 'float' of 10,000 dollars to keep the account open. The funds would always be collected in cash – and that was where the trail ended. All the withdrawer had to do was to walk into another bank, or perhaps several other banks, and lodge the cash in new accounts. It was impossible to find out any more. Once the money was lodged in the other bank or banks, it could be transferred to anywhere in the world. The trail to the Chameleon was broken into fragments and, like Humpty Dumpty, could not be put together again!

The FBI were not able to be of much assistance over Sheldon Incorporated. Yes, the company was going bust, and yes, it was suspected of being a 'front' for Mafia funds, but nothing could be proved. It looked like JB Finance had been set up years before for a long term 'sting' operation, and in all probability the EEC would have been involved in yet another rip-off, in Denmark.

The Dublin address of the phone number that Richard Gordon had contacted over the gun was raided by armed members of the CIB. Along with the murder weapon, a selection of other hand guns and rifles were found. Eamon Boyle, a known Dublin villain who lived at the address, had set himself up as a quartermaster to the Irish underworld. He 'rented' the guns out to whoever had the funds to pay the high rental he asked. The forensic department were having a field day, matching up several of the weapons to armed robberies where shots had been fired and to three murders, including that of Jimmy Douglas. The weapons had all been hidden in secret compartments in the floor of the attic. Having ripped up the floor and found the collection of weapons, the CIB discovered that three weapons were missing from the stockpile. A single shot .22 rifle with a telescopic sight, a sawn-off, double-barrelled shotgun, and a Browning automatic. Each weapon had its own resting place, surrounded with moulded foam padding which lay empty. Boyle refused to confirm that the weapons actually existed, let alone who he had rented them out to.

Mooney decided it was time that Clark was brought in from his 'house arrest' and for Colloney to be freed from Port Laoise jail. Now that the Chameleon knew they were after him there was nothing to be gained from secrecy any more. The CIB now had enough to get Colloney out officially and Clark put away to await his trial. Intending to take part in bringing Clark in himself, Mooney and Cowboy were about to leave his office when the phone rang. It was Detective Constable Des Keogh, assigned to stay with Clark. Chameleon had just phoned the house in Malahide!

'Clark took the call, then clicked his fingers at me to listen in,' Keogh explained to his boss, when they reached the Clark residence. 'I picked the extension up and for a moment there was silence on the line. Then Clark said "Are you still there?" and I heard a sort of chuckle, and the line went dead. That was it, Boss.'

'Okay, Des, thanks a lot. Ask Clark to come in, will you?' Keogh nodded and left the study to find him. Clark walked like a broken man, shuffling along, shoulders slumped, his eyes darting nervously from one man to the other. He had cut himself shaving that morning and a small piece of toilet paper was still stuck to the cut. Cowboy started to feel a twinge of sympathy for the man, until he reminded himself that because of him a friend was dead and another man had been in jail for years for something he had not done, tormented all those years by the thought that his best friend had been a pervert who had abused his daughter. Whatever Clark had coming, he deserved.

'Good morning, Mr Clark. Please sit down and tell us exactly what happened. How did you know it was Chameleon who called?'

'I just knew it,' Clark replied, his voice low and hesitant. 'I answered as normal, then this voice said "Mr Clark, it would appear that our previous business arrangement has gone wrong somewhere along the line." I knew, just knew, that he was referring to . . .' He stopped, looked over at Cowboy before continuing, lowering his eyes from Cowboy's stare. 'I knew he was referring to the death of Inspector Douglas. I snapped my fingers at the young detective, indicating that he should pick up the other phone. "Where are you?" I asked. At the same time I heard a sort-of "click" on the line. It must have been the extension being picked up. He was silent for a moment or two, then he just . . . chuckled? At least that's what it seemed like, a chuckle. Then he hung up. I'm sorry, Commander Mooney. I did try my best.'

'I'm sure you did, Mr Clark. It can't be helped. We should have thought of this sooner, that he might try to contact you. Would you be willing to stay here a few more days, with the lines tapped, just in case he calls again?'

'Anything you say, Commander. I'll do anything I can to help.'

'Okay,' Mooney replied, rising to his feet. 'I'll arrange for what's necessary and I'll also have a few men posted here, including Sergeant Johnson, just in case.' Clark, knowing he was being dismissed, left his own study, going upstairs to his bedroom.

'What d'ya reckon, Cowboy?' Mooney asked after Clark had closed the door behind him.

'I reckon the bastard's in Dublin, that's what I reckon. He's here, Frank, I know it. I can feel it in my water.'

'I agree. But will he try and contact Clark again, that's the 64,000 dollar question? All we can do is hope he will. I'll arrange for some more men to be here, twenty-four hours a day, for a week. You're in charge. But if we have nothing after a week, then that's it. I pull the plug.'

Cowboy knew that his boss was talking sense. A week was being generous, over-generous in view of the fact that the Chameleon was on guard and most likely understood that Clark was actually being guarded by the police. If I were him, Cowboy thought, I'd be long gone and living on the other side of the world.

But he wasn't long gone. He was sitting in a café in O'Connell Street, having made the phone call to Clark, thinking about what his next move should be. The same thought that had run through Cowboy's head ran through his. Get out. Get away. It's all finished. Twenty years of being the best in the business was over. He wanted it to be over, didn't he, he argued with himself. Yes, but not this way, not without knowing how his cover had been blown. A perfectionist in everything he did, it niggled him not knowing what had gone wrong, what mistake he had made. And it had to be *his* mistake, because all those he employed hadn't the faintest idea who he was. Quite apart from being annoyed about it, he was beginning to enjoy pitting his mind against whoever it was that was leading the investigation against him. He smiled to himself, remembering a conversation he had had with the Englishman, Gordon, when he had set up the one and only job he had carried out in Ireland. Gordon had said it would be easy. The Irish were like the Polaks in the States. Thick. He wondered if Gordon still thought of them as 'thick'! But loose ends were loose ends and they had to be seen to. Finishing his coffee he paid the young waitress and walked out into the street, heading towards the bridge and his room at Jury's Hotel.

Cowboy sat in the kitchen of the Clark residence sipping a mug of coffee, reading *Manhunter*, a novel by Michael Slade, about a serial killer on the loose in Vancouver. It had been recommended to him by a friend and he was finding it interesting and exciting. He seldom read books other than Westerns, or biographies of famous people of the Wild West, but he was engrossed in this one when the phone rang. He looked at his watch. Just after two in the morning! The phone that was ringing was Clark's own personal, unlisted number, in the study.

Cowboy had moved into the Clark residence that afternoon accompanied by three other detectives. All the telephone lines, four in all, had been tapped into. The sophisticated equipment they now used would allow them to trace an incoming call from anywhere in the world. The days of using delay tactics, of keeping the caller talking for as long as possible while an engineer made the trace, were gone. Once the connection was made between two phones then the trace could be made. Des Keogh was dozing in another chair in the kitchen, a tape recorder and a set of headphones resting on the table beside him. Two other detectives, Nicky Kane and Bert McCann, were asleep in one of the guest rooms on the first floor. Cowboy put the book face down on the floor and turned to look at Keogh who was waking himself from his slumber and putting on the headphones. He looked at Cowboy and shrugged his shoulders. Who could be calling Clark at this hour of the morning? They'd know in a moment, when Clark came down to answer the phone.

The persistent ringing woke Clark from his troubled sleep. Climbing out of bed he wrapped his silk dressing gown round his silk-pyjama clad body and went down to his study. Dorothy, asleep in her own bedroom, would ignore the call in any case. The ringing phone was his, and only those he had business dealings with knew the number. It was the number Clark had given Chameleon as a contact number when he had left the message on the answering machine in Hong Kong, shortly after he had received the bogus blackmail letter. Cowboy was standing at the kitchen door as Clark came down the stairs.

'Try and act as normal as possible, Mr Clark. Take a few deep breaths before you pick up the phone, okay? There'll be no tell-tale clicks on the line this time.' Clark slowly nodded and opened the door to his study.

The phone lay on his desk, by the window. Moonlight lit the room through the open drapes at the window. Pressing the light switch the main overhead light came on as he walked up to the desk and picked up the phone.

'Hello?'

'This is New York calling.' It was the voice of a bored female telephone operator. Clark relaxed. 'I have a personal call for a Mr William J. Clark.' Clark turned as he heard Cowboy approach the door to the study, remaining in the hall. Clark shook his head at the detective and turned to look out the window once more.

'This is William Clark speaking, operator.'

'Just a moment please,' the telephonist replied. There was silence for a few moments.

'The call is for William *J.* Clark,' the woman said, breaking the silence.

'For God's sake woman, that's me. I *am* William J. Clark.'

The window disintegrated with a loud crashing noise and Clark clasped a hand to his chest as he crumpled to the floor, the phone bouncing off the desk, hanging by its lead. Cowboy flicked the switch on the wall turning the lights back off. He heard Des Keogh running along the corridor behind him.

'Stay back, stay back. Get Kane and McCann and call the Castle. Call an ambulance as well. Clark's been shot.'

He heard the muffled reply of 'Oh fuck' as Keogh ran up the stairs to waken the other two detectives and to make the calls. Cowboy wriggled across the floor on his stomach. He searched for a pulse in Clark's neck, but found none. The man was dead. He picked up the hanging phone, with the operator still asking if Mr Clark was there.

'Who is this speaking?' Cowboy demanded.

'This is the operator.'

'The operator where?' he queried.

'New York. Can you tell me what is going on, sir? I have a caller on the line who wishes to speak to a William J. Clark.'

'Listen to me, operator, and listen very carefully. I am not playing a trick on you. I am Detective Sergeant Johnson of the Irish Police. William J. Clark has just been shot dead. Try and keep the other caller on the line at your end and call your police department. Get them to wherever that person is calling from and ask them to hold that person. Do you understand? Please. This is urgent. I *am* a police officer and a man *has* just been murdered.' There was a moment's pause on the other end, then the operator spoke again.

'Okay, detective. I believe you. Keep this line open for me, don't hang up. I'll get my supervisor to call the police.'

Cowboy then heard her muted conversation. 'Hello caller, I have William J. Clark on the line. He wants a name please. Hello caller? Hello? Hello? Hello caller, are you still there?

'Hello, police in Ireland. I'm sorry. The other caller has rung off. There's nothing I can do. I'm sorry.'

'Do you have any idea where the call came from, or who made it, operator?'

'Sorry. It could have come from anywhere in the city, and most likely from a phone booth. Is this William J. Clark really dead?'

'I'm afraid he is, operator. Good night.' With that Cowboy hung up.

'Bollocks,' he cried, pounding his fists on to the carpet.

'You okay, Cowboy?' The enquiry came from the door of the study. Crouched by the door were the other three detectives.

'I'm okay, I'm okay, but Clark's dead. Ever heard of a bullet that can travel 3,000 miles?'

'Nah!' came the reply.

'Well, that's how Clark got hit. From fucking New York!'

Two ambulances had been and gone, one to take the body of Clark, the other to take Mrs Clark, who collapsed when told her husband was dead. She had been shocked, disbelieving, when he had told her what he had been arrested for, but somehow she had been sure she would overcome that. But his death was different. It was so final.

Armed CIB detectives from the Castle had turned up in three cars, but they were of no use now. When Frank Mooney arrived he agreed with Cowboy that they should be sent back. There were too many people around the house as it was and the Chameleon had carried out what he had set out to do. He was long gone by now. When the trace came through on the call it confirmed it *was* international – but came from a public phone booth in Hong Kong, not New York! Cowboy remembered that Buffalo Bill had said that in the beginning the Chameleon's contact had been an oriental woman, believed to be Vietnamese. Cowboy had a very strong suspicion that he had just spoken with her! And where did all messages for the Chameleon go? Hong Kong.

'Jesus,' Cowboy roared. 'What a clever, conniving, ruthless bastard this Chameleon is. He gets his woman to call Clark on a person to person from Hong Kong, gets her to make sure it's him on the line, pops him, and fuckin' gets *me* to confirm his hit! Jesus!'

'What was it everybody has been telling you, Cowboy? That this guy is the best there is. Well I don't think there is any doubt about that, is there?'

The two men were sitting in the kitchen, mugs of tea and coffee on the table between them, as they waited for first light. They didn't expect to find much in the way of clues, but they intended looking. The shot had come from the back of the house, towards the beach area.

'None whatsoever, Frank. None whatsoever.'

They found the weapon 200 yards from the house, lying by a clump of dune grass, just where the lawn ended and the beach began. It was a single-shot .22 rifle, with a scope sight attached to it. There was no doubt in either of the detectives' minds that this was one of the missing guns from Eamon Boyle's hoard. They also found a field telephone handset – the kind used by telephone engineers when testing lines – connected to the line leading into the house. Chameleon had been listening on the line and, when it was confirmed that the man he could see standing in the light was Clark, shot him. He had taken the shot, awaited confirmation his target was dead, then dropped the rifle and disappeared. The loose sand held no clues in the way of footprints in which direction he might have gone. Nor did the rifle and handset offer any clues. Both were clean of any prints. Neither detective had expected to find any. Once again, his trail disappeared.

CHAPTER SEVENTEEN

Dublin, October 1994

THE NEWSPAPERS HAD A FIELD DAY with the revelations. 'HIT MAN IN DUBLIN' screamed one. 'THE COWBOY IN SHOOT-OUT WITH KILLER' was another, erroneous one. 'COLLONEY CLEARED OF MURDER AND OUT OF JAIL' screamed yet another. Mary Colloney had phoned Cowboy and asked if he would accompany her to Port Laoise jail to pick her husband up. She knew her husband would want to thank him for what he had done. Cowboy had declined, saying that he was sure that the pair of them would really rather be alone on the great day. But he felt good about it. A good man, sent to jail for a crime he hadn't committed, was free, and the bad guy, or at least one of them, was to be buried in a few days.

The newspapers made a big thing about how the investigation had been started by Cowboy, and they all carried his photograph and his history, along with photographs of Frank Mooney and the late Detective Inspector James Douglas, of Scotland Yard. With the trail of the Chameleon dead, Cowboy had worked on a full report for Mooney. Copies of the report would go to both Interpol and member countries of the International Police Federation, as well as the FBI in the States. Cowboy, with full agreement and backing from Mooney, wanted to bring to the attention of as many police forces as possible the way Chameleon had operated. He pointed out that any case in which the murderer had returned to the scene of the crime within a short time of the crime actually being committed, should be suspect. He had no control over what happened after that, but he felt he had to do all he could to see if others, like Colloney, could be re-investigated. Within the week the case file on The Chameleon was closed, and Cowboy was assigned to a new team. Life was as close to being back to normal as was possible.

Cowboy woke, sweating, and looked around him. The room was in darkness and Marlane lay on her side, away from him, fast asleep. Their love-making had, as always, exhausted both of them. Wiping a hand across his forehead he eased himself out of bed. Naked, he walked to the kitchen, opened the fridge door and took a swig of orange juice, straight from the jar. What had woken him, he wondered? A noise? No, silence prevailed throughout the apartment. Then he smelt it, and a shiver ran down his spine. The smell of Chinese spices. A face started to weave its way in and out of his mind. It was happening again. Taking the jar of juice with him he went into the living room and sat in the armchair, the room in darkness. Willing himself to relax he began to breathe slowly and deeply, inhaling through his nose, exhaling slowly through his mouth. With eyes closed he tried to imagine a gate, set into a high wall. Mentally opening the gate, he was opening his mind to the image that had woken him. The image, the face, was hazy at first, like looking at somebody through a fog, but as the mist parted he recognized his friend, Jimmy Douglas. Somebody else was present, just behind Jimmy. As the mist cleared further he saw the face of his father.

His belief in survival after death proved to his own

satisfaction years ago, Cowboy was neither scared nor mystified by what his mind could 'see'. He accepted these messages as readily as he would one from Frank Mooney. The face of his dead father was smiling, reassuring him, while Jimmy's showed concern, the lips moving. Cowboy understood the difficulty in communication from the etheric world, especially from one who had only recently crossed over, as Jimmy had. But the message must be important for him to 'come through' so soon. Words formed in his mind.

'NOT GONE ... STILL THERE ... CAREFUL ... CAREFUL ... DANGER ... CHAMELEON'

With that the image began to fade, as though somebody had thrown a stone into a clear pond, the ripples breaking the image up. But Cowboy had got the message. The Chameleon had *not* left Ireland. He was still around. He had one more job to do – and Cowboy was the contract. This was not a contract that Chameleon was being paid for. No, this one was personal. This was to be a freebie.

For over a week the Chameleon had been studying up on Detective Sergeant Cowboy Johnson. The nickname amused him. Most of the policeman's history had been published several years previously, in the newspapers, when he had been kidnapped by a terrorist organization, The Popular Front for the Liberation of Ireland, a group that no longer existed. The long article had given details of his wealthy family background, his scholastic achievements, the death of his father, his early career in the Gardai and eventual transfer to the Criminal Investigation Branch. Great emphasis had been placed on Cowboy's private life – his luxury apartment in Ballsbridge, the black Porsche he drove, the long list of girlfriends, a list which ended when he met the young model Marlane Davis. The current reports, on both the death of Clark and the killer known as the Chameleon, gave a full account as to how Cowboy had started the hunt, after his first trip to Denmark.

The Chameleon, who prided himself on leaving nothing to chance, enjoyed the irony of how his existence had become known to this man. He remembered the job he had taken in the Soviet bloc. Who could possibly have foreseen that two drunken Russians would ever get to know of it, and would then blab in front of a future escapee to the West! And to top that, there was the accidental meeting between the Danish policeman and Cowboy. And all of it happening just as he made the decision to retire! He found himself admiring this Irishman who had hunted him so doggedly. But admire him as he did, he also realized that the only way the case would ever end, the only way he could retire for good, was with his own death. And so he set about planning it, and he planned to involve Detective Sergeant Cowboy Johnson in that finale. First he had to make some phone calls.

'I'm telling you Frank, he's still here, still in Ireland, still in Dublin. He hasn't gone yet.'

'Cowboy, don't be stupid. He's long gone. Killing Clark was his final job here. Not knowing what Clark knew or didn't know, what he had or had not told us, he was just clearing out the closet. Why should he stay? There's nothing here for him. He's gone. End of story, case closed. It happens, Cowboy. You win some, you lose others. All we can ever hope is to keep a little bit ahead.'

'Please believe me, Frank, he's here. And he does have one last job to take care of. Me.'

'Don't get paranoid on me, Cowboy. Why should he

kill you? You don't know diddley squat about him, except rumours. If he stood in front of you now, you wouldn't be able to point a finger and say "That's him". Who the fuck would want to a pay a million to get rid of you, except me?' Mooney smiled, trying to use humour to bring Cowboy to his senses. He knew what a 'gut feeling' was, he understood it, knew that all good cops got them. It was the feeling you got when something was just not right, but you couldn't put your finger on why. Frank Mooney had had enough such feelings in his long career to understand, but this seemed to be something entirely different. There was no logical reason for this Chameleon to target Cowboy. None whatsoever. In fact, it would most likely be the first, and last, stupid move the man would make in his life, and he had not survived as long as he had by being stupid.

'Look, Cowboy, take a few days off, eh? You've worked long enough at this one and you've got a great result. I know we didn't get him, but you got Colloney and the Danish guy out of nick. Who knows how many other cases may get re-opened as a result of your report. You're due some leave. Take it. If Lane's free, why don't the pair of you go off somewhere nice, where there's some sun. He's gone. I promise you.'

Cowboy looked across the desk at the man he admired most in the world. The man who had become a father substitute, a man he was possibly closer to than he had been to his own father. But even to him he could not explain how he knew that the killer was still in the city, and that he was the designated target.

'Maybe you're right, Frank,' he replied, resigned to the situation. 'Maybe a few days off will do me a world of good.' A few days off would leave him free to work on this in his own time. At least this way he wouldn't have to make any excuses to anybody about his movements.

'Great. Take ten days. Now get the fuck outta here, okay? Give Lane my love.'

'Sure.' Cowboy got up and walked out without looking back, closing the door gently behind him.

The trouble with 'going it alone' was, he found, simply that. Going it alone. Sean, in Denmark, sympathized, but there was little he could do to help. As far as the Danes were concerned the killer had gone. Fries had walked free, thanks to Cowboy's intervention, coupled with the information that came to light during the bank's investigation into the life of Peter Schantz. From the amount of cash found in several bank accounts, most of them unknown even to his wife, it was obvious Schantz had been involved in illegal activities. Fries had been compensated by the bank and was back in business. He told Sean that neither he nor Cowboy would have any use for money in his establishment. As soon as he opened up the hotel side of his business he intended inviting Cowboy and 'a guest' to a proper Scandinavian holiday. Sean repeated, almost word for word, what Mooney had said: Chameleon had no need to remain in Ireland, nor to go after Cowboy. He was long gone.

Marlane had to go on a five-day shoot in Spain, doing a spread for a new range of cars. She tried to talk Cowboy into going along with her, but he made an excuse to get out of it. He was relieved she was going to be away for a while. Not because he didn't want her around, but because he felt she would be safer. It was three days after her departure that a courier delivered a small parcel, addressed personally to him at his apartment.

When he opened the red-bordered cardboard envelope, two packets of photographs slid on to the coffee table. Intrigued, Cowboy opened the first one. It was a series of pictures of himself and Marlane, taken over the past week, before she had left for Spain. There were shots of them leaving his apartment, both together and alone. There were shots of Lane entering her own apartment at Doyle's Corner. Shots of him getting in and out of his car, of them entering and leaving restaurants. Cowboy felt a chill of fear run through him as he realized what was happening. Opening the second one he found that it contained photographs of Marlane and of Frank and Marjory Mooney.

Leaving the photographs on the coffee table, but taking the cardboard envelope they had arrived in, he went to the Courier Express office. Showing his warrant card he asked for information on the sender. He was told that a gentleman rang from the Shelbourne hotel. The name given was McAllister and he was registered in Room 101. He had paid cash for the delivery. Leaving the courier office, Cowboy drove to the Shelbourne and asked for Mr McAllister. He had checked out. He had only stayed the one night. The only external phone call that had been made from his room had been for the courier. The other two calls had been to room service. The gentleman had little luggage with him and had paid cash for his stay.

Back at his apartment Cowboy went through the photographs once more, spreading them out on the coffee table. What did the bastard want? The photos were obviously a message telling Cowboy that he, along with Marlane, Frank and Marjory, was being watched. Chameleon had pinpointed the people Cowboy cared most about and was saying 'I know where you live'. What should he do? Even as he asked himself the question, he knew the answer. Wait. He had no control over this game. The game and the rules had been invented by the Chameleon, and he would be making the next move.

It came late that night, just as Cowboy was about to go to bed. He was in the bathroom when he heard the phone ring. Stepping out of the shower and grabbing his dressing gown he padded barefooted into the living room.

'Hello?'

'Get my message, Cowboy?' There was a hint of an American accent in the voice at the other end. There was also a hint of laughter in it too. For a moment Cowboy was silent, not knowing how to answer.

'Come on, Cowboy. Don't fall asleep on me now. You've been very very good at all of this, up until now. Speak to me.'

'What the fuck do you want?'

'I want to end the game, it's the only way to do it, isn't it?'

'If you lay a hand on the girl . . .' Cowboy felt bile rising in his throat.

'You'll what?' the other interrupted. 'Kill me?' The man chuckled down the line. 'Listen, Cowboy, if I wanted to kill the girl, or Mooney, I could have done it any time. You know I could, so stop worrying about them. I have no intention of harming either of them. I just wanted to get your attention. Have I got it?'

'Oh you've got that, all right. What else do you want?'

'I've told you, Cowboy. I want to end it, one way or the other. You're the sheriff, I'm the outlaw – that's something you understand, isn't it? Those were good days, eh? Men knew where they stood then, didn't they? A man's word was his bond and a handshake was as good as a contract. Each man stood for what he believed in. But you know and understand all of this, don't you. That's why they call you the Cowboy, isn't it? I'm calling you out, Cowboy. It'll be just you and me, nobody else. We'll go like the old days, the fastest draw walks away. What d'ya say?'

'How do I know I can trust you?' Cowboy asked.

'Because I'm giving you my word. It is the one thing I've lived by these past twenty-odd years. I've never broken it.'

Cowboy believed him. It seemed illogical to believe, to trust, a man who had been a professional killer for so long, yet Cowboy did believe him.

'Come on, you know you want to do it, don't you Cowboy? Your interest in the Wild West is more than just reading about it and the collection of memorabilia you have in your apartment.' Cowboy heard him chuckle. 'Yes, Cowboy, I've visited you when you were not at home. You've got a nice place and a nice collection. But back to the business at hand. How many times have you asked yourself what it would be like to step out on to a dusty street at noon to face another man down, eh? Haven't you asked yourself "Could I do it?". Well now's your chance to find out.'

'Why?' Cowboy asked. 'I mean, why didn't you just disappear, leave. We still don't know who you are, and you know that. You could be long gone. Why this?'

'Would you believe me if I said that I thought you deserved it? Perhaps not, but you're the first, what I would call, honest cop, to make the connection and work on it. I've had dealings with other, so-called agencies of the law, supposedly there for the protection of the people. Most of them were as crooked, if not more so, than some of those they paid me to remove.'

'There has to be more than that.'

'Well, I suppose it's because I know you'll always be on my back. This is one you won't leave alone, Cowboy, isn't it. The case may be closed, but not for you. I had intended to retire after my trip to Denmark. Just fade away. But that's not the way it worked out, and the reason for that is you. What's your answer, Cowboy?'

Cowboy knew that if he didn't accept the challenge this time, then it would happen at some time in the future. This was a gunfighter who would not back down. 'Okay. Where do we meet?'

'Good man. I knew you'd see it my way. Have you got a piece, or would you like me to provide you with one? I've had a look at those on your wall. Not much use, are they?' There was another chuckle down the line.

'I've got one,' Cowboy replied.

'Good, I thought you might. Then the place is the Phoenix Park, by the Wellington Monument – or, under the circumstances, would you prefer The Fifteen Acres?' Once again Cowboy knew that Chameleon was teasing him. In eighteenth-century Dublin this place was used as a duelling ground. Chameleon had done his homework exceedingly well.

'The Wellington monument will do fine.'

'Good. Then that's the place, and the time is tomorrow night, 3.00 a.m. Please don't disappoint me and come with friends, Cowboy. I've said your girl and Mooney are safe, and they are – but don't fuck with me, okay? This is you and me time, and nobody else. Do we have a deal?'

Cowboy almost felt the chill that had crept into the other man's voice as he issued his warning.

'We do.'

'Then it's "*Adios, amigo*", until then.' With that the line went dead.

Cowboy replaced the phone and sat on the sofa, his mind in a turmoil. He had just been invited to a gun-fight, just like in the old days of the Wild West, and he had accepted. He shook his head, almost in disbelief at what he had done, yet he knew that this was how the ending *should* be. The only difference was the timing. Usually it was high noon, with each protagonist aiming to have the sun behind himself, and in the eyes of the other. This time it was going to be in darkness. Making his way to the bedroom he got into bed. It was some time before he fell into a troubled sleep.

By 10.00 p.m. the following evening he was ready to leave. He had begun his preparations early in the morning by moving the mattress from his bed and opening the safe built into the base. From it he removed a small wooden box that contained the hammer firing pins of three of the hand guns that were in glass fronted boxes, mounted on his living room wall. The Chameleon hadn't been as thorough as he thought he had been. He had a collection of replica models of hand guns made famous in the West, but three of them were in fact the real thing. For safety reasons he had removed the firing pins and kept them locked in the safe, substituting flat-headed hammers in the guns. He picked the one that was famed as having 'won the West' – the Colt .45 Peacemaker. Beside the gun collection on the wall was an original Colt advertisement. 'God created Man. Samuel Colt made him equal.'

As he stripped and oiled the weapon, Cowboy was thinking of one gunfighter in particular, Doc Holliday, famed for his part in the shoot-out at the OK Corral. Holliday had been a dentist back East, who had contracted tuberculosis when TB was a killer, and had been advised to go West to prolong his life. As well as dentistry work he had made his living as a gambler. What made him so awesome as a gunfighter was the fact that he did not care if he lived or died when he stepped out to face another man down. Every gunfighter who made his name wanted to survive – but Doc Holliday had the edge over them with his death wish.

Strangely enough Holliday was one of the few, the very few, who actually died with his boots off. He had survived the legendary gunfight, when he stood side by side with the Earp brothers, and died in a TB sanatorium a few years later. Cowboy was under no illusion about the Chameleon. From the conversation they had had on the phone, Cowboy placed him in the same category as Holliday. Chameleon didn't care if he survived the coming gunfight.

He sat on the sofa cleaning the pistol and checking the action for several hours. Cock the hammer back, aim, 'click'. Cock the hammer back, aim, 'click'. Cock the hammer back, aim, 'click'. Time after time he loaded the pistol with the small brass dummy rounds. They saved the firing pin dropping on to an empty chamber, causing a possible 'suspension' in the pin, defecting it. By ten he was feeling cooped up in the apartment, and, strangely enough, he felt hungry. He had debated with himself what he should do about Marlane. She was due back the following evening. Would he be there, or not? How would she feel if he were not? How would she feel if he did not return, ever? Before he left the apartment he decided to write her a note. He could always destroy it tomorrow, if he came back. It was short, but to the point.

My Darling Lane,
From the moment I first set eyes on you, I fell in love with you. Each day that has passed since then has only intensified my feelings. Please always remember that. Until we meet again, and you know I believe that we will, in another 'world', stay safe. My love will always look over you.
Yours, for *ever* and *ever*,
Cowboy.

Deciding against taking the leather gunbelt he loaded the Peacemaker with five rounds, leaving the pin resting on an empty chamber, and slid the gun into his raincoat pocket. Checking the lights were off and the alarm on, he left the apartment, made his way to the small underground car park then drove off into the night.

It was almost 11.30 p.m. when Marlane returned. The shoot had finished earlier than expected, mainly due to the good weather and light, and she had caught a late plane out of Barcelona. She wanted to surprise Cowboy. Paying off the taxi driver she made her way to the apartment, cursing quietly as the alarm 'buzzed' its forty-five-second warning before it would activate. Fumbling with her keys she found the correct one and switched it off. Flicking lights on as she walked through the living room on her way to the bedroom she didn't notice the letter resting on Cowboy's desk. Finding the bed empty and unmade she was puzzled. Where the hell was he? Damn the man for spoiling her surprise, she thought, going back into the living rooom. Noticing the two packets of photographs on the coffee table she flicked through them, mystified as to who could have taken them, and why? Spreading them out she remembered where she and Cowboy were when they were taken, but she could not remember anybody they knew being there at the same time. In any case neither of them seemed to be aware that they were being photographed. And why were there also photographs of Frank and Marjory? Placing them back into their protective envelopes she went to put them on Cowboy's desk and found the note. As she read it the blood drained from her face. This was no 'I'll see you in a day or two I love you' note. This was something . . . something like . . . like a . . . suicide note!

'Oh my God,' she gasped, her hand flying to her mouth, the letter dropping from her fingers. For God's sake, why should he want to kill himself? It couldn't be money – he had more than enough. It couldn't be because of her – she loved him, so very, very much. What could it be? Her eyes darted about the room as though the answer to her questions could be found there. Suddenly her gaze flew backwards, resting on the empty gun case. She had to get help. Somehow, someone, had to help her. Grabbing the phone she tapped in the home number of Frank Mooney.

After years of experiencing late night calls, Mooney picked up on the third tone, wide awake.

'Yes,' he growled.

'Frank. It's me. Marlane. Something's gone wrong with Cowboy. There's a farewell note to me, and there's a gun missing from his collection. Please help me, Frank. Please. We have to find him.'

'Marlane, stay calm. I'm on my way over, okay? Don't panic. I'll be there as quickly as I can.' Without waiting for her answer he hung up. Peeling off his pyjamas he started to dress hurriedly.

'What's wrong, Frank?' Marjory asked, waking as she heard Marlane's name mentioned.

'It's Cowboy. Marlane's just got back and found a farewell note from him, and a gun missing from his collection.'

'But they're only replica guns aren't they? That's what he told me when I asked him about them.'

'Me too – but I've often wondered about that.'

'But why would Cowboy want to . . . want to . . .' Marjory found she could not even say the words.

'He wouldn't – and that's the problem, Marj. But he's been a bit funny recently. Over that last case, this . . . this . . . *fuckin'* Chameleon. Cowboy reckons the

235

geezer's still in town, and that he, Cowboy, is on the list. Call the Castle and tell them to get my car and driver over to Cowboy's place pronto. I'll take the car and get over there, I'll get somebody to drive it back here for you.'

'Don't worry about that Frank, just get to Marlane and find out what's happened.' As her husband dashed down the stairs still buttoning his shirt she was on the phone to Dublin Castle.

'It's okay, Lane, it's okay, I'm here.' Holding the sobbing girl in his arms, Frank scanned the room and noticed the empty gun-case on the wall. Easing her back on to the sofa he asked her to tell him what had happened since she came back.

'I wanted it to be a surprise for him. I'm a day early, Frank.' She blew her nose into the handkerchief he had handed her before she continued. 'I came in, found he wasn't here, saw the photos, then the note and then the gun missing.'

'What photos?'

'Those. There on the desk, beside the letter.'

The moment he saw them, Mooney recognized instantly what they were – surveillance photographs. He picked up the phone and dialled the Castle.

'Garda, can I help you?'

'This is Commander Frank Mooney of the CIB. I want an APB put out immediately for Detective Sergeant Christopher Johnson of the Dublin CIB. He's driving a 1987 Porsche 930 turbo, colour black, registration number . . . just a sec, Marlane, what's the number of his car?'

He repeated the number down the line to the mystified Garda at the other end who had instantly recognized Mooney's voice.

'What's the charge, Commander?'

'Make one up, but find him, and stop him, is that understood?'

'Yes, sir.'

'Did my wife call in about my car and my driver?'

'Yes, sir. He's on his way to you now.'

'Right. The moment Johnson is found I want to be told. Contact me on the car radio. Got that?'

'Yes, sir.' Mooney hung up.

'What's going on, Frank? Is Cowboy in trouble, or something.'

Frank sat at the desk and ran his fingers through his thinning hair.

'I'm afraid he might be, Lane. When you said that Cowboy had left a farewell note for you and that a gun was missing, I couldn't believe he was going off somewhere to kill himself. But when I saw the photographs I clicked.'

'Then what *is* it, Frank? What's he up to?'

'Those photographs, unless I'm very much mistaken, were taken by this killer, this Chameleon. Cowboy came to me a few days ago and said that he had a feeling that the man hadn't left Ireland, but was still here, and that he, Cowboy, was his next target. I told him the man was long gone, and to take a few days off and rest up.'

Marlane's hands flew to her mouth once more. 'Oh, my God!' she whispered, her eyes large, staring at Frank.

'The photographs were a message. He's let Cowboy know that either he does what he's told, or one of us gets killed.'

Marlane started to sob into her hands, her body shaking. All Frank could do was hold her and let her cry. He had no words of comfort to offer.

*

The Phoenix Park is one of the world's largest enclosed urban parks with a circumference of seven miles, and covering 1,760 acres. It contains the Presidential Palace of the Irish Republic, Áras an Uachtaráin, the Residence of the Papal Nuncio, the Pope's Ambassador to Ireland, the residence of the United States Ambassador, the Zoological Gardens, St Mary's Hospital, and the Headquarters and training establishment of the Garda Síochána. As well as mile after mile of open parkland, the large area known as 'The Fifteen Acres' – which in reality covers two hundred acres – contains football pitches (Gaelic and soccer), hurling grounds, a polo ground and even a cricket ground.

Herds of red deer roam freely, safe from any hunter. Roads criss-cross the park and benches are plentiful along the miles of pathway. The Hollow, a crater-like hole, used to be a well-known meeting place for lovers in the summers of the early sixties. The Army and Garda bands often give open-air concerts in the park bandstands. On this particular night it also contained a professional killer known only as Chameleon.

It was just after 2.30 a.m. when Cowboy drove his car through the entrance from the North Circular Road, slowly skirting the Garda Headquarters to his right, where it had all begun for him, years earlier. He could still remember his passing out parade and the Chief Constable asking him if he had any ambitions. 'To join the CIB,' he had replied. Well, here he was, back again, a Detective Sergeant in the CIB, heading for an old-fashioned, Western gunfight. Driving slowly along Fountain Road, across Chesterfield Avenue on to the Wellington Road, he pulled over on to the open grassland and parked the car. He walked the last 200 yards towards the area surrounding the Wellington monument, built by the British to honour the Iron Duke.

Standing well in from Wellington Road, the immediate area was dark and desolate. Behind it were the railings of the park, and beyond them was Conyngham Road. The open ground surrounding the monument was bordered by thick, close-grown bushes, several feet tall. The light at the monument was out of order and the two road lights, spaced before and after it were not strong enough to illuminate the area. The monument stood in shadows. Cowboy's double-breasted raincoat was open, his hand resting on the now cocked pistol in his right-hand pocket. Stepping out of the shadows on his side of the road he slowly walked towards the meeting place.

'That's far enough, Cowboy.' The voice came from the bushes to the right of the monument. He turned in that direction.

'Step out,' Cowboy replied. 'I want to see your face.'

The answer he got was the flash from a gun and a split second later the round hit him, pushing him backwards, like a blow from a great weight. His legs buckled under him. Falling, he threw himself on to his left side, the gun still held in his right, his finger resting along the trigger guard, away from the trigger. He was amazed not to feel any pain as he hit the ground. 'Bastard,' he said softly, 'the bastard couldn't even keep his word.' He heard the sound of the bushes being pushed to one side. The Chameleon was coming to finish him off. 'Shite. What a way to go!'

Parked on the intersection of O'Devaney Gardens and the North Circular Road, sipping tea from a flask, the two uniformed Gardai argued for several minutes before they radioed in. A black Porsche had passed them five minutes ago – but the registration number, one maintained, was wrong. He checked his folder. 'Look,' he pointed, the folder held down towards the dashboard and the long, thin, flexible light that illuminated it. 'It says "406". That one was definitely "694". It ain't the one.'

'And I'm telling you it was an '87 Turbo. I still think we should call in and check again. It's too close.'

'Fuck it, go on then. All you'll get is a bollocking, I'm telling you. But go ahead, Terry. You call it in.'

Terry, worried about *not* calling it in, and about making fools of the pair of them, eventually called his Control.

'Alpha Charlie Bravo here. Please confirm registration number of black Porsche belonging to Detective Sergeant Johnson.'

Both men groaned as the number was confirmed as '694'. 'Oh, shite,' Bill mumbled as Terry got back on to Control.

'Alpha Charlie Bravo, confirmed sighting of vehicle on the North Circular Road, heading for the Park. Repeat. Confirmed sighting of vehicle belonging to Detective Sergeant Johnson, entering Phoenix Park by North Circular Road Gate.'

Mooney, accompanied by an insistent Marlane, had just turned down on to Essex Quay when the call came over the radio. Without waiting to be told, Detective Joe Henderson turned on the car's siren and put his foot on the accelerator, heading west towards the park. Having already called into his office to give instructions to the uniformed Gardai and the CIB officers on duty, both Mooney and Henderson were armed with Browning automatic pistols. 'This is Commander Mooney. I want squad cars at all exits to the park. All cars to be stopped and drivers identified. Detective Sergeant Johnson is to be held. Any other suspicious driver to be held also. Armed CIB officers to back up uniformed Gardai. An unknown, male suspect, armed and highly dangerous is believed to be within the park perimeter.'

The quiet night air was broken by the sound of sirens wailing as cars from all directions converged on the vastness of the park. A second car appeared behind them as Henderson turned right across the Liffey by Heuston Station, left on to Parkgate Street, right again and up Infirmary Road towards the entrance gate Cowboy had used. The car behind them drove on a few yards at Parkgate Street, stopping to block the entrance to the park at Chesterfield Avenue. As they drove up Infirmary Road, touching ninety miles per hour, the patrol car at the gate moved out of the way. Mooney's car swerved in through the gates, tyres screaming and spinning, moments in front of a second unmarked police car speeding up the North Circular. Other cars were stopping at the Cabra Gate, Ashtown Gate and Castleknock Gate, all accessed off the Navan Road to the North. To the South, further along Conyngham Road, the gates at Islandbridge and Chapelizod were being blocked, as were the Knockmaroon and White gates. While the perimeter was being sealed by uniformed Gardai patrol cars, armed CIB detectives drove into the park.

Approaching the first fork at Fountain Road, Mooney stuck his hand out the window, indicating to the second car behind him, that they should take the right hand fork, alongside the Garda Síochána headquarters along the North Road. The flashing headlights of the car behind confirmed his instructions. Beside him in the back seat Marlane hung on tightly to the arm strap above the passenger door, thankful of the rear seat belt that was preventing her from being thrown all over the car. As they shot past the intersection from the Wellington Monument, Marlane spotted the car.

'There, Frank. Over by those trees.'

Henderson also heard her and spotted the car. Hand-brake on, right foot pressed down on the foot brake, the car changed direction in a split second. As he came out of the turn, Henderson lifted his foot from the brake and pressed it on to the accelerator. A few seconds later they squealed to a halt by Cowboy's car. In the darkness the monument stood tall and proud.

'The Wellington Monument,' Mooney roared into the radio. 'All cars converge at the Monument.'

Lying on his side without moving Cowboy watched the dark shadow of the man approaching him. He lay perfectly still, his right hand clutching the Peacemaker, still in his coat pocket. He let the man get to within thirty yards before he squeezed the trigger. The recoil as the pistol roared ripped the pocket free of the coat. As he fired, Cowboy rolled over to his left, screaming out loud from the pain as the thigh wound scraped on the ground. Turning back to face the man he cocked the gun a second time and fired. The man, still standing but staggering from the first hit, fell backwards in a heap as the second round hit him in the chest. Cocking the gun for a third shot Cowboy crawled towards the prone body, conscious that he could be faking. But he wasn't. As Cowboy leaned over him he could see the blood pumping from the two gaping holes in the man's chest. As he ran his hand along the neck to feel a pulse he felt a texture that was not skin. Further down the neck he felt the ridge where the texture ended, and the skin began. Dragging his wounded leg a few inches further, he leaned up over the dead man to look at his face. Staring back at him were the features of Arne Fries, the Dane. With his fingers back down on the neck he round the ridge and pulled. It was a struggle but the mask finally began to peel off. He stopped as he heard a sound in the bushes across the road. He cocked the pistol once more,

242

resting the small of his back against the dead body, his gun aimed towards the sound. Was there somebody there? He couldn't see. He waited, listening for the sound a second time, but there was nothing. It must have been the wind blowing through the bushes. He suddenly felt very cold and perspiration broke out on his forehead. Shock was setting in. 'Jesus,' he thought, 'I could kill for a fag.' Seconds later his hand was inside the side pocket of the dead man's jacket, extracting a packet of Marlboro cigarettes and a Zippo lighter. Inhaling deeply on the cigarette he grinned as he realized he *had* killed for a fag!

'Fuck you, Chameleon, The Dublin Kid was the best shot, if not the fastest.'

The man in the bushes smiled and slid the light intensifier night-sight back into his pocket, silently easing his way further into the darkness, away from the area.

Cowboy heard them before he saw them. Like the bugle charge of the 7th Cavalry coming to the rescue, siren after siren blared out into the night. The area was immediately bathed in the headlights of several cars as they squealed to a halt by the monument. Suddenly she was beside him, crying and calling his name over and over.

'Cowboy, oh Cowboy, speak to me, speak to me you bastard.' She grabbed the lapels of his coat and shook him, positive he was dead from the amount of blood that covered him. Through her tears she felt his hand weakly grab hold of her wrist. 'For God's sake woman, stop before you *do* kill me,' he whispered, a smile on his face.

Now she was crying and laughing, kissing all over his face, holding his head gently between her hands, all the time telling him how much she loved him, needed him, and how she was going to kill him when she got him back home. Frank loomed over him, then dropped down on one knee. 'Where're you hit, son?'

'Hi, Frank, lovely to see you. I'm not sure. Thigh, I think. He's dead.'

'I can see that. What'd you use? An elephant gun?'

Cowboy tried to lift the Peacemaker up, but the weight was too much for him. 'There's a mask there somewhere, Frank. He was made up to look like the guy he set up in Denmark, Arne Fries.'

'Okay, son. Take it easy. The ambulance will be here soon. I'll leave you with the nurse here until then, okay?' He grinned at his wounded colleague, then stood up and walked away.

As he reached his car Henderson approached him. 'Yank Embassy's been on the phone, Boss. Want to know what the hell's going on. What should I tell 'em?'

'Tell them that Carlos the Jackal escaped from France and has been sighted in the Park. That should keep the buggers up all night.'

'Sure, boss.' Henderson walked back to the car to pass the message on that everything was okay and that the Embassy had nothing to fear. There had been a slight problem, but the CIB had taken care of it. In the distance they could all hear the sound of the approaching ambulance.

EPILOGUE

Dublin, October 1994

ONCE AGAIN THE NEWSPAPERS HAD A FIELD DAY, with most of the tabloids going for 'Gunfight at the OK Corral' type headlines.

The dead man's identity, however, remained a complete mystery. His fingerprints were sent to both the FBI and to Interpol, but neither had anything on file. Through world-wide contacts in the International Police Federation a similar request was made with the same result. There was no police file anywhere in the world on the dead man. No passport was found on the body and apart from a wad of US dollars and some Irish punts the only other documents were five bogus American Express cards in five different names. His Hertz hire car was found in the park. Picked up the day before at Dublin airport it had been paid for by one of the Amex cards in the name of John Mc-Allister – the name he had used while staying at the Shelbourne Hotel. There was no trace of him entering the country, despite an extensive search through the videos taken at the Arrivals or Departures gates at the airport. The driver's licence that had been verified at the time of renting the car was not on the body, nor was it ever found. From the details provided by Hertz it too proved to be bogus. Nobody at the Shelbourne Hotel recognized the photograph of the dead man.

The gun he had used, a Browning automatic pistol, was traced as being one of the three missing weapons from the Eamon Boyle collection. Cowboy owed his life to faulty ammunition and a defective barrel. Tests carried out on the weapon showed that in all probability the killer had been aiming for Cowboy's chest when he fired, but hit him in the thigh instead. Cowboy's wound was not as serious as first thought. The bullet had gone straight through the fleshy part of his thigh without hitting bone or artery. He would be out of commission for some time but he would recover completely.

The *South China Morning Post*, one of Hong Kong's leading English language newspapers, ran the story of The Chameleon. Alongside the story was a photograph of the dead man. Nobody recognized him.

In the Hong Kong Toy Emporium, on the Jaffa Road, the man known as Mr Li read the article with a sense of loss – loss of income. Over the years he had created many masks for The Chameleon, but as far as he knew never once met him. His contact had always been the woman – and of her he knew nothing.

In the big house in Kowloon the woman was packing up. She had spent days supervising the packing of crates. On top of one of the packing cases was a small, framed, watercolour of a multicoloured flower that grows wild in the jungles of her old homeland. She never went anywhere without it, and it would be packed into her own suitcase when she left in a day or two. The crates were all going into an air-conditioned storage depository until required. Beside the watercolour lay a copy of the *South China Morning Post* with the story and photograph of The Chameleon. She didn't recognize the photograph either. Beside the newspaper was a folded telegram which read 'ANGEL. DON'T BELIEVE ALL YOU READ

A week after the shooting Mooney paid a visit to Cowboy in hospital and brought him up to date on their findings, or rather lack of them, as Mooney put it.

'He remains as big a mystery in death as he did in life, me old son. But there you have it. He made one mistake, like they all do, eventually, and you're alive and he's dead.'

'And you believe that, do you, Frank?' Cowboy had listened to everything Frank had told him, and one thing did not ring true. Something about the shooting – he wasn't sure what – had been bothering him for the last couple of days. Now he knew what it was.

'What do you mean?'

'That after twenty to twenty-five years as the, *the* most successful killer-for-hire, he makes a simple mistake – like not testing the weapon? He tested the weapon, Frank. He tested it and made *sure* it was faulty.'

'Are you trying to tell me that he committed suicide? Are you sure the bullet didn't hit you in the head instead of the leg? He made a mistake, son, and died because of it. If he'd wanted to kill himself he could have smoked his gun.'

Cowboy turned his head away and looked out of the window of his private ward. Frank did not, could not, understand. Or could he?

'He's not dead, Frank.'

'Oh, for fuck's sake, Cowboy. Come on. Wise up. The Chameleon is dead, and the case is closed, finito, the end. Got it?' Frank was beginning to get annoyed. 'What do you think he did? Hired somebody to die in his place?'

'That's precisely what he did do, Frank. No . . .' he

247

held his hand up to stop Frank replying. 'Let me finish first. For twenty-five years this man has been at the top of his chosen profession. Then, out of the blue, just as he's about to retire, we get on to him. For the first time in his career he is in danger of being caught. You reckoned he would just disappear and we'd never find him. I told you he wasn't gone. He couldn't go, and leave things as they were. If he was still alive, we – or somebody else – might find him. The only way to finish the game was if he died – and that wasn't his intention. Do you honestly believe a man of his calibre would forget the fundamental rule of checking the weapon? Bollocks, Frank. How long has he had those weapons, the rifle he killed Clark with, and the Browning? Long enough to have been out in the Wicklow Mountains testing both of them until he was sure, ab-so-fucking-lutely sure they fired true. No, Frank, he did exactly as you just suggested. He hired somebody else to take his place, doctored the weapon and ammo in some way, and made sure the poor bastard didn't have the time to test the gun. You're forgetting one other thing about this man, Frank.'

'And what's that?'

'Part of his MO was providing a patsy. He just provided one for his own death. He's alive, Frank – but this time he *is* long gone.'

'Sometimes I think you read too many books, Cowboy. The case is closed – and I'm outta here before I'm tempted to finish the job this guy started . . . killing you.' With those final words Frank stormed out of the room. Cowboy understood the other man's anger. But he also knew that although Frank would continue to state that the Chameleon was dead and the case *was* closed, what Cowboy had just told him would continue to niggle at the back of his mind. Cowboy knew that the case was finished. There was no way he or anybody else would be able even to begin to trace him now.

Two weeks after the shooting, a large basket of fruit was delivered to Cowboy in his hospital room. Along with it was a card which read 'From Billy the Kid to Pat Garratt, best regards and get well soon.' He understood the message immediately, and knew who it was from. Billy the Kid had been shot and killed by Sheriff Pat Garratt, a man he had trusted as a friend. However, Cowboy also knew that there were some who believed that wasn't how it happened. They believed that Garratt had faked it all, allowing his friend to wander off into the heartlands of Old Mexico, where he lived to be an old man.

The fruit had come from the Fruit and Flower Shop in the main hall of the hospital. He called down and asked who and how it had been ordered. It had been an Interflora request from Singapore. No name had been given, other than the two on the card. Cowboy placed the phone back on the hook. He couldn't help but admire the cheek of the man. Chameleon knew that Cowboy would understand the message, but that there was nothing he could do about it. It was checkmate, game set and match to the Chameleon, and he wanted to make sure that Cowboy knew that. He looked at the fruit basket and a weary smile flittered across his face. Sometimes, he knew, the baddies did win. Such was life.